MURDER IN THE PARK

Also by Jeanne M. Dams from Severn House

The Dorothy Martin mysteries

A DARK AND STORMY NIGHT
THE EVIL THAT MEN DO
THE CORPSE OF ST JAMES'S
MURDER AT THE CASTLE
SHADOWS OF DEATH
DAY OF VENGEANCE
THE GENTLE ART OF MURDER
BLOOD WILL TELL
SMILE AND BE A VILLAIN
THE MISSING MASTERPIECE
CRISIS AT THE CATHEDRAL
A DAGGER BEFORE ME
DEATH IN THE GARDEN CITY
DEATH COMES TO DURHAM
THE BATH CONSPIRACY

MURDER IN
THE PARK

Jeanne M. Dams

**SEVERN
HOUSE**

First world edition published in Great Britain in 2021 and the USA in 2022
by Severn House, an imprint of Canongate Books Ltd,
14 High Street, Edinburgh EH1 1TE.

Trade paperback edition first published in Great Britain and the USA in 2022
by Severn House, an imprint of Canongate Books Ltd.

severnhouse.com

British Library Cataloguing-in-Publication Data
A CIP catalogue record for this title is available from the British Library.

ISBN-13: 978-0-7278-5045-4 (cased)
ISBN-13: 978-1-4483-0715-9 (trade paper)
ISBN-13: 978-1-4483-0714-2 (e-book)

All Severn House titles are printed on acid-free paper.

Typeset by Palimpsest Book Production Ltd.,
Falkirk, Stirlingshire
Printed and bound in Great Britain by
TJ Books, Padstow, Cornwall.

ACKNOWLEDGMENTS

The Oak Park of my story, set in 1925, may have sheltered a good many unpleasant people, but the Oak Park of today is a different place. In my journeys there to do research, I found the villagers unfailingly kind and helpful. Rachel Berlinski, operations manager at the Historical Society of Oak Park and River Forest, was of the greatest possible help, finding me all the facts I needed and a good many I didn't even know would be useful. Ed O'Brien, local history librarian at the Oak Park Public Library, helped me view copies of Oak Leaves, the local newspaper at the time (and still), and showed me two wonderful books I was able to find and buy, a pictorial and an oral history that were invaluable in getting the feel of the village in the 1920s. When I wanted to see Grace Episcopal Church, which was closed because of the pandemic, its archivist Marilyn Wardle not only showed me around but made and emailed me copies of church bulletins and newsletters of the time. Don Gianetti, a parishioner at St Edmund Catholic Church, was able to show me the church and tell me stories about his father, who was a parishioner there not too long after the period in which I was concerned. When I was able to tour Pleasant Home, the mansion built by John Farson, Theresa Czarnilk, the docent who led my tour, later sent me a video she made about that remarkable man. A local expert on Ernest Hemingway, Scott Schwar, gave me many insights into Hemingway and his family and arranged a tour of his birthplace, now a house museum run by the Ernest Hemingway Foundation of Oak Park. The first person I met in Oak Park, Mary Rinder, is a lovely lady with many charitable interests who introduced me to Scott, told me about the Historical Society, and in general took me under her wing. She and Scott have become good friends with whom I shared an ice cream date at Petersen's. The staff at the Carleton Hotel, where I stayed for both visits, were pleasant, helpful, and efficient.

Three other people deserve special thanks. Pedro de Jesus, who is the Manager of Client Services and Analytics for the Ravinia festival, assured me that Ravinia was a going concern in 1925, and scanned and emailed me copies of the programs for that summer, so I could send my characters to the right performances. Finally, my friends of many years, Augie Aleksy and his wife Tracy, have cheered me on since the beginning of the project.

Augie owns the delightful bookstore Centuries and Sleuths in neighboring Forest Park. He showed me the books I would find most useful for research, put me in touch with a Capone historian, and told me wonderful stories. And Tracy took me on a tour of Oak Park neighborhoods, pointing out Frank Lloyd Wright houses, Hemingway locations, and so many other points of interest.

Of course, any mistakes I've made are entirely my own fault, and I apologize for them to my kind mentors.

ONE

Oak Park, Illinois. June, 1925

I t was Ginger who started it.

Elizabeth was looking for her favorite summer dress, rummaging through the trunk where she was sure she had put it last fall when the weather got too brisk to wear it. The cat was joining enthusiastically in the search, jumping into the trunk again and again, burrowing and disarranging the contents.

She clapped her hands sharply. 'Stop it, Ginger! Go play with Charlie, or find a mouse, or something.'

He jumped out with a flick of his orange tail, giving her a look that made it quite plain he was going because he wanted to, not – certainly not – because of her command.

He had made a sorry mess of her carefully organized belongings. Out-of-season clothes had been neatly folded at the top. Now they were in a rumpled mess, and falling half out of the trunk. The summer dresses would have to be ironed all over again, and poor Susannah had quite enough to do, helping Mother prepare for the garden party on Saturday. Young Mary wasn't much good at ironing. And I've never picked up an iron in my life, thought Elizabeth, but I suppose I'm going to have to try. It's getting really hot; I can't go around in woolens much longer.

She began to pull out the dresses she would need right away, the simple tunics with few of the awkward frills or pleats that would be so easy to ruin with a clumsy iron. Thank goodness her taste ran to the tailored look. The dresses were last year's and fashions were changing, true, but she didn't care a lot what she wore to her usual round of charity events and committee meetings and hospital visits. There were better things to spend her money on than new clothes that she didn't need. And who cared what she looked like, anyway?

Ginger had scrabbled all the way to the bottom of the trunk, pulling out some papers that she had forgotten were there. She pulled out the folder to tidy everything back. A few things fell out.

And there they were, the two pieces of paper that had changed her life forever.

The telegram had come first. Flimsy yellow paper with the message hastily scribbled by the telegraph operator as he decoded the clicks coming through on his receiving set. 'Deeply regret to inform you . . . killed in action November 10 . . .'

The day before the war ended. Hours before. Not even in a battle, just a stray shot by a German soldier determined to kill one more of the enemy before all was lost.

They has been married exactly six months the day the message arrived.

She had just begun to sleep without the horrible nightmares, without the trembling. Had begun, not to heal, but to believe that healing might one day be possible, when the second message had arrived, the letter from Will. Long delayed by the chaotic conditions in war-torn France, it was a paean of joy. The war would be over in days, it said. The Kaiser was going to abdicate. All over but the shouting. He'd be home as soon as he was mustered out. 'Can't wait to see you, my darling Liz! Give Skeeziks a pat for me, won't you, and tell him his dad will be back before he even finds his way into the world!'

She didn't need to open the envelope now, to read the words. They were seared into her brain.

The cruel irony of those happy words had dropped her into a trough of depression so deep that no one could reach her, not her friends or her parents or her pastor. One well-meant attempt to cheer her ended in the hysterics that caused her to go into labor, much too soon. The doctors couldn't save the baby, and nearly lost Elizabeth, too.

'Leave me alone!' she had said fiercely to one nurse who tried to make her eat, once she was able to sit up. 'Why should I eat? I have nothing to live for. Let me die!'

The nurse was bitterly weary. She had spent a long shift looking after wounded soldiers, men fighting for their lives with the same determination they'd shown against the enemy in France. 'That's a wicked thing to say,' she had burst out in a fierce whisper. 'Here you are, feeling sorry for yourself because you lost your baby! You can have another baby; you weren't badly damaged. And yes, I know you lost your husband, too. Does that mean it's all right for you to commit suicide, just throw away all the effort your doctors and I put in trying to keep you alive? Suicide is a sin, you know! Or if you don't, you should! And not only a sin, but cowardly!'

Elizabeth remembered that she had turned her head away, burrowed into her pillow to try to shut out the harsh words, but the nurse had continued, still in that furious undertone.

'You're all set to die in the comfort of your nice private room, you with all your family money, while those men out in the ward are trying with all their might to live, to be useful people again, when some of them have lost a leg or an arm, some have lungs that won't give them enough air, some . . . oh, I won't bother! You're nineteen years old and rich and they tell me you're smart. You could do great things for the rest of the world, but no, you'd rather give up because it's easier. Well, go right ahead and die, then! You make me sick!'

Sitting there on the closet floor, Elizabeth remembered that speech as if she'd heard it yesterday, and once again felt hot with shame. That nurse had saved her life seven years ago.

Her first reaction, after the nurse had stormed out of her room, had been sheer blazing fury. How dare she! A nurse was supposed to be sympathetic, caring, soothing. She, Elizabeth Walker Fairchild, was a seriously ill patient who should be treated with respect.

Why? asked some inner voice. Have you earned her respect?

Elizabeth was, as the nurse had said, intelligent. She was also honest, even with herself. Through the long night after the nurse had delivered her scalding tirade, she lay sleepless in bed replaying over and over what she had been told, and by morning she had made her decision. She asked for some breakfast, surprising the day nurse, and from that moment on made steady progress. Elizabeth never saw her furious angel again, never knew her name, but from then on, she was a model patient, doing as she was told, trying her best to eat, taking her medicine.

'Elizabeth!'

Her mother's voice sounded irritated. 'I've been calling you and calling you. Dinner's ready, and you're going to be late for your meeting if you don't hurry.'

Startled out of her reverie, Elizabeth looked at her wristwatch. Two hours lost to pointless woolgathering, old, painful memories stirred by two pieces of paper. She should have thrown them away long ago.

'Coming, Mother!'

She picked up the telegram and the letter, ready to tear them up, but something made her drop them back in the trunk. Stupid, she thought, just plain stupid. And now you've no time to iron something to wear tonight.

She picked up the pile of clothing she had set aside, took everything to her room and dumped the garments on the bed, and then hurried downstairs.

'Why, you haven't even changed!' Her mother looked horrified at her daughter's attire, an old, black, woolen dress, far too long for today's fashions and adorned here and there with cat hair.

'My summer things are too wrinkled to wear. This will do. It's only a committee meeting. I'll brush it before I go.' She helped herself to salad.

'You'll do no such thing. What are servants for?' Mrs Walker picked up the small bell that sat at her place, and when the maid came in, said, 'Mary, please ask Susannah to drop what she's doing and come here. Tell her I'm sorry to interrupt her work, but I have a small chore for her that can't wait.'

'Yes'm.' Mary dropped a clumsy curtsey and left the room, narrowly escaping tripping over the cat.

Elizabeth continued eating.

'When are you going to stop being so careless about your appearance, Elizabeth? These things matter. Even if you're so determined about not wanting anything to do with men, you have a position to maintain in this community.'

'Leave the girl alone, Mildred,' said her father, breaking his usual meal-time silence. 'She's not a child. She has her own life to live. Let her live it the way she wants.'

'I know she's not a child! That's just the point. She's fast becoming an old maid, and people are beginning to talk. I'm simply trying—'

'You sent for me, ma'am?'

'Oh, Susannah. Yes, we need your help. Elizabeth needs a summer frock to wear to a meeting this evening, and there isn't a fresh one. Can you iron one for her, please?'

'That Mary'll spoil the chocolate sauce if I don't watch her every minute.'

Susannah was a large colored woman of decided opinions, and Mrs Walker was, truth to tell, a little afraid of her. 'Yes, I know, Susannah, and I'm truly sorry to call you away from your work, but this is urgent. The silly child has left things to the last minute. She must leave for the guild meeting in less than an hour, and she has simply nothing to wear.'

Elizabeth slid back her chair, leaving most of her meal untouched on the plate. 'I'll go up and show you which dress, Susannah. I'm sorry I can't do it myself, but I wouldn't even know where to begin. Excuse me, please, Mother.'

'You just bring it down to me in the kitchen, Miss Elizabeth,' said Susannah once they were out of Mrs Walker's earshot. 'Stairs don't like me much these days. And your mama got no call to treat you like a child that way. You're a full-grown woman, even if you got no husband, and twice as useful in this world as she ever was.'

A well-trained servant would never have dared say such a thing, or if it simply came out, she would have apologized. Susannah, well aware of her importance to the smooth running of the household, said what she thought and apologized to no one.

'I hope I am, but there's no point in arguing with Mother. I used to try, but her views about a woman's place in the world are stuck back in the nineteenth century somewhere, and she's not going to change them. I'll go get that dress.'

Susannah snorted and headed for the room off the kitchen where ironing was done.

Elizabeth expected her meeting this evening to be extremely boring. Most of them were. St Katherine's Guild consisted mostly of well-to-do middle-aged women and was at present engaged in dreaming up fundraising projects for their church, Grace Episcopal. Elizabeth thought privately that if every member simply wrote a check for an amount commensurate with her financial standing, the church would be generously funded. She had learned, however, not to voice such opinions. St Katherine's had always had fundraising projects, and would continue to do so, world without end, amen. Elizabeth's role was to sit silently while suggestions were made and endlessly discussed, and to volunteer her services in carrying out the projects once they were decided. She would probably end up as treasurer for the current project, the selling of bronze doorknockers. These, replicas of one of the carvings near the font, had been cast locally and were expected to sell like the proverbial hotcakes, for use as paperweights where door knockers were not required.

Elizabeth thought them double-ugly, but she would buy at least one. Almost every other parishioner would do the same, and a decent interval would elapse before the castings began to appear in rummage sales in aid of this or that cause.

At least the meeting would pass the evening and tire her out. Perhaps she would sleep.

She woke early the next morning with a sense of dread. Nightmares had haunted her sleep. She could remember none of them in the light of day, but the weight of pain and fear lingered.

There was no point in staying in bed. She wouldn't sleep. There was little point in getting up, either. The day would be spent at home, following her mother's orders. The garden party was now only two days away. The servants had done it all before, for years, and knew quite well how to organize the work, but Mrs Walker would insist on stage-managing the whole affair and would insist on Elizabeth's entirely unnecessary aid. There would be quarrels and storms of temper, and at some point Susannah would threaten to quit. Then Mother would come down with one of her sick headaches and take to her bed, and peace would reign again. Until that happened, Elizabeth's role was to soothe and cajole and keep her father well away from the fray. It was all so dreadfully familiar.

And so unnecessary, she thought as she dragged herself through the morning routine of bathing and dressing. She put on her coolest dress – bless Susannah, who had somehow found time to iron several of them – ran a comb through her hair and heaved a sigh as she went downstairs.

Her father was finishing his breakfast. He laid aside his *Chicago Tribune* with a sigh. 'Another killing. Two more gangsters. When will all this stop?' He sighed again. 'You're up early, Bets. Coffee?'

'Too hot for coffee, Dad. Too hot to eat, even.'

'It's going to be one of those days, sweetheart. Best get some food into you. There's cantaloupe, and Susannah made biscuits.' He passed the basket.

She poured herself some orange juice and took a biscuit. 'You're up early yourself. I thought you didn't have school today.'

'Not for the students. They're home studying, getting ready for their exams next week. But there's plenty for the teachers to do, and I thought I'd be better out of the house while—'

The sound of Mrs Walker's voice drifted into the room.

'Oops! I'm off, sweetheart. Try not to work too hard.' And he was out the French doors and onto the terrace, closing the doors quietly just before his wife came into the room.

'And where does he think he's going?' demanded Mrs Walker.

'He's off to school, Mother. It's a Thursday, remember?'

'Of course I remember! He said school was closed.'

'For the students. Not for the teachers.' Her mother began to speak, but Elizabeth cut her off. 'Now, what would you like me to do first?'

The day proceeded according to tradition. The sudden heat made everyone cross. Susannah's usual threat came earlier than usual, actually before lunch, which made Mrs Walker's headache also set in earlier than expected. By the time everyone sat down to a cold lunch, the lady of the house was in bed with all the shades down, an electric fan humming away, and an ice pack on her head.

'Maybe now we can get somethin' done,' muttered Susannah as she helped herself to more potato salad at the kitchen table. 'And no need for you to be wearin' yourself out, neither, Miss Elizabeth. Nor to come in here to get whatever you was wantin'. That's what that bell is for.'

'Now, Susannah. You know I like to save you steps when I can on days like these. You've got enough to do without waiting on me. In fact' – she pulled out a chair and sat down at the kitchen table with her glass of water – 'I'd rather stay in here with you all. It's lonely in there, all by myself.'

'Your mama wouldn't like you stayin' in here with us colored folks,' Susannah pronounced. Mary and Zeke, the gardener, nodded solemnly.

What my mother doesn't know won't hurt her. She didn't say it aloud, but she was sure Susannah read her mind. The subject was changed.

'You gonna go sing tonight, lovey?'

'Yes, it's the last choir practice of the year. Maybe by eight-thirty it won't be so hot.'

'You singin' something good, or just that dull old stuff you usually do?'

It felt good to laugh. 'Our music is old, as you say, but we like it, even if it isn't as lively as what you sing at your church.'

'You right about that, for sure. More like a dirge than praisin' the Lord, if you ask me.' Susannah stood up. 'But it'd be a weary world if folks was all alike. Now, Miss Elizabeth, ain't no need for you to be workin' this afternoon. The three of us can do it all blindfolded, and there's another day for the last-minute stuff. You go out and enjoy yourself.'

'It's so hot,' Elizabeth began, but Susannah cut her off.

'Honey, if you was fat like me, you'd know what hot is. Just you wash your face in cold water and go shoppin' or somethin'. Go on, shoo, get out from under our feet.'

Elizabeth got up obediently and went into the dining room. Susannah had been giving her orders since she was a baby and Susannah was her nurse. Mother had always ordered her around, too, but there was a difference. Susannah's commands were born of love and kindness.

She went out on the terrace. A light breeze made it somewhat cooler there in the shade. Ginger wandered out and wanted to sit on her lap, but she shooed him away. 'Too hot for today, buster.' She thought about her father, sitting in his broiling classroom, and the servants, toiling in the steaming kitchen and out in the brutal sun, getting ready for that redundant party.

The charity chosen this year to reap the benefits, the Hephzibah Children's Association, was a worthy cause, to be sure. They would appreciate the money that was raised and would put it to good use. But as with the other parties and sales and benefits for worthy causes, the donors would have been just as happy simply to write a check without having to attend a function, especially in dressy clothes in June.

One must not, in Oak Park, deviate from tradition, Elizabeth reminded herself. The Walkers had been giving this party for twenty years. They would doubtless continue to do so until Mrs Walker dropped dead.

Meanwhile . . . Elizabeth roused herself from her lethargy. There was actually something useful she might do this afternoon. Her father's fiftieth birthday was coming up soon, and she wanted to get him something special. Mother would doubtless insist on a big party, the kind Dad so disliked. But at least Elizabeth could give him something that would have special meaning for him. She'd been thinking about it for weeks and had finally decided on a watch, a lovely old pocket watch of the sort that he preferred to the modern wristwatches. She was sure she had seen just the thing in the antique shop window downtown.

And oh, heavens, she heard her mother's querulous voice from an upstairs window. She was awake! Time to get away. She ran around the back way, nipped up to her room for her handbag, and slipped out just as Mother came down the stairs.

TWO

The antique store was only a few blocks away, and Elizabeth would ordinarily have walked, but the heat rose from the sidewalk in waves, and the streetcar line went right past the house. It was hot in the car, too, but at least the motion brought a semblance of a breeze.

The car stopped in front of the new Carleton Hotel, and Elizabeth got out. The shop, Anthony's Emporium, was right across the street. The bell over the door tinkled as she walked in.

'Why, Mrs Fairchild! How nice to see you.' The little man pushed his gold-rimmed glasses back up on his balding head and beamed.

'And you, Mr Anthony.' She warmed, as she always did, to the greeting from this sweet man. He said it as if he meant it. 'I hope business has been good.' *And I hope you're doing well, yourself.* But she didn't say that out loud. Too personal.

'Yes, indeed. New houses and apartment buildings are going up all over the village, and they all need to have furniture and tableware and ornaments, all the lovely things that make a house a home.'

Elizabeth raised an eyebrow. 'And they buy those things from you? I'd have thought they'd want hideous modern furniture, all glass and aluminum and sharp angles to bump into.'

The shopkeeper made a face. 'Some do, of course, but there are still people in the world who understand real design and superb workmanship, people like you. Look, there's something I'd like to show you. I bought it at an auction in Virginia two months ago, and it arrived only this morning. I haven't shown it to anyone else yet.'

He led the way to the back of the shop, where in a storeroom, taking up most of the space, was an exquisite highboy. 'Gosh, I've never seen one so beautiful,' breathed Elizabeth. 'Look at the details. Those finials – and I've never seen a scroll top like that. Cherrywood?'

'Yes, with white pine and poplar. It was a master cabinetmaker and carver who created this.'

'When? And where?'

'Connecticut, around 1770. It's a lovely piece. Want to take it home?'

Elizabeth laughed. 'I would in a minute if I had my own place, but my mother's taste doesn't run to Queen Anne, I'm afraid.'

'Ah well, I'm not sure I can ever bear to part with it in any case. It's by far the loveliest thing I've ever bought.'

'You're in the business of selling lovely things, don't forget. Someone will come along who will prize it just as you do.' She hoped. This dear man deserved a worthy buyer for something this splendid.

He sighed and pushed his glasses back up again as they walked back into the shop. 'But you didn't come in to talk about my love of beautiful things. How may I help you today?'

'I had my eye on that watch in your front window. The gold one. My father—' She stopped as a look of dismay crossed Mr Anthony's face.

'Oh, I am so sorry, so sorry! If I had known, but I sold it yesterday. To a stranger, new in town, I think. He was rather rude, not the sort of customer I prefer, so I named a price well above what it was really worth, hoping to discourage him, but he paid it without question. He was . . . was quite insistent. If I had only known, Mrs Fairchild!' He was nearly in tears.

Elizabeth could read between the lines as well as anyone. The insistent customer, the man with plenty of money to throw around – it didn't take too much imagination to guess what sort of man he was. These days there was a great deal of money to be made in Chicago in one way or another, many of them illegal, and when a man living in Chicago got rich enough, he might well buy one of the beautiful houses in Oak Park. The village tried to ignore their presence, but the bootleggers and gangsters were there in their midst, living in their neighborhoods, shopping in their stores. The 'insistence' might have involved a suspicious bulge under the customer's jacket. She smiled at the distraught little man who cared so much.

'Don't worry, Mr Anthony. I was wanting it for my father's birthday, and that isn't until the middle of July. Do you think you might find another pocket watch by then? It wouldn't actually have to be gold. It was just that he'll be fifty, and that's sort of special.'

'And traditionally celebrated with gold. I'll find a gold watch for your papa, Mrs Fairchild. I know someone, a friend, who has several very nice ones. I will send him a note today, and by tomorrow I will have an answer. Saturday at the latest.'

'That's very kind of you, but there's really no hurry.'

'No, no!' He waved his hands excitedly. 'I have disappointed you. You are my favorite customer, my friend. I must make that right. Tomorrow, or Saturday, but I think tomorrow.'

After that, of course Elizabeth couldn't leave the store empty-handed, so she chose a small, highly decorated china clock of the sort her mother loved.

'It isn't actually Meissen,' said Mr Anthony anxiously. 'It is of the right period, though.'

'I'll take it. Mother will be exhausted when I get home. This may make her feel better.'

'Yes, she will like it, I think.' There was the very faintest emphasis on 'she'. The shopkeeper knew that Elizabeth preferred clean lines and sparse decoration, as he did himself. They both smiled. There was very little those two didn't understand about one another.

'Thank you, Mrs Fairchild,' he said with a courtly bow, when he had swathed the clock in layers of tissue paper and fitted it gently into a box. 'You wouldn't rather have this delivered? It is fragile.'

'No, it's better if I take it with me. Mother has been working hard all day and will enjoy a treat.'

'Ah, yes, the garden party. To benefit the Hephzibah this year, isn't it? It is a great deal of work, I know. I cannot be there – Saturday is a working day for me – but I will make a donation, of course. And I will let you know about the watch.'

They parted with a mutual exchange of courtesies, and Elizabeth went back out to the broiling afternoon.

She had just missed a trolley, and the wait for the next one, in the heat, suddenly seemed unendurable. She looked at her watch; there was no need to rush home. Her mother would be livid at what she would view as her daughter's dereliction from duty, but a few more minutes would make no difference. She would get something cold to drink in the hotel.

The lobby, paneled in dark oak, was cool and pleasant. Ceiling fans revolved, creating a welcome breeze. The desk clerk directed her to the dining room, where tables were set for dinner, with starched white napery, gleaming silver, vases full of flowers. The maître d'hôtel approached her, menu in hand.

'I don't want a meal,' she said with a smile, 'only a glass of lemonade.'

'Of course, madam, right this way.' He led her to a small table near the window. 'I'll send your waiter over straight away.'

He came, bearing a large frosty glass on a silver tray, and behind him came another man, bearing a large smile.

'Afternoon, Elizabeth,' he said with a little bow. 'May I join you?'

'Of course. It's good to see you, Fred.'

'Waiter, I'll have one of those, too. And something to nibble. Peanuts?' He raised an eyebrow at Elizabeth, who nodded.

'Didn't expect to run into you downtown,' Fred remarked. 'Thought you'd be slaving away getting ready for the big do.'

'No, Mother didn't actually need me, so I came down to buy a birthday present for Dad.'

Fred glanced at the parcel she'd put on the table.

'No, that's for Mother. It's just a treat, since she's been working so hard. Poor Mr Anthony didn't have what I wanted for Dad, but he said he could get one in a day or two.'

'Why "poor" Mr Anthony?'

'Oh, Fred, he was so sweet, so sorry he couldn't help me.'

'You were getting your father an antique?'

'A pocket watch. He likes them better than wristwatches. He's even more old fashioned than I am.'

'You're not old fashioned. Just sensible. And conservative.'

'Conservative in some ways, yes. These days, that counts as old fashioned. I could really use a few new clothes, but everything seems designed for flappers these days. I don't flap.'

'And thank the good Lord for that.' He paused for a handful of peanuts and changed the subject. 'Have you seen the Ravinia schedule for this summer?'

'Yes! Two of my very favorite operas, *Barber* and *Butterfly*.' The outdoor Ravinia festival was one of the highlights of the Chicago area summer, and Elizabeth loved it.

'And *Barber* is the first thing of the season. I'll get tickets, shall I?' asked Fred.

'Oh, please do. I'll look forward to that. Such a silly plot, but the music is glorious.'

'All comic opera plots are silly. And all tragic opera plots are the same: betrayal in one form or another, usually a man betraying a woman.'

'Yes.' Elizabeth looked out the window. 'I must go. The trolley's just coming. It was lovely seeing you.'

She was gone before he could get to his feet.

When she got home, she went straight to the dining room, where her mother could be heard ranting about something. Better to take her scolding first thing and attempt to stem the flow with her gift.

'Where have you been? The busiest day of the year, and you choose to go off gallivanting somewhere! And me with my head so bad I thought I would die! We're not half done with the work, and you don't even seem to care. I don't know what people will think on Saturday when they find the house still a wreck and the garden half tidied.'

There were many possible replies: that all the work would be done, and well done, by their hard-working servants; that she, Elizabeth, could have contributed nothing in any case; that there was a whole day left for preparations; that Susannah herself had sent her off. The arguments were pointless. Elizabeth simply waited until her mother ran down and then produced her gift. 'I went shopping and found this. I thought you might like it.'

Stopped in mid-tirade, Mrs Walker clung to her mood of righteous indignation. 'What is it? I don't have time to deal with it now.'

'Open it and see. I think you'll like it,' she repeated.

'Oh. Well.' Her mother picked up the box and looked at the label. 'Oh, from Anthony's! Is it an antique?'

'Careful. It's fragile.'

When the clock was released from its cocoon of tissue paper, Mrs Walker decided it was time to stop sulking. 'Oh, my! What a pretty thing. It will be just right for the mantel in my bedroom. Or, no, I'll put it in the living room first, so our guests can see it. A fine piece of Meissen! Florence Baker will be green with envy.'

Elizabeth didn't point out the mistaken identification, nor did she wait for any word of thanks. The gift had accomplished its purpose. She smiled and went up to her room to get ready for choir practice.

Friday morning dawned even hotter than the day before, and yet more humid. The sky, though still blue, had a solid look to it, somehow. 'Thunder before tonight,' Susannah predicted grimly as she passed Elizabeth in the downstairs hall. 'Your mama's gonna have a conniption fit.'

'Oh, dear. Maybe it'll blow itself out before tomorrow.'

'Mebbe.'

Susannah went on about her business, her brow furrowed, her lower lip protruding. Elizabeth sighed. The weather was always a worry. Mid-June in the Midwest was a chancy time to plan outdoor activities. If the heat wasn't oppressive – as it often was – there was always the possibility of a storm, and Oak Park specialized in rip-snorters. The threat meant that the big tent couldn't be put up today, to be blown away, but would have to await tomorrow's weather. And if there was a storm or even just rain, the whole event would have to be moved indoors, where all those people would make the heat even more unbearable.

She moved to the dining room, wishing she could go to Alaska instead.

Her father was at the table reading his *Tribune*, as usual. He looked up at her with an expression she couldn't read. 'Sit down, my dear. I'm afraid there's some very sad news.'

She sat. 'But what . . .?'

'There's no easy way to say this, Bets. Our friend Mr Anthony was murdered last night.'

THREE

Elizabeth paled but said nothing. Her father looked at her, deep concern shadowing his face. Her mother walked in just then.

'I swear, if it isn't one thing, it's another. I don't know what we'll do if we get a thunderstorm. I don't know why I kill myself every year for this party! And you two never lift a finger—' She stopped.

Elizabeth was still standing, her hand on the back of a chair, her face the color of chalk. Mr Walker was watching her, paying no attention to his wife. 'What? Seen a ghost or something?'

Elizabeth left the room. Her father sighed. 'There's been bad news. Mr Anthony was killed last night, struck down at his shop. He was a friend. Elizabeth is understandably upset.'

'Oh. Well. What a shame.' Mrs Walker paused. 'But there's no need to treat it like a death in the family or something. He was a shopkeeper. Why's she moping around like that?'

Mr Walker was silent for a moment before he said, 'Mildred, there are times when I fail to understand how your mind works.' He pushed his chair back and stood. 'I'm off to school before the storm breaks.'

A faint flash of lightning was followed by a distant peal of thunder.

'But the party—' she called after him. Too late. He was gone.

The storm was typical. The thunder and lightning became almost continuous. Rain pelted down, splashing mud from every flower bed. Fierce winds shredded the peonies in which Mrs Walker took such pride, and a brief hailstorm shattered the roses.

Mrs Walker spent the morning wringing her hands, while Susannah and Mary worked furiously in the kitchen, preparing dainties for the party. Much of the food could be made ahead and stored in the Frigidaire. Since none of the outside work could be done in the rain, the kitchen work took its place, though Susannah disapproved of the diminished quality of such food. 'Ought to be fresh,' she muttered as she sliced and chopped and rolled out dough. 'It'll be no better than store-bought. Mary, you get those eggs out of the water right now, or they'll be boiled hard as rocks. Didn't your mama teach you nothin' 'bout cookin'?'

Elizabeth stayed in her room, and apparently something Mr Walker had said kept her mother from bothering her, so she was free to think, and to mourn.

Dad had called Mr Anthony a friend. God help her, that was true. She had let herself become friends with the little man. In a way, she had loved him. Hadn't she learned the terrible lesson: love hurts? The only way to be safe was to keep clear of emotional entanglements. How had she forgotten? Keep everything light, never let feelings go deep. She had tried so hard to keep distant from everyone, and she had failed, and now this new pain.

She loved Dad. She couldn't help it, because he loved her so. With Mother it was easy. Mother loved no one but herself, so she aroused no love in anyone else.

She loved Susannah, for the same reason she loved her father. Love inspires love.

What would she do if anything happened to those two dear people?

Fred wanted her to love him. She knew that, and she was carefully, studiously, pushing him away. Her love of music enticed her to accept invitations to accompany him to concerts, operas. It was dangerous, she knew. Music stirs the soul. If she weren't careful . . . well, it wouldn't hurt to go with him to *The Barber of Seville*. Nothing there to kindle a flame. *Madama Butterfly* was more problematic. That lush, gorgeous music, the tender joy of the beginning, the heartbreak of the ending . . . no, it would be best to find an excuse not to go with Fred to *Butterfly*. If she were to break down in tears, as she had been known to do, Fred would comfort her, and then . . .

Here, alone in her room, she could indulge in the luxury of tears, and it was with reddened eyes that Susannah found her when she brought up a sandwich and some iced tea at lunchtime.

'You grievin', honey, but you'll feel better if you eat somethin'. And don't know if you noticed, but the storm's over and the sun's out. Time your sun came out, too.'

She sat up. 'Thanks, Susannah, but I can't eat.' Her voice came out hoarse and rusty.

'That big lump you can't swallow. I know, honey. When I lost my two sweet babies—'

'I didn't know you lost your babies, too.' Elizabeth was ashamed. She had never bothered to learn anything about this woman who had lived in her house for so long.

Susannah sat on the bed, which creaked under her weight. 'Not like you. You never had your baby chile. I had mine for a while. A boy and a girl. They was four and six when the diphtheria took 'em. 1885, that was. A bad year for diphtheria. Still bad, even now. They say they got a way to prevent it now, but it don't sound too good to me. Hope they still workin' on it.'

'So your children got diphtheria,' Elizabeth prompted.

'Real bad. Couldn't hardly breathe, poor babies. We was livin' in the South then, down in Miss'sippi. Hot, honey, you wouldn't believe. Wasn't nothin' we could do for those poor babies. They just . . . died. My husband and me, we thought we was gonna die, too.'

Elizabeth reached out and took the calloused, wrinkled, brown hand. Tears trickled down both faces.

'Now don't you start cryin' for me, Miss Elizabeth. I done my cryin' back then, this is jus' memory. I hurt bad, though. Long time before I could eat proper, on account of that there lump in my throat. I got thin, believe it or not.' Susannah looked down at her bulk, smiling through her tears. 'It was my Billie got me out of it. Told me I couldn't go and die, too, or who'd look after him and the other kids. We had my sister's girls livin' with us at the time, and we was so scared they was gonna get sick too. Billie said we had to make sure they had good food and all, to keep 'em healthy. Well, that was like cold water in my face. So I pulled myself together, the good Lord knows how, and we all survived, and then we moved north, and when Billie died I started workin' for your mama. That was jus' before you was born, and lookin' after you was a joy.

'Don't never forget, honey, there's always somebody worse off than you, and there's always somethin' the good Lord's got for you to do, 'stead of just grievin'. Grievin's right and proper, but it's gotta stop sometime.' She squeezed Elizabeth's hand and stood. 'You drink that tea now, and eat somethin' if you can. The sun's come out, like I said before. Gonna be a fine day for your mama's shindig tomorrow. Gotta get back to work 'fore she gets after me.'

Susannah opened the window before she stumped out of the room, and a fresh breeze wafted in, making the curtains sway. It smelled sweet, the scent of rain, of moist grass, of thirsty plants raising their drooping heads again. Elizabeth got out of bed and looked out. The peonies wouldn't recover. Their petals lay in sad watery heaps that Zeke would have to sweep away before the party. Their gaudy beauty was over for the season. But the roses had plenty of buds. They would bloom again.

And the heat would come back, and they would open out too soon, and it would get too dry, and they would droop again. Elizabeth sighed. That was the way of life, wasn't it? The beauty lasted for only a fleeting moment and then was snatched away.

There was a commotion in the hallway, the sound of running feet and a loud yelp. Then the disturbance erupted into her room.

Charlie was chasing Ginger. Or the other way around; Elizabeth couldn't quite tell, as they began to run in circles. Gray fur and orange fur bristled; tails were bushed. They raced over her bed, then under it, with hisses and growls. Then Charlie came out on one side, Ginger on the other. Both sat and began to wash, Charlie giving attention to his whiskers, Ginger to his tail. Some sound from downstairs caught the attention of both of them. They paused in their ablutions, ears pricked, heads up, then stood and padded out the door, side by side, hostilities forgotten.

And that was life, too, Elizabeth mused. Enormous effort expended to no apparent end, and then suddenly suspended for no apparent reason. Humans might try to understand why cats behaved in that way, but how could they, when their own actions were often as meaningless?

Why would anyone want to kill a harmless, pleasant man who loved beautiful things?

Could it have anything to do with the gangster who bought Dad's watch?

At that thought, she pulled herself up with a jerk. The gangster existed only in her imagination. And the watch was her father's only in her dreams. And furthermore it was futile to speculate about a crime she knew absolutely nothing about.

Absolutely nothing, she thought again. She hadn't even read the newspaper account. She'd just fallen apart, like a little idiot. She didn't know where Mr Anthony had been killed, or how, or when. Nothing. Probably by this time the police had the culprit in jail.

She shuddered. Murder wasn't something that happened in Oak Park. Chicago, yes. It had become almost commonplace there, rival gang leaders shooting each other every few weeks. But not in calm, peaceful Oak Park. The gangsters living here behaved themselves, for the most part, at least on their home ground. There were no taverns in Oak Park, that was the reason. No territory to fight over. No alcohol to escalate arguments into brawls and brawls into murder. So how well prepared were the local police to deal with a case of murder?

Her throat was suddenly dry. She drank Susannah's iced tea, now only cool, and took the glass and the sandwich downstairs.

Only Mary was in the kitchen, washing dishes, dozens and dozens of Mother's finest Haviland plates and cups and saucers.

Elizabeth looked in at the door, then backed softly away to the stairway, where she started walking heavily, loudly, toward the kitchen. It wouldn't do to enter quietly and startle Mary. If she dropped a plate, Mother would accept no excuses, and would rant until the poor girl was in tears.

Elizabeth waited until Mary's hands were empty before tapping on the door frame and stepping in. 'Oh, Mary, what an awful job! Are you almost done, I hope?'

'Just about, Miss Elizabeth. They's just the glasses to do yet, and they ain't as bad to do as them plates. The glasses, they's heavy, but not near as slippery. An' I ain't allowed to dry 'em, so I just has to wash an' rinse and set 'em out on towels. Miz Susannah, she polishes 'em till they looks like diamonds. They's so pretty, miss.'

'It's such a lot of work for you.'

'I don't mind, miss, only if I wasn't so scared I'd break somethin'. I likes pretty things.'

Then and there Elizabeth made a mental note. 'Something pretty' went down against Mary's name on her Christmas list. Of course her parents gave the servants gifts of cash at Christmas, but Elizabeth had just that moment decided that she would chip in something more personal for each of them. She'd ask Susannah what might please Zeke, and as for Susannah herself, she'd sneak a peek into the housekeeper's room and see if she couldn't get an idea of her taste.

Shame rolled over her in a wave. Twenty-six years she had lived under the same roof with Susannah, and she had only today learned of the great sorrow of her life. And she still didn't know what sort of present might please this woman who was more of a mother to her than her own ever had been. What a selfish pig I am! she thought.

'Was there somethin' you was needin', Miss Elizabeth?'

'No, I was just hoping to find this morning's *Tribune*. Have you seen it?'

'I was gonna throw it away, seein' as Mister had finished readin' it, and Missus wouldn' want it lyin' around with the party comin' up, but Miz Susannah wouldn' let me. She said as how you'd be wantin' to read it, so I put it away in the pantry.' Mary hesitated. 'I'm real sorry about your friend, Miss Elizabeth. Real sorry.'

Elizabeth's throat suddenly closed up again. 'Thank you,

Mary,' she managed to say, willing the tears not to wash down her cheeks.

Her will wasn't strong enough. The tears escaped, and Mary saw. 'Oh, miss,' she said, her own voice choked. 'I—I'll get the paper for you.'

FOUR

The household being in its customary pre-party uproar, Elizabeth took the *Tribune* up to her room to read in peace. It was not very informative. With murders a dime a dozen in Al Capone's Chicago, Elizabeth thought scornfully, probably the death of one unimportant man in little Oak Park didn't rate a lot of coverage.

But that one man was important to her, and to a lot of other people in Oak Park. She skimmed through the story, discarding 'local color' and mining for nuggets of fact. There weren't a lot. The body had been found in the alley behind the shop after midnight, by another merchant just going home.

Who? Why was he leaving his place of business so late? No answers to those questions. She read on.

Mr Anthony had been stabbed. No mention of the nature of the weapon, or the location of the wound or wounds. No estimate of the time of death.

'Police assume the murder resulted from a robbery attempt.' End of story.

Why that assumption? Had anything been stolen from the shop? Were any suspects being pursued?

In disgust, she threw the paper aside. *Oak Leaves*, the local newspaper, would undoubtedly have more information, but it was a weekly, not due out until late tomorrow afternoon. Meanwhile, who would be able to tell her more?

Other shopkeepers, that's who. The people who worked nearby. The man who found him. The *Tribune* didn't know, or perhaps didn't care, who that was, but everyone downtown would know.

The only trouble was she didn't really know any of the other merchants. The manager at their bank knew her and her family, of course. Their wealth ensured that bankers would be friendly, even obsequious. But bankers were notoriously close-mouthed, not only about their customers but about everything else. Besides, the few times she had talked to the manager, he had treated her with perfect courtesy but a distinct air of 'there, there, child, just leave it all to me'. If the exact words were never spoken, the condescending smile spoke volumes.

No, not the bank. As for the other merchants, she was at a loss. She shopped for her clothing and shoes and so on in the city, usually at Marshall Field's or Carson Pirie Scott. Chicago was readily accessible by rail, and safe enough in the daytime, so long as she stayed out of certain neighborhoods. The speakeasys were where most of the problems arose, and of course she'd never go near one of those.

Groceries and other household necessities were ordered by telephone and delivered. The servants would know the delivery boys, and probably had a nodding acquaintance with the clerks who took the orders, but no one else in the house even really knew the stores existed, except as names on accounts to be settled every month.

A tap on the door. Mary opened it and peeked in. 'Miz Susannah wants to know if she can fix you somethin' to eat. You ain't had nothin' all day, Miss Elizabeth. She got in some real pretty raspberries to make tarts for the party, and they'd go down real good with a little cream, she said.'

'Tell her thank you, but I couldn't – Mary!'

Startled, Mary pulled back and gulped. 'Yes'm?'

'It's all right. I didn't mean to sound so . . . anyway, did you take in the grocery delivery today, or was it Susannah?'

'It was Miz Susannah, miss. She wanted to check it over and make sure they didn't forget nothin'.'

Elizabeth slid off the bed. 'Where is Susannah?'

Mary retreated a bit farther. 'In the kitchen, miss. She told me to fetch whatever you wanted. She's awful busy, miss.'

'I'm sure she is. You don't need to tell her. I'll find her myself, so you can get back to other chores.' She smiled to take the sting out of what amounted to an order. 'I know you're run off your feet. I'll tell Mother you deserve some time off when all this is over. Now, scoot!'

Mary scooted.

Elizabeth combed her hair and smoothed her dress, which looked as if she'd slept in it. Well, she had, more or less. Once more she was ashamed of herself. Lying in bed all day feeling sorry for herself while the servants worked their heads off and endured the nagging of Mother. She could at least have diverted some of that irritation. Well, it wasn't too late.

As she went down the stairs, she could hear her mother's voice outside, berating the men who were putting up the tent. The pavilion, Mother called it. 'You've got that rope too tight! It has to be able to give with the wind. And if you move back one more inch, you're going to be stepping on the snapdragons. Can't you be more careful?'

The men were trying to ignore her, but the nervous, high-pitched voice was grating, even if one shut out the meaning of the words.

Elizabeth took a deep breath and moved out onto the terrace. 'Mother!' she called.

Mrs Walker spun around, planting one foot directly on the snapdragons in a muddy flower bed. 'Now look what you've done! What is it? Can't you see I'm busy?'

'You look so tired, I thought you might like to sit down with a glass of iced tea. It's much cooler in the shade, and I can keep an eye on this operation for a little while.'

'You've gotten over your sulks, then? I thought you were going to lie around all day.'

Elizabeth gritted her teeth but managed to reply civilly. 'I'm much better, thank you. Now you just go and sit down on the terrace in the shade. Or better yet, under the maple tree.' There was no view of the tent from that side of the house. 'There's a lovely breeze, and I'll bring you some tea.'

'And some aspirin. My head's ready to split.'

As she gave her mother her arm to lead her off the field of battle, Elizabeth saw Zeke shoot her a look of gratitude.

She got her mother settled, hurried to the kitchen for a glass of tea with plenty of ice, stopped at the bathroom cupboard for the aspirin, and was back outside in double time, bringing along a magazine she had picked up at random. 'Here you are, Mother. And I thought you might like something to read, so you can relax and forget all about your work for a little while.'

'My head's too bad to read.' But she took the magazine.

Elizabeth headed for the tent, exchanged a word or two with Zeke, and then set off by a roundabout route for the kitchen.

Susannah was moving as fast as her bulk would allow, from the table where she was rolling out pastry, to the oven, to the pantry. Her face shone with sweat; the baking was heating the room to broiling point. Mary and the girls hired as temporary help were running around following Susannah's orders and getting in each other's way.

The look Susannah gave Elizabeth was not welcoming. 'Glad you're feelin' better an' all, Miss Elizabeth, but I'd be obliged if you'd stay out of my kitchen. You want anything, you tell Mary. And you, Sally Mae' – turning to a hapless girl struggling under the weight of a tray full of china – 'don't you go carryin' all them dishes at once! You'll drop 'em for sure!'

'I don't want to bother you, Susannah, but I just wanted to ask—'

A cry of pain sounded. Susannah turned and glared at another of the temporary helpers. 'Nancy Smith, ain't you got more sense than to pick up a hot cookie sheet with your bare hands? Now you've gone and dumped half of 'em on the floor!'

She turned back to Elizabeth. 'Sorry, honey, but you can see I can't talk now.'

Elizabeth saw. She smiled at Susannah, who had already turned her attention to another disaster in the making, and backed out of the kitchen.

Now what? Susannah could have told her what the word was on the street about the murder. But now was no time to ask.

Well, what about Zeke? She wasn't as close to him as to Susannah, but he got out more, living not in the house, but above the garage, which was the old stable. He might know something. They chatted now and then about flowers, but she really knew almost nothing about him, save that he was an excellent gardener and a pleasant man.

And how long had he worked for her family? Twenty years? More? The wave of shame was becoming familiar.

Again she used a circuitous route to the back garden. On the off-chance that her mother had not fallen asleep in her shady, comfortable retreat, she wanted to preserve the illusion that she had been 'supervising' the tent operations all along.

The tent was finished. Zeke was going around methodically checking the ropes as the rest of the men leaned against trees, mopping their brows. Even though the air had cooled after the storm, working in the sun was hot. They nodded respectfully to her as she passed.

'Zeke, can I get you all some iced tea?'

'Thank you, Miss Elizabeth, but Susannah sent Mary out with nice cold water a little while back.'

'Good. Can you all rest for a little now?'

'No'm. There's the tables and chairs to set out yet.'

'Can that wait for a minute or two? I . . . there are some things I need to talk to you about. I know it's a bad time, but I don't know who else . . .' She trailed off because she was afraid she would cry if she continued.

Zeke's eyes showed sympathy. 'It'll be about Mr Anthony,' he said. It wasn't a question.

Elizabeth nodded and cleared her throat. 'I . . . the paper says so little. I thought you and the other men might have heard . . .?' Her throat closed up again.

'I'm real sorry, Miss Elizabeth. I know you was real friendly with Mr Anthony. But white folks don't tell us much, you know. Susannah'd know more than me. And lordy me, here comes your mama. Best git movin'.'

There it was again. That line drawn between Zeke's people, Susannah's people, and hers. She'd never paid much attention to it before. Now it was getting shoved in her face.

She plodded back to the house and tried to think, but there was no peace. At last she picked up a book at random and walked to the far back of the garden, where a rustic swing was sheltered by an elm tree. The seat was still wet from the earlier rain, but it didn't matter. It was quiet enough to think.

Her thoughts weren't productive. There must be some way to find out what had really happened last night, but she couldn't come up with a single idea. Her mind kept showing her pictures. Pictures of that gold watch she'd wanted for Dad. Pictures of the highboy Mr Anthony had been so proud of. Pictures of his small shop full of beautiful things, things he would never touch and handle and love again.

She was very glad when her father came home from school, later than usual, and they could think about a catch-as-catch-can supper.

FIVE

I t was not a comfortable meal. Susannah was far too busy to prepare her usual delectable food, so they dined on cold ham and bits of leftovers, served by Mary with even less efficiency than usual. Mother talked incessantly about the carelessness and laziness of the servants and the extra help hired for the day. 'Heaven only knows what they would have been up to if I hadn't been there to keep an eye on them. Seems like nobody knows how to work these days.'

She did not moderate her comments when Mary was in the room, and her voice was loud enough that it could be heard in the kitchen, Elizabeth was sure. Heaven only knows, she thought silently, why the servants don't leave, the way she treats them. Neither she nor her father responded to the rant but ate in silence the little food they could swallow and left the table as soon as possible.

Mr Walker headed for the terrace and beckoned Elizabeth to follow him, while Mother went off in a huff. Probably to her bedroom to conjure up another headache, thought Elizabeth.

'I wanted to talk to you, sweetheart. Are you feeling any better?'

The tears threatened again. 'I suppose, Dad. But it's all so awful! I tried all day to find out what actually happened, but Susannah is the only one around here who might have heard anything, and she's been too busy to talk to me.'

'Yes, of course. Well, I have some information, but I'm afraid it's not good.' He sighed. 'There are times when I wish I were a drinking man. Or a smoker. I could use something to take the edge off all this. However . . .' He waved his hand.

'I could get you a cup of tea, Dad.'

'Too hot, but thank you, love. And there are things I must tell you before your mother gets back.' He sighed again and continued. 'I learned a good deal from the other teachers today. Most of us had our tests prepared, and with no students we had time on our hands. Of course the talk was all about poor Mr Anthony.'

'What *happened*, Dad? The *Tribune* said almost nothing.'

'And they got some of even that little wrong. His body was found much earlier than reported. The grocer next door went out to the alley to throw away some trash a little after seven, just before he quit for the day, and saw the poor man lying there by his back door. Apparently he went over to see if he could help, but Mr Anthony was plainly dead.'

'So why did the paper say it was after midnight?'

'That was when the police were called.'

'What! Why did he wait so long? I thought with a crime like that, the police wanted to get started as soon as possible.'

'He was afraid. These are terrible times, my dear. And the grocer knew that Mr Anthony is – was – Italian. His name was really Antonelli, Enrico Antonelli.'

Elizabeth didn't have to have it spelled out for her. An Italian was a dangerous person. He might be connected with the Mob. Probably not, she thought. Mr Anthony was a decent and honest man. But did he earn enough in his small business to go out and buy an expensive piece of antique furniture? That highboy was worth a small fortune. Could he have come by that money in some dishonest way?

And even if there was no Mob connection, to be Italian in Oak Park was to be suspect, to be unwanted. An Italian was Catholic and therefore undesirable in the eyes of many people. Oak Park was deeply conservative and almost entirely Protestant. And then there was the Walosas Club.

Nobody in Oak Park was unaware that the meaningless and apparently harmless name designated an active chapter of the Women's Ku Klux Klan. Community opinion was divided. Many thought the organization performed an important role in keeping the community 'pure', free from the influences of foreigners and their religions, and from all non-white people (among whom were counted Italians). Even the Negro servants of the well-to-do were viewed with suspicion if not outright hostility.

Others in the village, including Elizabeth and her father, viewed the Klan and all its works as anathema, spreading hatred and intolerance and capable of almost any atrocity. Including murder.

'Do you think,' she almost whispered, 'that it was the Klan? Is that why the grocer was so afraid?'

'The Klan or the Mob, what's the difference? The man is dead, and his death could well tear this village apart. The one side is going to accuse the other. And I'm afraid there's worse, Bets.'

She held her breath. What could be worse than civil war in their beloved village?

'A friend of mine is about to be accused of the murder,' he said heavily. 'You know him. Our music teacher, Mr Briggs.'

'No! He's such a nice man, and such a fine musician.'

'He is. He is also Italian.'

'With a name like Briggs?'

'His father was from Peoria, but his mother is Italian. She's a widow now, and Paul Briggs is her only support. He's Catholic and spent a lot of time with Mr Anthony and his family. That's enough to make him guilty in the eyes of some in this community.'

Elizabeth sank back in despair. It was all only too true. With a convenient suspect ready-made, the police were unlikely to look much further. Oh, they'd make a token search for evidence. Unlike the police in Chicago, a force well-known to be corrupt and in the pockets of Al Capone and the Mob, Oak Park police were decent, and competent to deal with their usual run of petty crime. But they were a small force, ill-prepared to deal with murder.

'They can't – that mustn't happen!'

'It ought not to happen,' her father corrected. 'But there's no way to stop it, I fear. Briggs is almost certain to be arrested soon. I'm going to visit his family tomorrow to see if there's any way I can help not just his mother, but his wife and children.'

Elizabeth stood. 'And I,' she said with determination, 'am going to visit Mr Anthony's family. Do you know anything about them?'

'Briggs says he left a wife and daughter. There were two more children, but they died in the influenza epidemic. Now the poor woman has lost her husband, as well.'

'And her means of support.'

'The church will help, sweetheart.'

'St Edmund's? But their parishioners aren't rich. What can they do?'

'They will band together, as people do in a crisis.'

'Well, I'm still going. Tomorrow afternoon. It will give me a good excuse to get away from the party. And I'll take a basketful of party food. There's always way too much, and Susannah will be glad to let me pack some up.'

'You won't tell your mother where you're going?'

'Of course not. And I won't tell her what you're up to, either.'

They exchanged a look as of rueful conspirators.

Saturday morning dawned clear and pleasant. It would certainly be hot by afternoon, but the unbearable heat and humidity had departed for a while.

The house was astir early, of course. The temporary help had returned and were making a good deal of noise as they completed final arrangements for the party. Mary had put out place settings and a large coffee urn in the dining room, along with a basket of assorted pastries and another of fruit. Breakfast on this frantically busy day was self-service, and not to be lingered over.

Mother was nervous and even shorter-tempered than usual. Elizabeth knew from experience that the only way to cope was to obey her commands immediately, apologize for imagined mistakes, and say as little as possible. She trotted back and forth on unnecessary errands, meanwhile trying to stay out of the way of the servants who were doing the real work. Mary and Susannah had also learned how to survive. They nodded agreement to Mrs Walker's every word and then went off and did what they knew really needed to be done.

The party would go well. It always did, thanks to Susannah's firm hand. With any luck Elizabeth would be able to slip away unobserved when the proceedings were well under way. By the time everything was over, she hoped, Mother would be in a good mood, stroked by everyone's compliments on the house, the garden, and the hospitality, and might not notice her daughter's surreptitious return. Mr Walker always left after he had helped greet everyone, so he didn't have to sneak away. Today he'd be visiting the Briggs family, but Mother wouldn't know that.

In odd moments of leisure, Elizabeth tried to find a home address for Mr Anthony. Antonelli wasn't listed in the telephone directory, and the only listing for Anthony was the shop. Probably the family didn't have a telephone. Many people still didn't. A phone line wasn't cheap, even a party line, and anyway, if the Anthony family lived at any great distance from the center of town the wires might not have been run out to their neighborhood. She thought about calling St Edmund's, but the Walker phone was in the hallway close to the kitchen door and people were going in and out constantly. Privacy would be impossible, let alone enough quiet to hear. No, she would just have to go to the church as soon as she could get away and hope someone would be there to answer her questions.

St Edmund's was a beautiful church, at least outside. Gothic in appearance, it had been completed only fifteen years before, and might never have been completed at all had it not been for John Farson. Almost a legend in Oak Park, he had been the richest man in town for years, and one of the most liberal-minded. In the late 1890s he had built a large and luxurious home, the most magnificent Oak Park had ever seen, and when the Catholics were struggling to build their church in the early years of the twentieth century, Farson allowed the parish to use his mansion for a big fundraiser. Most of his neighbors, some of whom were aghast at the idea of a Catholic church in their utopian community, kept their mouths shut. After all, Farson supported many worthy causes, and it didn't do to quarrel with a man with that much money.

Elizabeth wished Farson hadn't died ten years ago. He had been a friend of her father's and often visited the house, so she had met him. She'd been a child, of course, and hadn't been allowed to sit in on any of their discussions, but she retained an impression of a pleasant man who had cared very little what anyone else thought of him, so long as he could live with himself. He would, she thought, have had no tolerance at all for the Walosas Club, and would have put a quick stop to the arrest of Mr Briggs for no reason except prejudice.

However, John Farson had gone to his reward long ago, and she intended to try to put a spoke in the wheel of injustice if she possibly could.

She had to dress for the party. Her mother criticized her choice of clothing, her modest accessories, her hair, her face. 'I'm embarrassed for you to be seen in that old thing! It's at least two years out of date. Anyone would think we couldn't afford to dress you properly. And it isn't as if you didn't have nice pearls to wear instead of those old beads. What will people think?'

Elizabeth bit off her reply that, like John Farson, she didn't care what people thought. She simply murmured something that might have sounded like agreement and was grateful when Mary interrupted with a nervous question about a silver serving tray. Then guests began to arrive and she was expected to mingle for a few minutes.

Having greeted some neighbors, she stepped aside and watched the spectacle, for spectacle it was. The women were all middle-aged and dressed like flappers. Beads, fringe, layers of floating voile and lace, all of it draped over bodies that required severe compression to create the boyish silhouette the styles demanded. The dropped waists, on the other hand, worked well, since few of the women had actual waists anyway. Gray hair was bobbed and hidden under cloche hats. The women were posturing and posing, speaking in strangled 'society' voices as they assassinated characters left and right. From the comments she overheard, she surmised that many of them were members of the Walosas, though she had never met anyone who identified herself as such.

Elizabeth shuddered. Mother never cared about her guests' political views, only their social standings. That was so important that Zeke, poor dear, was stationed at the garden gate to make sure none of the 'wrong sort' got in. From that vantage point, he could hear much of the conversation, references to unsatisfactory servants, veiled insults to 'darkies' and foreigners, and some not so veiled. His face remained impassive. He had probably, she thought, had to tolerate much worse.

The few men present, who were probably husbands of those hyper-conservative women, looked hot and uncomfortable in their business suits and stiff, high collars. Dragged along as escorts and chauffeurs, no doubt. As Elizabeth watched, one of them slipped behind a bush and laced his punch from a pocket flask.

That broke her resolve to remain inconspicuous and uninvolved. She stepped up to the man. 'Excuse me, sir, but this is a law-abiding household and one in which no alcohol is used. I'll ask you to give me that flask.'

'And just who are you, missy, to be ordering me around?' His words were a little slurred. This latest nip was apparently not his first.

'My name is Elizabeth Walker Fairchild, and my mother is your hostess. The flask, please.'

'Be damned if I will! This is a free country, and I'll not be bossed by some uppity girl!'

His voice had risen. The scene was beginning to attract attention, but in typical crowd fashion, people turned, looked, and then distanced themselves from the embarrassment.

The man with the flask moved nearer, near enough that Elizabeth could smell his breath. She had dealt with enough drunken college boys to recognize the scent, and the attitude. She stood her ground. 'Sir, you know my name. Will you give me yours?'

'Be damned if I will. Like to give you somethin' else though, honey-pie.' Another step closer. 'Seems like you don't know how to be nice to important people. Seems like you need a little lesson.'

Elizabeth's back was against the shrubbery, and fear was beginning to creep in, when two people approached the scene, one from each direction. On her right was Zeke, on her left a woman she didn't know. Neither could be seen by the drunken lout.

Elizabeth shook her head slightly at Zeke. He nodded and stayed where he was. The presence of a black man could only make things worse. If the lout's ire was aroused by a determined woman, how much more by Zeke?

Then the woman came nearer and spoke, sharply. Not to Elizabeth, but to the lout. 'Herman, you're making a spectacle of yourself and embarrassing me! Put that flask away and apologize to Miss Walker!'

Elizabeth didn't bother to correct her name but murmured something and edged away. Zeke followed her. 'You all right, Miss Elizabeth?'

'A little shaky, but yes, I'm fine really. Thank you for trying to come to my rescue. I—I discouraged you because the man is an obvious bigot. And he's drunk.'

'Yes, miss, I could see that. And you thought he'd lose control at the sight of me.'

'I was afraid he might. Prejudice is a horrible thing, Zeke. So is a double standard. These people pretend to be in favor of law and order, but here's one of them, openly drunk in a village where alcohol can't be sold and drinking it is mightily frowned upon. And when his wife comes to scold him, her only worry is not that he's breaking the law, but what people will think. It makes me so *mad*! Hypocrites, the whole bunch!'

'That they are, Miss Elizabeth. They's a lot of hypocrites in this town. Most of 'em in that ladies' club.'

'The Walosas? I thought those two might be mixed up with that.' She nodded in the direction of the couple, who were now leaving the garden.

'You right about that. I've run into both of 'em a time or two. They's trouble.'

'Have they given you any trouble?' she asked sharply.

'Not me. I know how to do with mean white folks.'

'But you shouldn't have to! There should be laws—'

'Now, Miss Elizabeth, don't get all het up. We's used to it,' he said with resigned dignity. 'Got to get back to my work, if you're sure you all right.'

The hubbub had died down. Mother had apparently not noticed any of it, thank heaven. Elizabeth took several deep breaths, pulled herself together, and slipped out of the garden into the kitchen, where she begged a basket of food from Susannah and escaped.

She knew where St Edmund's was, though she had never visited there. Protestants were no more welcome in Catholic churches than the other way around. She had seen pictures, in newspaper accounts of weddings. It was to her Episcopalian eyes somewhat gaudy. The statuary all over the place certainly hinted of idolatry. But, she thought, to each his own. She'd worship the way she wanted; let others do the same. What really mattered, anyway, wasn't what one said on Sunday mornings but what one did the rest of the week, and by that standard, she was beginning to feel uneasily, she fell quite a bit short.

It was a rather long walk from her house to the church, which had been built in the part of town where its parishioners lived. The houses there were not as big or as attractive as her own. The lawns, though neatly maintained, were mere scraps compared with the gracious gardens Mrs Walker so gloried in. The day was growing very warm, and her basket got heavier and heavier. Elizabeth realized she would have been smart to change her shoes. True, her party shoes had lower heels than were fashionable, but the soles were thin and not suited to a long walk. Oh, well. If they fell apart, she could buy more. Unlike, she suspected, many of the residents of this neighborhood.

The rectory was next door to the church. Elizabeth walked up to the front door and knocked.

It was answered by a bustling sort of woman in an apron, wiping her hands on a towel. Elizabeth swallowed, suddenly unsure of herself. 'My name is Elizabeth Fairchild. I'd like to speak to the rector, please, if he's in.'

'Come in, dear, and sit down.' She gestured toward the parlor.

'Father's leaving in a few minutes, but I'll ask if he has time to talk to you for a little while.'

Elizabeth had imagined having to explain herself to the housekeeper, but evidently she was schooled to ask no questions. People probably came to the priest with all sorts of troubles. With a sudden qualm, Elizabeth wondered if she had been taken for a young woman 'in trouble' in the commonly used sense of the term. Oh, dear.

Footsteps descended the stairs and a man walked into the room. He had thick black hair and was wearing a long black cassock. 'I'm James Cole, the pastor here.' He extended his hand. 'What can I do for you, Miss Fairchild?'

'It's Mrs Fairchild,' she said, 'but that doesn't matter. I don't want to take up your time, but I'd like to pay a visit to Mr Anthony – I mean Mr Antonelli's family, and I don't know their address. He was a friend, and I'm so sorry about his death. I hoped there was something I might do to help.'

The priest looked at her searchingly. 'Have we met? I don't believe I recognize your name. Perhaps you attend Ascension?' The other big Catholic parish in town.

'No, I'm an Episcopalian. I attend Grace Church.'

'Ah.'

The single syllable spoke volumes. There had been a time in the not-too-distant past when the rector at Grace had not behaved very cordially to the Catholics in town, had in fact openly opposed the building plans of the Ascension parish. Though that attitude had since changed, or so Elizabeth hoped, she was sure bitterness still lingered.

She blushed. 'I know what you're thinking, Father, but my church isn't like that anymore. And even if they were, my opinions are my own, not dictated by anyone else. I try to respect everyone's right to practice their religion in the way that seems best to them.'

A clock on the mantel chimed the half hour.

'And I respected and liked Mr Anthony, as I knew him, and I would like to call on his family.' She looked the priest straight in the eye.

'I'm sorry,' he said. 'I should not have jumped to conclusions. I know your rector. He's a good man. It's just that . . . ah, well. What's past is past. As a matter of fact, I'm on my way to visit Mrs Antonelli myself. There will undoubtedly be a houseful of friends there, but if you wish to come with me, you're welcome.'

'I brought some food for them, but I wouldn't want to intrude on a private pastoral visit,' she began, but he smiled.

'Mrs Fairchild, as a friend of Enrico Antonelli, you will be welcomed. They'll probably hand you an apron and put you to work in the kitchen. There will be only a few Italians there, his family and close friends, but you'll find everyone warm and friendly.'

She managed a smile. 'Well, I don't know any Italian except opera lyrics, and I don't really know exactly what they mean, so if you're sure you don't mind . . .?'

He held the door for her and followed her out.

SIX

'I don't have a car,' said Father Cole, looking at her shoes, 'but it's not a long walk.'

'I know they're terribly impractical, but I didn't want to take time to change.'

'You were going to a party? Excuse me, that's none of my business.'

'I was leaving a party, my mother's garden party.'

She hadn't meant to get into that. Darn! Now the priest would think she was just a wealthy woman playing Lady Bountiful. She watched his face change.

'You're Mrs Walker's daughter?'

She admitted it. 'Again I can imagine what you're thinking, but my mother's values and mine do not always agree, Father. And I have just had an idea. I do want to see Mrs Antonelli and let her know that I liked— no. Why am I so shy about it? In a way, in the way of friendship, I truly loved her husband. He was almost my closest friend. We shared a love of beauty. For the sake of that love, I want to help his family. But if you think they might resent it, or be embarrassed, suppose you tell me what they might need, and I can supply it through the church, anonymously.'

She couldn't read his look, but she plowed ahead. 'My money is my own, Father, a bequest from a great-aunt. There's quite a lot of it, and I'm free to do with it as I like. In this case, I would like to help my friend's family.'

He said nothing for a long block.

She broke the silence. 'My mother comes from a wealthy family, as you probably know. She is . . . well known in philanthropic circles in Oak Park. My father is a teacher, as you may also know. He has little money of his own, but his ideas about how to spend it are similar to those of his friend John Farson. As are his attitudes about people, all people, not just those of his own class or holding his own beliefs. I take after my father.'

'I can see that you do. I will talk to Mrs Antonelli about her needs. This is where she lives.'

It was quite a nice house, not large, but pleasant. Flowers bloomed profusely around the foundation, and everything was spotlessly clean. The windows gleamed in the sunshine and one could see that the curtains inside were snowy white. The front door stood open; a babble of voices issued from it.

Elizabeth hesitated. This home was so very different from hers. What would the people be like? Even if not Italian, these people were probably all Catholic. She knew very few Catholics. Would they resent her? She could feel perspiration beading on her forehead, and not just from the heat.

If she had been alone she might have turned tail for home. But Father Cole smiled and gestured her inside, and she had no choice but to go ahead with it.

He was entirely accurate in his predictions, she realized. He introduced Elizabeth to the first woman they encountered. She smiled briskly and said, in unaccented English, 'Friends of Father Cole are always welcome here. We're just fixing some food for Luisa, and for visitors. Why don't you bring your basket in to the kitchen and we'll find something for you to do.'

Elizabeth hoped her smile looked genuine as she followed the woman into the crowded kitchen.

The basket was unneeded, Elizabeth saw. Food covered every surface. Fried chicken. Salads of every imaginable kind, including gelatin molds beginning to puddle in the heat. Meatloaf. Desserts from rice pudding to elaborate cakes.

The basket was kindly received and unpacked. An apron was produced. 'Don't want to get anything on that pretty dress, do we? This is big enough for two of you, but it's protection. Now let's see. Here are a couple of nice plates. Let's set out some of these cookies. My name's Carter, by the way, Thelma Carter. Fairchild, Father Cole said?'

'Yes, Elizabeth.' She looked at a pan of brownies cut into neat squares, uncertain about how to extract them.

Mrs Carter tutted. 'Oh, dear, now where's a spatula? Or a knife might work better for the first one or two. Here, let me tackle those and you can do these molasses cookies. Though you'll need a spatula for them, too. They look pretty well stuck to the pan.'

She rummaged in a drawer and found a broad knife and a spatula, and the two set to work.

Elizabeth tried not to look as awkward as she felt. Susannah had never allowed her to help in the kitchen. 'Mrs Carter, are you a parishioner at St Edmund's?'

'No, dear, just a neighbor. And you?'

'I'm . . . I was a customer at Mr Anthony's . . . Mr Antonelli's shop. I . . . we were friends. He was going to find me a watch to give to my father for his birthday.'

Now what on earth had prompted her to say that last? She felt her chin trembling and applied herself with new vigor to the stubborn molasses cookies. One flew off the cookie sheet onto the floor.

Mrs Carter picked up the cookie and kindly ignored the tears that threatened. 'You don't know the family, then.' She went on dealing with the brownies.

'I didn't even know he had a family until today.' She couldn't say any more. A tear trickled down her cheek, and then another. Impossible to pretend any further.

'My dear, it's all right, but try not to cry on the cookies. Salt won't improve them.'

Elizabeth pulled her handkerchief from her bodice. 'I'm sorry. It's just that I saw him only two days ago, at the shop, and he was so happy. He'd just bought a lovely piece of furniture, at an auction, I think, and showed it to me.'

'Then you can think about that, how happy he was on the last day of his life. Now. We've done the cookies, and this kitchen is getting very warm.'

That was an understatement. With all the women moving about in the small room, the temperature approached broiling point.

'Why don't you wash your face, if you can get to the sink? Then you can go pay your respects to Luisa. Mrs Antonelli. Father has probably finished talking with her.'

'Mrs Carter, you've been very good to me. I'd like to ask you
. . .' She hesitated. 'Do you think you could come outside with
me for a minute? It really is hot in here.'

'Let's use the back door,' the woman replied.

There was a breeze in the small back yard. Elizabeth fanned
herself with her hand and took a deep breath. 'The fact is, there's
something I need to find out. You see, I have no idea how well-
fixed Mrs Antonelli is. Now that her husband's gone, will she
have enough to live on? I'm sorry to be so blunt, but I'd like to
help her if I can. The only thing is, I don't know what she might
need.'

'You have money,' said Mrs Carter after a pause.

'Well – yes.'

'I thought you looked as if you'd never worked in a kitchen in
your life.' It was said matter-of-factly. 'Fairchild, you said?'

'Yes. My maiden name was Walker.' She sighed. It had been
nice for a little while to be anonymous, to be treated like anyone
else.

'I see.' A pause. 'And your husband?'

'I'm a widow. My husband died some years ago, in the war.
We were married for only a few months, and he was in France
almost all that time.' She, too, paused. This was being a difficult
conversation. 'Mrs Carter, I don't want you to think . . . whatever
you're thinking. I asked Father Cole to sound out Mrs Antonelli
about what she might need, but I'm not sure she'll be open with
him. I want to help her, but anonymously. I thought perhaps through
the church.'

She took a deep breath. 'I'm not just some rich woman trying
to be kind to the poor. It's not like that at all. I have far more than
I need. I work with all kinds of charities, but Mr Anthony was my
friend. I liked him a lot. And I'm a widow, like Mrs Antonelli
now. I had plenty of money when my husband died, but I felt very
alone. I—I lost my baby, too, so I had even more reason to grieve.

'Mrs Antonelli is in a different situation. She has her daughter
and her church and her friends. Look at all the people here to
grieve with her and wish her well and look after her! But she may
not have the money to supply her needs. I don't know that; I'm
guessing. I know the church and her friends will do all they can,
but I'm in a position to do a lot more, and I truly want to help.'
She made a 'that's all' gesture. 'I think I'd better go in and say a

few words to Mrs Antonelli, and then go home. My mother will
be wondering where I've gone.'

'Oh, yes, today is her big party, isn't it? That's why you're so
dressed up.'

'Yes. I had to make an appearance. And I really must be getting
back.'

Mrs Carter put out a hand. 'Not before we get one thing straight.
My dear girl, I wasn't judging you, just trying to size you up. Not
all rich people are self-righteous snobs, any more than all poor
people are deserving and trustworthy. I've learned a thing or two
after being on this earth at least twice as long as you. Don't worry.
The family has always been moderately well-off, but things will
be different now. I'll ask around, find out what Luisa needs, and
I'll let you or Father Cole know. I may not belong to that church,
but I know how much good they do in this neighborhood.' She
gave Elizabeth a pat. 'Don't try to see Luisa now. You'd just cry
again, and she doesn't need any more of that. Go home and placate
Mama. You're a good girl.'

Elizabeth left, feeling about five years old.

SEVEN

Elizabeth approached her home feeling as though she had
been gone for hours. She had visited another world and
forgotten her own for a while. It was disconcerting to return
and find the garden party at its peak, with her mother presiding
in full glory. 'There you are, dear,' she said in the sugary tone she
used in front of guests. 'We were all wondering where you'd gone.
Stuck with your nose in a book, probably.' She laughed the tinkly,
artificial laugh that always reminded Elizabeth of chalk squeaking
on a blackboard.

'Of course,' said one of the women nearby. She was jammed
into a waistless dress at least two sizes too small, and her feet
overflowed her shoes. 'We all know what a scholar your daughter
is, don't we?' Her tone was not pleasant, nor was the accompanying
titter. Too brainy to get a man, it said.

Elizabeth longed to make an equally nasty reply, something

along the lines that she preferred stuffing her head with learning to stuffing her stomach with too much food. Either that, or tell them where she'd really been, making a condolence call on an Italian Catholic family.

She did neither, but bestowed a meaningless smile on her mother and the other women and turned away. 'Such a shy girl,' said the fat lady, just loud enough for Elizabeth to hear.

Suddenly shaking with anger, she wondered how much longer she could continue to hide her feelings from these rich, hypocritical women, who smiled so sweetly while stabbing each other in the back. She wished she *had* told them where she'd been, wished she could have watched their faces as the shock penetrated. Disbelief, followed by horror, followed by utter blankness as they refused even to believe such unthinkable behavior. Then they'd leave the party, first in little groups of three or four, then in a stampede as the word spread in sibilant whispers. 'My dear, you can't imagine . . . obviously disturbed . . . her poor mother . . .' The party would be ruined. Her mother would rage at her and then retire with her worst headache ever.

And then her poor father would come home to the disaster and would bear the brunt of it. It was his fault, the tirade would begin, his fault that Elizabeth was so hard-hearted and peculiar. He refused to support Mrs Walker in her efforts to find another husband for the girl. She couldn't understand either of them. And on and on, until Mother finally made herself really sick and had to be ministered to, far into the night.

No, she couldn't have spoken the truth. But she continued to contrast the two households she had seen this afternoon. Mrs Antonelli had been surrounded by loving friends, genuine people, their voices loud with real grief and real comfort. Then there was this gathering of her mother's friends, the elite of Oak Park society, their well-bred voices saying nothing as they sipped fruit punch and nibbled at expensive little treats and checked to see whether anyone else's clothing and jewels topped theirs, all the while concealing the petty hatreds and squalid little jealousies that hid behind their polished façades.

She went in the house and up to her room to change into a practical dress and comfortable shoes. Leaving by the back way, she walked quickly up a side street to Mrs Hemingway's house.

Elizabeth had never cared a lot for Ernest. Though they had been in the same class in high school and graduated together, they had never been close. True, he was extremely good looking and could be charming when he wanted to be. He had a fine mind and was a good student, especially in English classes; he read voraciously and edited the school newspaper, but he was noted more for aggressively male pursuits like boxing and football. Elizabeth preferred music and had become attached to Ernest's mother when she first began her piano lessons. They were at ease together, although Elizabeth (along with almost everyone else in Oak Park) stood somewhat in awe of her commanding personality. It was possible that Mrs Hemingway was at the garden party, but unlikely. She and Mrs Walker didn't get along well, as both liked to run things and resented competition.

The neat maid who answered the door led Elizabeth to the spacious room where Mrs Hemingway taught piano and voice lessons and staged the occasional concert. The older woman was alone in the room, seated at the piano playing an unfamiliar tune. She looked up in surprise. 'Have I forgotten a lesson? Surely not!'

'No, no! I'm so sorry to interrupt you. Are you composing something new?'

'No, just revising an old tune that doesn't quite work. What can I do for you?'

'I just wanted to talk to you. But if you're busy . . .'

'Never too busy for you. Let's go to the parlor and be comfortable.'

They had barely taken their seats when the maid appeared with a tea tray, set it down and vanished.

'If you've been playing the good daughter at that party, you must be ready for some proper tea.'

'Thank you, I am more than ready. But I didn't stay at the party for more than a few minutes. I've been to a wake.'

Mrs Hemingway put down the teapot with a thump that rattled the china on the tray. 'Tell me!'

'I went to pay a condolence call on Mr Anthony's family.'

Her hostess considered that in silence while she added milk and sugar to Elizabeth's cup and then her own. 'You didn't tell your mother.' It was not a question.

'Of course not. She would . . . no, I didn't. I haven't told anyone except you. I knew you'd understand.'

'I knew you were his friend. I didn't know you were close to his family.'

'I'm not. I didn't even know his real name, nor that he was Italian. I should have guessed, I suppose, but I never did. The fact is, when my father gave me the details, I thought his family might well need some help after his death, monetary help, I mean, so I went to talk with their priest. But he was on his way to the Antonelli house, a pastoral call, and invited me to come with him.'

'Here, drink this.' Mrs Hemingway handed over the teacup and offered a plate of tea cakes. Elizabeth refused the cakes but drank the tea thirstily.

'You were quite right. My throat was dry. Anxiety, I suppose. It wasn't a comfortable visit.'

The older woman waited, sipping tea.

'It was like stepping into a different world,' said Elizabeth. 'Not just the difference of means, though that wasn't quite as I expected. The Antonellis weren't rich, but they were comfortable, in a nice house. No, it was the people. The house was crowded with friends and neighbors, people from the church, and I suppose family. A few of them were speaking Italian. It looked as if they'd all brought food. It was . . .' She struggled for a word. 'There was a warmth. There was . . . love.'

'And that made you uncomfortable.' It was said drily.

'Yes, because it was unlike anything I'd ever known. It was real.'

Mrs Hemingway snorted. 'As opposed to the nice, sedate, sterile gathering that was taking place at your home at that very moment.'

'Exactly.' She was silent for a moment. 'I've never really known people who let their emotions show. In public, I mean. My father . . . but not when other people are around, and not so—so noisily.'

'That, my dear girl, is probably one reason you love opera. The emotions are all there on the surface, and often very noisy indeed. And don't forget that your favorite composers are all Italian.'

Elizabeth smiled for the first time that day. 'I hadn't thought of that. Maybe that's why I liked Mr Anthony so much. I mean Mr Antonelli. He could be enthusiastic. He positively glowed the last time I saw him. He'd purchased a new piece, a lovely highboy, and he couldn't wait to show it to me.' Her eyes filled with tears, remembering the joy that was so soon ended forever.

But Mrs Hemingway was frowning. 'A highboy is an expensive piece of furniture. It was a really fine one, you say?'

'I'm not an expert, but he is. Was. And he knew all about the workmanship, the age, everything. He said it was the loveliest thing he'd ever seen.'

'Then how did a small-time dealer like him find the money to buy it? Oh, yes, he would have sold it for a sweet profit, but he had to acquire it in the first place. Where did that money come from?'

'I don't know. Maybe . . . maybe he was allowed to pay part of it, and the rest when he sold it.'

'Sweetheart, you may be able to buy stocks on margin, though it's a fool's game, but not antiques. Cash on the barrelhead. You've never been involved in business or finance, have you?'

She shook her head. 'My mother does all that.'

'Yes, of course,' said Mrs Hemingway drily. 'Well, I can tell you, any small business has a tough time making it, but especially antiques. The cost of inventory is exorbitant, and the return anything but guaranteed.' She paused. 'Besides the highboy, did you notice anything of special value in the shop when you were there? When was that, by the way?'

Elizabeth had to stop and think. 'Thursday. The—the day he died. It feels like much longer than that.'

'The day he died! Was he acting any different? Worried? Afraid?'

'Just happy about the highboy. And then a little distressed because he didn't have what I'd wanted to buy.'

'And what was that?'

Elizabeth explained. 'And he didn't really want to sell the watch to that man, but the customer insisted. I think—' She broke off.

'You think the customer was – shall we say – not quite honest?'

'I think he was a gangster, if you want to know. And I have no real reason to believe that. It's just a feeling.'

'And later in the day, the poor man is murdered. Elizabeth, I think you should tell the police about that customer.'

Elizabeth shrugged. 'I thought of that, but what good would it do? They've already made up their minds. Dad says they suspect Mr Briggs, who's a good friend of the Anthony – I mean Antonelli family. He'll be arrested today, Dad thinks.'

Mrs Hemingway stood and began to pace. 'Briggs! That's absurd! Briggs is a fine musician, a singer as well as a pianist. He's wasted at the high school. He should be singing opera, not trying to teach adolescents! Why is he a suspect? It's ridiculous.'

'He's Italian. And Catholic. And knows the family well. In this town . . .'

She let the sentence trail off. There was no need to continue. Mrs Hemingway knew Oak Park as well as she did.

Elizabeth knew she sometimes exaggerated the hypocrisy of the village. Its people were no worse than most people. They wanted to remain in their snug, comfortable houses and cling to their snug, comfortable lives. Where was the harm in that? Let the foreigners do whatever outlandish things they wanted to do, so long as they kept to their place. Which was not next door to the 'real' Oak Park citizens, upright people who went to church (Protestant) on Sundays and spoke English and never touched a drop of alcohol. At least not in public. But those Catholics – why, they even had wine in church!

There was a long silence. 'You think the police won't do anything,' said Mrs Hemingway at last.

'Why should they?' said Elizabeth bitterly. 'They have a suspect right under their noses. Looking for someone else would only stir up trouble. Around here, there's plenty of trouble just waiting to be stirred up.'

'The Mob, you mean. Though there's never been much trouble with the Mob here. Probably because Oak Park is dry. There aren't any taverns to fight over, no places for the bootleggers to make money. But if the police were to open an investigation into the death of an Italian man, who had contact with a possible gangster just hours before his death, what would happen?'

Mrs Hemingway let the question hang in the air. They both knew the answer. Though the gangsters who lived in Oak Park were usually peaceable, they could make big trouble if they wanted.

'So they'll throw Paul Briggs in jail and let him rot there,' Elizabeth said finally. 'A musician, in a jail cell where they won't even let him sing, let alone listen to music. He'll die without it.'

'That's if they don't have him tried and convicted and hanged. That would be a quick death, anyway.'

'How could they possibly convict him without evidence?' Elizabeth protested. 'And there can't be any evidence, because he didn't do it.'

'Oh, my dear child, you can't possibly be that naïve. They can get all the evidence they need. Are you really not aware that there are people in this community who will lie their heads off to get rid of one more troublemaker?'

'The Walosas,' Elizabeth groaned. 'I'd forgotten for the moment.'

'Yes, well, I forget about them as often as I can, but that doesn't make them disappear. A lot of their rhetoric is just that, just talk, but it's dangerous talk, and they're dangerous people.'

'Their husbands can be dangerous, too.' She told Mrs Hemingway about the encounter at the party.

'My dear, what a nasty experience! I'm so sorry, and so glad Zeke was there.'

'It was the man's wife who hauled him off, though.'

'And that's my point. The men of the Ku Klux Klan are bigger and louder. They're the ones who organize parades and burn crosses and lynch people. But it's the women who keep them under control, at least when they want to. And it's the women who spread the poison, quietly, insidiously. They teach their children to hate. They cloak it all in sweetness and light. "We must keep our children safe from impure ideas. We want to bring them up as good Methodists." Or Presbyterians, or Congregationalists, or whatever. Have you never seen them in action at one of your committee meetings?'

'No. Our rector won't allow it at the church, as you may know, and none of my other meetings have speakers.'

'Then you're among the fortunate few. They love talking to women's groups, and church affiliation makes it all seem innocent, even praiseworthy. No, Elizabeth, never underestimate the influence of a group of determined women. They incite their husbands and the rest of the community to action. Terrifying action.'

Elizabeth had been growing more and more restive. Now she stood. 'Then who *is* going to do something about Mr Briggs? My father went to visit his family this afternoon, just to offer support, but that isn't enough. The poor man has to be given fair treatment. There has to be justice for him, and for poor dear Mr Anthony.'

Mrs Hemingway also stood. 'Then we're going to have to start the search for what really happened. We'll need help. Two women, even strong and influential women, won't have much impact.'

Elizabeth demurred. 'Influential? You are, but who am I?'

The older woman shook her head pityingly. 'You are the daughter of a wealthy family. You have money of your own. You are known to every charitable institution in this village. Of course you are influential! But we two are not enough. What about that young man of yours, the one who takes you to Ravinia and the symphony?'

'He – I – if you're referring to Fred Wilkins – he isn't "my

young man". He's just a good friend who loves music as much as
I do.'

'Right.' Mrs Hemingway's voice dripped with sarcasm. 'Of
course. He is also a rising young attorney. He certainly knows
people who know people. And he'll do anything you ask.'

Elizabeth said nothing.

Mrs Hemingway gave her a sharp look. 'And your father?'

'He'll do what he can. But my mother . . .'

'Yes, of course. I can deal with your mother if she gets out of
hand.'

How? wondered Elizabeth. One domineering woman trying to
stop another? Well, maybe.

'Now, we can't waste any more time,' Mrs Hemingway went
on. 'You go home and call your— Call Fred. I'll phone some
people I know. But Elizabeth . . .' She hesitated. 'Be careful. You
know this could be dangerous?'

'I do know. We're talking about hunting down a murderer. I'd
very much rather leave it to the police, but we both think that
won't work. I'll go cautiously. I wonder – would any of Ernest's
friends be likely to help? He has pretty liberal views, or at least
he used to. Of course I haven't followed his career since he left
Oak Park.'

Mrs Hemingway's face closed up, and Elizabeth realized she
shouldn't have talked about Ernest. What little she had heard about
him had not been such as would please a rather rigid mother:
rumors of heavy drinking, womanizing . . . Oh, dear.

'I have very little contact with his friends now. I doubt they
could help. Now please do try to take care.'

And exactly how, she mused as she walked rapidly home, does
one go about taking care when one doesn't know where the danger
lies?

EIGHT

The garden party was nearly over, a few stragglers just
leaving. Zeke had left his post at the gate. Elizabeth walked
into a silent house – the silence left behind when frenetic

activity dwindles to exhaustion. Her mother sat in her favorite chair in the parlor, eyes closed, shoes off, a glass of iced tea on the table at her side. Her mouth was open and she was snoring slightly.

She would hate to be seen like that. Elizabeth backed quietly out of the doorway and made for the kitchen.

The phone sat in the hallway. Elizabeth hesitated before picking it up. Saturday. Fred wouldn't be at the office. He didn't play golf. It was nearing suppertime; he'd probably be at home. And Elizabeth didn't know his phone number. She had never before called him; he was always the one to call her.

She took a deep breath, lifted the receiver, and dialed zero for the operator.

'Mr Frederick Wilkins, please,' she said, trying to sound calm and authoritative. 'I don't know his number.'

'That would be Euclid two-eight-four-two.' The operator sounded bored. 'I'll ring it for you.'

The receiver buzzed in her ear. Once, twice, three times. Maybe he wasn't home. Maybe she would be spared this embarrassment. Oh, but then what about poor Mr Briggs?

'Hello?' A cool voice, neither welcoming nor hostile.

A deep breath. 'Fred, this is Elizabeth.'

'Elizabeth! Is something wrong?'

Because I never call him, she thought, he thinks something awful must have happened.

Well, something awful *has* happened. Mr Anthony . . . 'Fred, I need to talk to you. It's nothing about my family; don't worry. But it is urgent.' She looked at her watch. 'I only have an hour or so before supper. Can I meet you somewhere?'

'Pleasant Home, the park?'

'That's perfect, unless something is happening there today.'

'I don't think so. It's early in the summer yet. Fifteen minutes?'

She agreed and put down the receiver. It would be good to shift some of the burden to Fred's shoulders. And it would be good to do it at the mansion John Farson had built, with its extensive grounds open to the public. Even though John had long ago departed this life, and the house was now owned by Herbert Mills, somehow Farson's sense of tolerance, of even-handed justice, seemed to pervade the park. It was a soothing place.

The heat of the day was less oppressive under the trees of the park. As mealtime approached, most of the children who played there had been called home, so it was quiet. Fred was there before her, waiting at the gate.

Elizabeth was startled and somewhat alarmed by how glad she was to see him. She tried to temper the warmth of her smile.

'You sounded upset on the phone. What's wrong?'

'As I said, it's nothing about me or my family.'

'Then it's Mr Anthony, isn't it?'

She frowned. She was, it seemed, becoming transparent. She much preferred to hide her feelings. 'Well, more about Mr Briggs,' she said, and was pleased that her voice was steady. 'You know that he's likely to be arrested?'

'Has been arrested,' Fred corrected. 'This afternoon. I just heard.'

She bit her lip. 'I suppose it was inevitable. I've talked it over with Mrs Hemingway, and we both feel that the police are unlikely to look any further, even though there's no evidence whatever to connect him with the crime.'

'I'm afraid there is, though,' said Fred. 'You haven't heard the latest. There are witnesses who say that Briggs went to the shop late Thursday afternoon.'

A knot tightened in her stomach. 'What witnesses?'

'Three very respectable women. They had thought about shopping there for some gifts but saw that the place had closed. They didn't think much about that; Anthony often closed early when he had a delivery to make or needed to attend an auction. They were surprised when they saw Briggs inside.'

'How do you know all this? I haven't seen today's *Oak Leaves* yet, but they wouldn't have had time to deal with events this afternoon.' The local paper would follow the case assiduously, of course. It was the hottest local news in years. But deadlines were deadlines, and they wouldn't put out an extra only hours after their regular edition.

'No. There's a full account of the murder, correcting a lot of the mistakes the *Trib* made, but nothing about an arrest. No, Mrs Briggs called the office. Her husband is going to need a good lawyer. Not me,' he answered her eager look. 'I'm too junior, and I've done very little criminal work. No, it'll go to Sanders. They called me because I'm going to have to take over some of the work Sanders is doing now.'

'That means you'll be putting in more time at the office.'

'Sadly, yes. I'll make sure to save time for Ravinia, though!'

Elizabeth dismissed Ravinia with a wave. 'I was hoping you might have some time to look into the murder. Fred, Mr Briggs didn't do it!'

'I agree it's unlikely. He's a mild-mannered sort of man, and a fine musician. But he was seen—'

'Seen by whom? Who were those women?'

His expression changed. He looked closely at her face. 'You're taking this very seriously, aren't you?'

'Yes. Fred, Mr Anthony was Italian. And Catholic. So is Mr Briggs. In this village that can mean that they are . . . are negligible. The police can tidy away the case as just one more instance of irresponsible immigrants getting into trouble. Nothing to do with the decent citizens of Oak Park.' Her distress had been replaced by anger. 'I don't gamble, as a rule. But this time I will bet you any amount you care to name that those "witnesses" are members of the Walosas Club, and that they are lying through their teeth.'

Fred looked at her even more intensely. 'If you're right, then there's one more thing they're lying about. You're not going to like this. Nor do I. Briggs isn't the only person those women claim they saw at Anthony's Emporium.'

'But then there's another suspect! Why would you say I wouldn't like it?'

'Because the other person they say they saw was you.'

'Well, I was there. But earlier in the day. You know exactly when I was there, because I saw you just afterwards. I don't see why this is a problem.'

'They say you went back. They say they saw you later, around the time Briggs was there.' He leaned forward, elbows on his knees, hands in the prayer position. 'Elizabeth, where did you go and what did you do the rest of that day?'

'Are you accusing me—' Her voice rose.

He slapped the bench. 'No! Don't be a fool! And keep your voice down.' He glanced from side to side. 'There are still a few people around. Of course I'm not accusing you of anything. I'm trying to determine how your time is accounted for from the time you left me until seven or so, when Mr Anthony was found. I hope you were with someone for every minute.'

'Of course I wasn't, not for every minute! And so much has happened . . . I'll have to think.'

'I saw you get on the trolley. Did you go straight home?'

'Yes, I wanted to give Mother the gift I'd found for her. I knew she'd be angry that I left, with the party coming up, even though there was nothing useful I could do to help. I gave it to her, and it did sweeten her mood a little. And then . . . I don't know.'

'It was choir practice night. What did you do between the time you got home and when you left for church?'

'I don't remember. There couldn't have been much time. I think I went upstairs to wash and change, because my clothes were positively sticking to me. And then we had a light supper, and then Dad drove me to church. I usually walk, but it was so hot, and I wanted to get there a little early. I'm singing a solo Sunday . . . oh, heavens, that's tomorrow! And I haven't looked at it or thought about it, and it's the last choir Sunday of the year, and—'

He patted her arm. 'Don't worry about it. You'll be fine. You always are. What are you singing?'

'"Come unto Him" from *Messiah*. Jennifer is leading off with "He shall feed His flock".'

'And you've sung *Messiah* so often you could do it in your sleep. The point is you were with people from the time you left me until you came home from choir at – when?'

'It was well after nine, I think. Later than usual, because of all the extra music for the last Sunday of the season, and we had to practice with the men's choir, too.'

'Did you walk home?'

'Yes. It was still hot, so we took it pretty slowly.'

'We?'

'Jennifer came with me. She only lives a couple of blocks away, and she wanted to talk about the music.'

'Good. So if it comes to that, you'll have no trouble proving exactly where you were the whole time.'

'Will it "come to that"?'

'Not if Sanders and I have anything to say about it.'

'But he's been hired to defend Mr Briggs, not me.'

'Yes, but you see, when he can prove that the ladies – I use the term loosely – are lying about seeing you there at the critical time, it also throws doubt on their statement about seeing Briggs.'

'We need more than doubt, Fred. We need to know who the actual murderer is.'

'That won't be easy to find out.'

'I know.' She sat in a depressed silence. 'But what I don't understand is why those . . . people – I won't call them ladies – why they should have made up the lies about me. They hate Mr Briggs because of his religion. What do they have against me? I don't even know any of them.'

'They know who you are, though. You're an Episcopalian, a member of a church that spurns them. You're known to be a liberal. Your father is known to be friendly with untouchables like Briggs. You have refused to remarry, and since marriage and family represent their ideal for womankind, you're a Bad Example. Your social position in the village is high enough that they are loath to attack you directly, but if they can blacken your name this way, they'll be delighted.'

She shuddered. 'It's . . . sick. It frightens me.'

'All hatred is sick, Elizabeth. These are dangerous people.'

She thought for a fleeting moment of telling Fred about the incident at the party but dismissed the idea. He would only get angry and protective, which was not useful.

She waved a hand in an ambiguous gesture. 'That's what Mrs Hemingway said. Even more dangerous than the men, she said. She also said they would produce evidence. They've been very quick about it.' She took a deep breath, raised her head and set her chin. 'And we must be just as quick to fight back. What do you think we should do first?'

He thought for a moment. 'The first move is mine, I think. I'll go to the office and talk to Sanders. He's bound to be working late, even though it's Saturday. I'll tell him just what you've told me about your activities on Thursday. That way he can pre-empt any unwise move toward you on the part of the police.'

'I think I'd better talk to Dad. He'll know about the false evidence if he spent the afternoon with the Briggs family, and I don't want him to hear from someone else what's being said about me. Then . . . well, I'll think of something. The man who found Mr Anthony might know more. He's a place to start, anyway. I wonder if the police even bothered to question him closely, since they were sure they had their man.'

'Probably not. And you're right, he's the place to start. But Elizabeth, I want you to make me one solemn promise. You must not talk to him, or anyone else you think of, alone. Take me with you, or someone from the choir, or Zeke – any able-bodied man.

I know you're an intelligent and capable woman, but you are also slender and not accustomed to violent physical effort. It's not just the Walosas you're up against, I remind you, though they're bad enough. Their violence is mostly verbal, I admit, but they have husbands and sons who may be less restrained. But behind all of this is someone who has killed once and won't hesitate to kill again. Promise me – no solo expeditions.'

She stood, very glad that she had not mentioned her nasty little encounter at the garden party. 'I promise. I do know, Fred. And I'm afraid of them all – the gangsters and the sweet hypocrites and all. But poor Mr Anthony is dead, and if no one else is going to seek justice for his murderer, I am. With help, yes. But I'm not going to stop until I've learned the truth.'

NINE

Elizabeth had no time to collect her thoughts before sitting down to supper. It was, to her relief, a simple supper that didn't keep her at table for long. Her mother was very tired, but in a self-congratulatory mood that kept her remarks focused on herself and the success of the party, and required little response from anyone else beyond an occasional murmur of agreement.

As soon as she could, Elizabeth asked to be excused and went up to her room, where she was joined shortly by her father. He sat down heavily on the bed. 'You've heard, I suppose. Mr Briggs has been arrested.'

'Yes. I talked to Fred just before supper. His firm is acting for the defense. You know about the "evidence"?'

Her tone added the quotation marks.

'No. How could there be any evidence? He certainly didn't do it.'

She explained. 'And Dad, before you hear it some other way, they tried to implicate me, too. I was in fact at the shop that afternoon, and I saw Fred right after I left. He made me remember every single thing I did after I left for home, and he's telling the lawyer who's acting for Mr Briggs. He thinks the fact that they lied about me will weaken what they say about Mr Briggs.'

'Possibly. Possibly. But there is another way to look at it, Bets. Did anyone, anyone reliable, see Mr Anthony alive after you left the shop?'

That stunned her. She drew in a sharp breath. 'I . . . don't know. I went across to the hotel after I left the shop to get something cold to drink, and Fred came in just after that. We sat at a corner window but I was watching for the trolley. I didn't see anyone go into the Emporium, but I wasn't looking that way. I can ask Fred. But Dad! Would anyone believe – *could* anyone believe – that I could stab a man? Not to mention the fact that I could have had no possible motive? And don't they know when he died?'

Her voice had risen as she stood and began to pace the room.

'Hush, dear. You don't want your mother and the servants to hear. Certainly I will speak to Fred and ask if he saw anyone enter the shop, or saw Mr Anthony through the window. But you keep forgetting that we aren't necessarily dealing with facts here. The police are concerned, most of all, with keeping the peace in our little community. They can do that most easily by going with the flow. They have a suspect. They're not likely to rock the boat.'

'Well, I am!' She kept her voice low, but it was as emphatic as if she had shouted. 'I will not let hatred and bigotry pervert justice! I'll rock any boats necessary—'

Her father held up a hand. 'My darling girl, think! You're not in the habit of going off half-cocked. You're an intelligent, self-possessed, calm woman. You must know what you're proposing to get yourself into. Money and social position can't protect you against everything, you know. What's happened to your usual cool judgment?'

She sank down onto the bed. 'I don't know, Dad.' The fight had gone out of her. 'I think it's because I really cared about Mr Anthony. He was my friend. I don't have many friends.'

'You've wanted it that way.' He said it calmly, as an obvious fact. 'You keep everyone at arm's length.'

'Well, yes, I suppose I do. I never made a conscious decision to be that way, but it's easier. Things don't hurt if you're just an observer.'

'No. You're spared a great deal of pain. Of course, you also miss out on a great deal of joy. I've worried about that, you know.'

'Yes, well now I've broken my rule. I allowed Mr Anthony to become a real friend.' She sounded bitter. 'And look at all the joy it's brought me.'

'Cynicism is just as good a barrier as detachment,' her father said evenly.

That did it. His understanding, his calm acceptance of her irresolute frame of mind, broke through her defenses. She threw herself into his arms and sobbed like a baby, looking to her daddy for comfort as she had at age five when she had fallen out of a swing and skinned her knees and elbows.

When she reached the sniffling stage, he supplied a large handkerchief and then a damp cloth to wash her face.

'Better?'

'I think so. Except I feel like a fool.'

'Best thing you could have done. And long overdue. You've kept a tight rein on your emotions for years.'

'I had to. I couldn't . . .'

'You thought you couldn't, which I suppose is much the same thing. Now.' He took her gently by the shoulders and held her away from him. 'You have some plans to make, and some decisions, but now is not the time to do any of that. I'm going to send Mary up with a cup of tea, and you're going to drink it and take a nice warm bath and go to bed. I know it's early, but it's been a trying day, and you need to be up early tomorrow for choir.' He kissed her and left the room.

She thought she ought to resent being treated like a child, but oh, how nice it was to be told what to do in that voice of firm kindness. Dad seldom took the reins in the household. It was simpler to let Mother control everything. She had the money, after all, and the dominant personality. But from time to time he exerted his authority, and when he did even Mother conceded. She remembered, as she lolled in her bath, the time when she was nine and Mother wanted her to take dancing lessons. She hadn't cared one way or another until she saw the dress she would have to wear, all frills and lace, with a ruffled petticoat and a big ribbon in her hair. She had refused, and there had been the most terrible scene until Dad stepped in and put his foot down. 'That doesn't suit her at all, Mildred. Either she wears something else, or you forget about the lessons.'

The lessons were never mentioned again. Instead her father enrolled her in piano lessons with Mrs Hemingway. That had led, when she was older, to voice lessons, and they'd been pure joy.

And just a few years ago, when she wanted to go to college

and try to put her shattered life back together, Mother had insisted that she enroll at Concordia. It was so close she could still live at home, and it would prepare her to become a teacher, a respectable job a woman could take until she got married.

But she didn't want to be a teacher. The thought of working with children was pure pain. And she didn't need a job; that bequest from Great-Aunt Emily, wisely invested, would support her comfortably for the rest of her life. What she needed was to get away from home, to nourish her brain, to restore the sense of self that she'd lost with the death of her husband and child. Mother refused to understand that. Dad quietly helped her apply to Northwestern, found her an apartment in the city, and turned a deaf ear to Mother's expostulations.

She went to sleep cradled in her father's love and understanding.

Morning came all too soon. Yesterday's memories and problems had come flooding back as soon as she woke, and glancing over the account of the murder in yesterday's *Oak Leaves* hadn't helped. By now she knew more about the crime than the newspaper reporters did, which was an odd and unsettling feeling. Elizabeth breakfasted on coffee. She never ate much before singing, though Susannah clucked and scolded and offered freshly baked cinnamon rolls. In any case, she was too upset about Mr Anthony to have any appetite. She accepted a second cup of coffee, though, and took it out to the terrace to do a little quiet vocalizing. She didn't want to wake the neighborhood. Most especially she didn't want to wake her mother, who was sleeping the sleep of the righteous.

What would Mother say when she found out that Elizabeth was planning to investigate Mr Anthony's death?

And she would find out. In a village like Oak Park, there was no such thing as a secret. The only reason she hadn't heard about it yesterday was the party, which had kept the gossips occupied all afternoon. The fact that today was Sunday would slow them down a bit, but phones would start ringing the minute everyone was home from church. It didn't bear thinking about.

'So I won't think about it,' she said aloud to the cats, who had followed her to the sunny terrace in hopes of a snack. They yawned in reply.

'Trying to wake up properly?' Her father came outside, bearing a cup and the coffee pot. He lifted the pot, eyebrows raised in question.

'No, thanks, I've had two already. Any more and I'll be flying to the balcony and singing three tones sharp.'

'Maybe I'd better have a couple more, then. I'm always flat in the hymns.'

'Dad, you don't sing flat. You get off into another key altogether. Several, before the hymn is done. But never mind. Your heart is in it.'

He sipped his coffee. 'You all warmed up? Got the high note?'

'I think so. I had to whisper out here. I'll wait till I get to church to let it out. It isn't all that high, only a G. I'll be all right.'

'Better than all right. You always are. And what about your troubles? All right in that department, too?'

'I still don't know what to do, exactly. But I'm ready to do it, when I figure it out. I'll face Mother when I have to.'

'I'll help if I can.'

'I know, Dad.' She smiled at him. 'You always come through when things get rough. I'll be fine.'

'Want me to drive you to church, or are you taking your car?'

'I'll walk. It's a beautiful day, and it'll settle me. I'll walk home after church, too. You don't need to wait for me.'

'Just be careful.'

She knew he wasn't warning her about traffic dangers or uneven sidewalks that might turn an ankle.

She wasn't dressed in her 'Sunday best', but in a simple cotton dress. She'd be swathed in cassock and surplice most of the morning, which would make it even hotter up there in the crowded chancel. The choir stalls had been constructed with the male choir in mind. The extra chairs needed for the women used every inch of spare space. She knew she'd be dripping wet before the morning was over. No point in ruining something nice.

She grinned to herself, remembering the old adage: horses sweat, men perspire, ladies glow. Well, she'd be glowing like a house afire.

She was very early, so she was able to get into her vestments without having to talk to anyone. Good. She needed to plan how she was going to answer the questions.

For there would be questions, and comments. Some people

would be kind. Some would pretend to be kind. 'I'm only saying this for your own good, my dear.' A few would be openly censorious. She had a good idea who the latter would be, and she might be able to avoid those harpies. It was amazing, she thought sadly, how much 'anger, hatred, malice, and all uncharitableness', in the words of the Litany, could be found in your average congregation.

She sat down at the piano, sang a few scales *sotto voce*, and then opened up her full voice in the first few bars of her solo for the morning.

'Splendid, splendid, my dear.' It was the voice of the choirmaster, the director of the men and boys' choir who this morning was also leading the combined choirs. 'Don't use it all up on practice!'

'No danger of that.' Her own director, the woman who led the women's choir, had come into the room. 'She can sing like that till the cows come home.'

The two directors didn't always get along well. Mr Whitcomb made an inarticulate noise expressing doubt and left the room.

Mrs Clayton came over to the piano and said in a low tone, 'Are you all right, Elizabeth? It might be a little . . . difficult this morning. If you'd rather not stay for church, we'll be fine with just Jennifer and the "Flock". You could go home and hide.'

'Thank you, Mrs Clayton. I'll be fine. I love to sing. Well, you know that. Music actually helps.'

'Soothes the savage breast?'

'Something like that. It's partly the sheer beauty of it and partly the concentration that drives out everything else. In any case, hiding is not my way of dealing with problems.'

'No. You prefer to pretend they don't exist. Ice them over, as it were.'

'Or freeze them out. That's what my father accused me of doing. And he was right.' She dropped her hands from the keyboard. 'I've made a resolution. I'm going to try not to react that way anymore. I've been an ice maiden for too long. Now I'm going to try to face my troubles. It's the only way to solve them.'

'It can hurt. A lot. And – it can be dangerous.'

'I know.' She played a few bars of the Chopin 'Funeral March'. 'I suppose everyone knows what I'm trying to do.'

'Probably. Oak Park is not a big place, and this murder is the most exciting thing that's happened here in years. The grapevine is working overtime.'

Elizabeth made a face. 'And spreading the usual lies, no doubt. Well, I'll just have to deal with it. Maybe I'll hold onto my frozen-face persona a little longer.'

Church choirs are known to be chatty organizations. Even on a Sunday morning, with the service imminent, the noise level in the rehearsal room was high when they had all drifted in. The woman clustered around Elizabeth, who smiled absently and said, 'You'll excuse me. I need to concentrate on this,' and buried her nose in her music. The men, just as curious, were more subtle. Their technique was to conduct conversations, in voices pitched just a trifle too loud, about the murder and her scandalous behavior in consorting with the Catholics. They hoped she would answer back. She didn't.

The boys went on being boys, rowdy and mischievous. This morning Elizabeth wasn't exasperated with them, as she often was. At least they took no interest in her affairs.

Mr Whitcomb stepped up to his music stand and tapped it with his baton. It was a moment or two before the silence was complete, but it did come. He was a good director and somewhat intimidating, even to the boys. A signal to the pianist and the warm-up began.

The choirs were well-trained and well-rehearsed. There was little for Mr Whitcomb to correct. A cut-off here, a dynamic level there. He took only a couple of bars of each solo, just to make sure the entrances were smooth, and took the boys through their descant on the closing hymn. Then they were ready to line up and process in, to the rousing 'Holy, Holy, Holy' always sung on Trinity Sunday.

Elizabeth was not unaware of the eyes that fixed on her as she walked up the aisle, nor of the nudges and exchanged glances in the congregation. But the music carried her along, as it always did. She didn't meet the staring eyes but feasted on the stained glass, the glorious east window over the altar. She didn't need to look at her hymnal; she knew this one by heart and even sang the alto for a couple of verses, just for fun. The procession was carefully timed so that both choirs, male and female, ended up at their places for the final 'Blessed Tri-ni-tee!'. A solemn 'Amen,' sung in four parts, and the service began.

It was indeed hot in the chancel. The stone church was normally comfortable, but this morning there were too many people crammed into too small a space, wearing several layers of clothing and working hard. Yes, thought Elizabeth, singing properly was hard work. And a lot of hot air was expelled in the process.

The service ran smoothly. The anthem sung by the combined choirs was tricky, but they had practiced it thoroughly, and it went without a hitch. The two Handel solos, during Communion, were lovely, and singing at that time meant that Elizabeth and Jennifer could go to the altar among the last of the congregation instead of earlier with most of the choir, which she appreciated. The ordeal of the day was yet to be faced, during coffee hour. She was happy to put off thinking about that as long as possible.

But at last the benediction was pronounced and the recessional hymn sung, and everyone was back in the choir room getting out of vestments and congratulating themselves on difficult music well sung and complaining about the heat. And, of course, converging on Elizabeth.

'You sang beautifully, my dear,' said one of the altos, a stout gray-haired woman who hoped she would be described as middle-aged. 'But then you always do. I hope it wasn't too hard on you, singing a solo when you must be so upset.'

Elizabeth took a deep breath. 'I'm not upset, Mrs Sloane. I'm angry.' She hung up her vestments.

Mrs Sloane was ready to offer condolence and dig for details. She was put off her stride. 'Angry? Oh, well I can see why you'd be angry at being suspected of such a nasty little crime.'

'I am not angry at foolish people's accusations, Mrs Sloane.' She knew how to project her voice. Though not loud, it carried over the babble, which quieted to listen. 'I am angry over the death of a good man, and the callousness of a community which accepts it as a "nasty little crime" and is willing to gloss it over. I am angry at suspicion directed at a man, a fine musician, whose only crime is being different. I am angry at everyone who prefers to look the other way. I intend to investigate Mr Anthony's murder, since the police seem unwilling or unable to do so, and I intend to try to help his family in any way I can. I'm sure most of you will be happy to contribute money and/or food to that cause. I'm on my way to speak to Dr Edsall about setting up collection boxes. Excuse me.'

She was out the door before the stunned silence gave way to a shocked chorus of recriminations.

She was trembling as she approached the sacristy, where the rector and his acolytes were getting out of their robes, trembling not with fear but with warm anger.

'I'm sorry to bother you,' she began.

'Never a bother. I wanted to thank you for your lovely singing, Elizabeth. That aria is one of my favorites.'

'Thank you. Mine, too. Do you have a moment to talk?'

Dr Edsall ushered her into his office, and she briefly explained her plan for collecting donations. He listened, shaking his head. 'It's a kind and Christian thing to do, Elizabeth, but I don't know how successful it will be. I'm happy to let you put out a box or two in the social hall, but some in this congregation can be—'

'Narrow-minded. I know. I'm doing it partly to shame them, and I admit it. I intend to half-fill the food box, and I'll use a big pickle jar for the money, so people can see what others have given.'

'Others, meaning yourself.'

'Yes, to start. It may not work, but there are lots of good-hearted people here, too. I think this church needs to show the Catholic community that we no longer harbor the prejudice of years ago.'

The rector nodded. 'Indeed. Let me know when you want to bring over your box and jar, and I'll be sure the church is open.' He stood. 'I'm afraid I have to go to coffee hour, unless there's something else . . .?'

Elizabeth stood. 'Just pray for us. We need all the help we can get.'

Later she wondered just what she meant with that 'we'.

TEN

Of course by the time she got home, her mother had heard all about her activities that morning. Though Mrs Walker was only a Christmas-and-Easter churchgoer, she somehow managed to hear all about what went on.

Elizabeth had decided what she had to do, but she managed to avoid Mother until after she'd washed and changed her clothes (damp with sweat, as she'd known they would be). She couldn't skip Sunday dinner. It was all cold, as suited the weather, but Susannah was back to her usual form. The meal was delicious and beautiful. It began with a Waldorf salad, to which Susannah had daringly added some walnuts, and proceeded through cold chicken and ham served with tomato aspic and potato salad and cold vegetables, to a Bavarian cream served with an apricot sauce and fresh strawberries.

Mother didn't get started until Mary had served them and left the room. 'Well,' she said in a tone that could curdle milk, 'I suppose you're satisfied. You've made me the laughing stock of the village. None of my friends will speak to me.'

Elizabeth said nothing.

'Three of them called me this morning. Three! On a Sunday morning! All telling me the horrible things you said at church.'

The obvious rejoinder was to ask how they told her anything, if they weren't speaking to her. Elizabeth continued eating her salad.

'I don't know how you can shame me so, after all I've done for you. You never do anything I tell you to, and now you go off on this ridiculous tangent, acting like a missionary or something. I certainly never brought you up to go hobnobbing with heathens!'

Dad opened his mouth to say something, but Mother cut him off. 'And you always side with her! I guess I'm good for nothing around here but to pay for everything and never get any thanks for it!'

Again Dad tried to speak. This time it was Elizabeth who held up a hand. 'This is my battle, Dad. Mother, we do appreciate all you do for us. No, let me finish. I realize I have become an embarrassment to you, which is why I've decided to live somewhere else for a while. Those new apartments on Pleasant Street are quite nice. That way everyone will understand that you are in no way responsible for my actions. Dad, would you pass me the chicken, please?'

Her proposal was so unexpected that it actually silenced her mother for a couple of beats, enough time for Elizabeth to slip a few slivers of chicken to the cats, who had stealthily crept under the table and were rubbing against her ankles.

It didn't take Mother long to recover her voice. 'Move away from home? Certainly not! I never heard of such a thing! Since you refuse to marry, your place is here.'

'I'm thinking of you, Mother. You and I have different views about many things, and I think it will be more comfortable for both of us if I stay away, at least for a while.'

'But what will people think!'

'They will think she is doing the sensible thing, Mildred,' said Dad quietly. 'I will miss you more than I can say, Bets, but you must do as you think best.'

She heard the quiver in his voice, and she was hard put to keep her own voice steady as she replied, 'Yes, I have to follow my own conscience. I'm sure you both understand I don't *want* to leave home, but in a place of my own I will have much more freedom to act as I must.'

'Freedom! I'm sure we never restrict your freedom! You go where you want, when you want. You even have your own car, a ridiculous expense, if you ask me.'

'And have I freedom to think as I want?'

Her mother took a sharp breath. Elizabeth wondered if she'd gone too far. She had not issued a direct challenge to her mother in years, not since her flat refusal to attend the many parties intended to help her 'find the right man'. The resulting scene still burned in her memory.

But she'd won her point in the end.

She went on eating the chicken, though it had turned to sawdust in her mouth, and drinking iced tea. This time she had given her mother a clear either/or: stop commanding my thoughts and actions, or let the community think you've turned your daughter out.

'Well, I'm sure I've never told you what to think. The idea! Of course you must act as you wish. I certainly won't stop you.' It nearly choked her, but she got it out. Anything was better than defying public opinion. She'd be able, somehow, to explain away Elizabeth's strange sympathies. 'You know we want you here. This is your home.' She managed to infuse the last statement with a little warmth, and Elizabeth smiled sweetly.

'It is, and I love it. And if that's the way you feel, Mother, if you're sure my actions won't embarrass you, I'll wait a while to decide about that apartment.'

'That's settled, then.' Mother couldn't quite keep the relief out of her voice. She picked up the bell and rang for dessert.

'You gave me a scare there, Daughter,' her father said later as they were lazing in the comfortable wicker chairs on the back lawn. Mother would have preferred wrought iron, which was prettier and more fashionable, and almost impossible to sit on. When the subject was raised, Dad had simply gone out and bought the wicker.

'I hoped I wouldn't really have to move,' said Elizabeth, 'but I meant what I said. And I still do. If it becomes impossible to live under Mother's thumb and be my own person, I'll have to reconsider.'

'Your mother can be very stubborn, but she knows which side her bread is buttered on. You have her between a rock and hard place, and she knows it. She'll behave.'

'I didn't mean to put her in an impossible position, Dad. It just happened. I couldn't keep silent any longer. You said I was frozen. I . . . somehow I've thawed.'

'And a good thing, too, but . . . I don't know if you've ever had frostbite.'

'Once, in college. We had that terrible winter – you remember – and I lost one glove. It was a long walk to one of my classes, and even though I stuck that hand in my pocket, it was completely numb by the time I got to class.'

'So you'll remember how much that hand hurt when it started to get warm.'

'I remember, Dad.' She smiled her understanding of the point he was making. 'It's my choice.'

'I'll help all I can, but—'

'But you're in a precarious position, and not just with Mother. You're a teacher. You have to behave as the community expects.'

'To a degree, yes. I've been at the high school a long time. They won't fire me if I become obstreperous, but they could make me very uncomfortable. However, school is almost over for the summer, so I won't have daily contact with the other teachers until fall. By that time this will all have blown over.'

She sighed. 'Not for the Antonellis. Or for the Briggses, unless they find the real killer soon.' She paused and then amended. 'Unless *we* find the killer. The police aren't trying.'

'We don't know that, my dear.'

'But we know this town. We have an image that must be preserved. Easy way out. Don't rock the boat. All the old clichés that boil down to no action!'

He shook his head at her vehemence. 'You are so sensible, so

adult in your manner and actions that I sometimes forget you're
still very young. Your heart is in the right place, but try to keep
it under the firm control of your excellent mind. Very few things
in this world are black or white. Try to look for the gray.'

'Oh, I know not everybody's like that. But it's those people
in the middle, those gray people who "don't want to be involved"
who make it possible for the extremists to have their way. I'm
just so angry, I'm furious with the gray, too! It helps to be
angry.'

'It's better than sorrowful, I agree, and can spur you to action,
but it can also interfere with your judgment. Have you a plan of
action, or are you going to go out and tilt at windmills?'

Don Quixote had been assigned reading in high school. She
smiled and looked down at the middy-blouse and skirt she had
donned after church. 'I don't notice any armor.'

'No, and that's part of the problem. You've cast off your frozen
armor, and on the whole that's a good thing, but you still need
the armor of clear thinking.'

'I don't seem to be able to think clearly,' she said after a
silence. 'I suppose you're right about those windmills. I tilted at
a few of them this morning, and probably accomplished nothing
except offending a lot of narrow-minded people. Did Mother tell
you what she was so upset about?' Dad shook his head, and she
related the scene in the choir room.

'You might also have made a few of them think, might have
opened those minds a crack. But it would have been better if you'd
thought about it first, instead of speaking out of fury. You do realize
you've exposed yourself to danger?'

'I suppose so. I hadn't actually thought about it.'

'Then I suggest you do!' He sounded exasperated. 'You know
I'm on your side, now and always. But for a very intelligent
woman, you can sometimes be very stupid! There is a murderer
walking these streets. You have publicly announced that you intend
to hunt him down. Ye gods, girl, do you plan to paint a target on
your back and stand on a street corner waiting to be killed?'

Elizabeth winced. Never before had her father spoken to her in
that tone. And she couldn't even resent it. He was quite right. She
swallowed hard. 'Do you think – what do you think I should do?'

'First, call Fred and tell him all you've told me. He's a lawyer.
He'll know whether you should request police protection, or

perhaps hire a bodyguard. Then you and he, and I if you want
me, will sit down and make some plans.'

'Of course I want you! But where? Mother . . .?'

'Your mother is a realist, Bets. Dearly as I love her, we have
different opinions about many things. That has led her to see
the family as us, you and me, against her, and I fear she will
continue to see it that way. But she will not oppose you, not
now. She knows you could carry out your threat to move away.
We can meet wherever you feel comfortable, whether here at
home or at Fred's office.'

'Then here, I think. In your study?'

'That's nice and private. Sounds good. Go call him.'

She was spared the trouble of asking the operator, once more,
for his phone number. As she headed toward the house, Mary came
out. 'Telephone call for you, Miss Elizabeth! Mr Fred, he want to
talk to you.'

It would be nice, Elizabeth thought as she hurried to the phone,
to be able to have a private phone call.

Bearing in mind the listening ears in the kitchen, Elizabeth kept
the conversation short. Yes, what he'd heard was true. Yes, she had
realized that. Could he come over to talk about it? Now? Good.

She hung up and went into the kitchen to request a fresh pitcher
of iced tea.

'Mr Fred, he likes lemonade better,' said Susannah firmly. She
was already cutting up lemons. Elizabeth, who preferred iced tea,
conceded.

Fred was there within ten minutes; he'd decided to drive, haste
being advisable. He knocked on the front door, which was open
to the fitful breeze. Elizabeth went to the door and was greeted
with a scowl.

She held up a hand. 'Don't say it. I know. Dad already made
the point. Forcefully.'

'Pity nobody drilled it into your head before you went and
painted a target on your back!' At least he said it quietly, with
one eye on the stairway.

'He even used the same analogy. We can't talk here. Mother is
taking a nap, and we don't want to wake her. Come with me.'

Susannah had already taken a tray to the study, with a big pitcher
of iced lemonade, the best Waterford tumblers, and a plate of her
incomparable icebox cookies.

Susannah was in favor of Frederick Wilkins.

Dad came in, shook hands with Fred, and sat down in his favorite chair. Elizabeth poured him a glass of lemonade. He thanked her. She poured one for Fred and passed the cookies. Fred made polite remarks about Susannah.

At last Dad cleared his throat. 'Yes. It's hard to know where to start, but I asked you to come here for a strategy meeting. I take it you know about the idiotic thing my daughter did this morning.'

Fred glanced at Elizabeth. She shrugged. 'I don't disagree with the adjective.'

'Then yes, sir, I did hear something about it.'

'So the first thing we need to work out is how to keep her safe. Not an easy task.'

'No. But there are some obvious precautions. For a start, the door was open when I got here. Do you always keep your doors unlocked?'

'Yes, of course. Everybody does in the daytime.' Elizabeth looked puzzled.

'Thereby making it easy for anyone who likes to enter your house. Like a man with a gun.'

'Oh!' Elizabeth looked around the comfortable room, at the Persian carpet on the floor, the blue draperies, the well-worn leather chairs that her father loved. It had always been a haven of peace. It was home. Now this haven, the very safety of her home, was threatened, and it was her fault.

'So locking your doors is the first step. You can't very well close all the windows in this heat, but I'm afraid the downstairs ones should be open only a crack. And I'd advise, sir, that you make it very difficult for anyone to open them further. Perhaps pieces of wood jammed between the top of the sash and the window frame would do it.'

'Hmm. I'll talk to Zeke about it. He'll have some ideas. What else?'

'Elizabeth, you're not going to like this, but I strongly suggest that you keep to the house for the next few days.'

She raised her head. 'No. I can't do that.'

'Daughter, think! At least half of your committee obligations are over for the summer. There's no more choir practice, no place you really must go.'

'You're forgetting, both of you, that the main object of this exercise is not simply to keep me safe, but to help me investigate a murder while taking no unreasonable risks. I have my own ideas about that, but I'm open to yours.'

'You are not a policeman!' Her father was getting worked up, something that seldom happened. 'You have no obligation in this matter. Yes, you were fond of Mr Anthony. We all were. Yes, you deplore what has happened to him, and you're upset because the wrong man has been blamed for it. But you have no way to make that right!'

'I think I do.' She spoke quietly, but with steel in her voice. 'I have lived in this village all my life. I know almost everybody. I have very few close friends, true. I've wanted it that way. But I am respected in most circles. I have a degree from Northwestern, with high honors. That helps make me persuasive. And – I hate to mention this, but it matters – I have money. I give generously to charity. I volunteer my time. In short, I can talk to people, and get them to talk to me. Surely that's the beginning of any investigation.'

Fred had been listening, his frown growing ever deeper. 'You're right, of course. You can talk to anyone you please. And in this close-knit community, how long do you think it will be before everyone in town knows what you're doing? Including the murderer? I'd give it a couple of hours, tops. You've already given him fair warning that you're after him. How do you propose to protect yourself?' He stood and began to pace. 'You know, of course, that men from Al Capone's gang, and the rival gangs, live right here in Oak Park? I can give you their addresses, if you want to know. These are men who have no respect for human life. If someone gets in their way, they gun them down. Do you think you can escape them?'

'No. But I've been thinking about this, and I have a plan. You are familiar with the precept "divide and conquer". How happy do you imagine the Italians in this community are with the fact that one of their own has been killed? And that another is suspected of his murder? And that their arch-enemies, the KKK, are spreading their propaganda about the suspect?

'Now, among those unhappy Italians are some gangsters, with connections to the Chicago Outfit. That segment of our society is not likely to suffer in silence. So I propose to start some rumors of my own, stories that will set the two factions against each other, the Mob against the Walosas. I think in the midst of the fight, the truth might come out.'

'But . . . but—' sputtered Fred.

'That could start a bloodbath, Elizabeth.' When her father used her full name, she knew he was seriously displeased.

'Not if both sides are forewarned, as well as the police. Dad, you know I studied history at Northwestern, including military history. And I'm a good chess player. I'm familiar with strategy and tactics. I doubt that many of the individuals in the gangs, or in the KKK, are very well informed about their adversaries. So, since neither of you seems to have any ideas, here's what I propose to do.'

She laid out her plan of action, in broad outline.

'I'll have to fill in the details as I go,' she finished. 'Each step will depend on how people react. But I think it will work.'

Fred's hair, usually carefully slicked down with brilliantine, was standing on end. He'd been holding his head and wildly rumpling his hair. 'If everyone reacts the way you think they will. If the gangsters don't decide to shoot first and think later. If, if, if. I think you're overestimating their intelligence.'

'Most of them, yes. The rank and file. But don't forget the gangsters have bosses. I don't know about some of the others, but Al Capone is no dummy. He knows where his advantage lies, and he won't let his goons go against his wishes. They're all terrified of him.'

'With reason,' said her father. 'As you should be.'

'I am, Dad. He may just be the most dangerous man in the country. But he's mostly interested in firming up his position in Chicago, making sure he's the boss of the bosses, the king. He won't take Mr Anthony's death, and Mr Briggs's situation, lying down, but he won't start a war over it. It's not in his interests.'

'You think.'

'Yes, Fred, I think. As for the Walosas, of course some of them are birdbrains. But their leaders have an agenda, and it doesn't include being wiped out by gangs. They'll play it to their advantage. Don't you see? The gangsters are going to be looking for the real killer, probably so they can execute him. And the Walosas and their husbands are going to be looking for him, too, so they can escape the wrath of the gang, while showing everyone how pure their motives are.'

'It's a terrible risk, Daughter. For everyone concerned, including you.'

'I know that, Dad. But it's something I must do. With your blessing, I hope. But even if . . .' She tried to swallow the lump in her throat.

'Of course with my blessing, child! Also with grave doubts, but I've known you for twenty-six years, and I know that there's no deflecting you, once you've set your course. Now I want you to tell us how Fred and I can help.'

ELEVEN

They had finished Susannah's first pitcher of lemonade, and most of the second one she brought unasked, before they had the rudiments of a campaign mapped out. The cookies were gone, and the small room had grown hot and stuffy, even with the windows wide open. A small electric fan on a table whirred noisily, moving the air around without noticeably cooling anyone.

'All right then,' said Elizabeth crisply. 'We can't do much today. It's Sunday. I want to begin with Mrs Hemingway, but that household observes the Sabbath pretty strictly. I'll call her first thing tomorrow, since you're so particular about me staying inside. You, Fred, will find out all you can about Mr Briggs's situation, and try to get bail set at some reasonable figure. I can come up with that, if necessary.'

'I doubt the judge will grant bail, though I know Sanders is pushing for it. There's pressure on the police to deal with the case quickly.'

'Then that's one thing Mrs Hemingway might be able to work on. That family has influence. I'd feel much better if Mr Briggs were free.' She made a note. 'Dad, do you think you could talk to the Briggs family again? They might be able to supply an alibi for Mr Briggs, or at least might tell you what he says about the whole thing. After all, he was a good friend to Mr Anthony. He would know who his other friends were, and maybe his enemies.'

'Have you considered,' asked Fred gravely, 'that Briggs might be a good deal safer in jail? If the murderer thinks Briggs knows anything useful, he certainly wants him where he can keep an eye on him, and keep his mouth shut.'

Elizabeth sorted out the pronouns, but she was still puzzled. 'I don't understand. How can anyone keep a prisoner from talking, to his lawyer at any rate? I thought they had to allow that.'

Fred and Mr Walker exchanged a look. 'Oh, my dear,' said her father. 'You have a good education in many ways, but you have a great deal to learn about this world. Did you not know that jails are hotbeds of intrigue? A criminal who wants to get a message to someone in jail can do it in any number of ways. And that message can be a threat to keep silent or else face punishment.'

She absorbed that. 'I see. And yet you say he would be safer in jail.'

'The intimidation he may receive there will probably be just that. It's possible, in a big prison, for threats to be carried out, but much harder in a small jail like ours.' Fred shook his head. 'But Briggs may not know that. He's a music teacher. He may not be any more worldly wise than' – Elizabeth gave him a sharp look – 'than your average ordinary citizen. If he does receive a threat, he might believe it. Don't forget he's a member of a small minority in this village, a minority that has sometimes been badly treated. He may be afraid of everything right now.'

Elizabeth shook her head irritably. 'We've lost the thread. If he's terrified in jail, how would it be worse for him if he were out on bail?'

'It could be much easier for someone who wished him harm to get to him,' said her father. 'We talked a little while ago about turning this house into a fortress. You hate the idea, I know, but it could be done. We have a solidly built house with good strong locks. We could hire guards. A determined criminal might be able to get in, but only with great difficulty. Mr Briggs lives in a very pleasant bungalow, about as burglar-proof as a doghouse.'

'Then the only thing to do is to hear his story right away,' said Elizabeth firmly, 'before anyone has a chance to silence him. Fred, does your Mr Sanders work on a Sunday?'

Fred looked slightly shocked. 'No one in Oak Park works on a Sunday.'

'I'll bet the crooks do. Fred, I want you to call him – no, go and see him and tell him it's crucial that he talk to Mr Briggs right away.'

'I don't know that I can – that is, I'm a very junior member of the firm, and on a Sunday afternoon—'

'Fred Wilkins, if you think you can't persuade him, then I will!' She stood. 'Where does he live?'

Fred knew when he was beaten. 'No, no, I'll go. I may not get anywhere, but I'll try.'

'You won't accomplish a thing if you go with that attitude!' Elizabeth took a deep breath and moderated her tone. 'You know perfectly well that you're a good lawyer. That means you know how to plead a case. You can be persuasive when you need to be. And in this matter, you absolutely need to be. Off with you!'

Mr Walker followed him to the door. 'She has more of her mother in her than she'd like to admit,' he murmured. 'Good luck.'

'I'll need it, sir.' He strode resolutely to his car. Mr Walker thought a moment, then closed and locked the door and returned to the study.

He found Elizabeth sitting at his desk, writing on a pad of yellow paper. 'Lists, my dear?'

'A plan of action. And an outline for my conversation with Mrs Hemingway. I'll have to stress the music aspect of it, I think.'

He watched her for a moment. Her straight, dark, bobbed hair shone in the late-afternoon sun, hanging down in two wings as she pored over her work. She paused a moment for thought and looked up. Her face was flushed with color; her eyes were bright.

Something about her father's scrutiny penetrated her preoccupation. 'What? Do I have a smudge on my face?'

'You have a glow on your face, Daughter. Odd, I never took you for a firebrand.'

She laughed ruefully. 'I guess I never before noticed a fire that needed to be lit. And I'm not sure I can get this one going.'

'Oh, I have no doubt about that. I'm not so sure you, or anyone, will be able to put it out.'

'I know. But it has to be done. A fire cleanses.'

'And destroys.'

They sat in somber silence until Susannah called them to supper.

There was little conversation. Mother, still constrained by Elizabeth's unprecedented behavior, couldn't find a neutral topic of conversation. Elizabeth and her father had said what needed to be said. It was a relief when Mother professed a headache and went back upstairs, and they were released from the uncomfortable meal.

Elizabeth questioned her father with a look. He shook his head. 'She'll get over it. She needs time to adjust.'

'And I suppose I do, too.'

'Yes.'

It was nearly bedtime before Fred called. His message was brief. 'He wasn't happy about it, but he went to the jail and talked to Briggs. I don't know what he learned. I did what I could.'

'You did what needed to be done, and I congratulate you. Thank you.'

It was not in her to wax lyrical, but Fred knew her well enough to understand. 'You're welcome. I'll call when I know more. Goodnight.'

There were unspoken rules about telephone calls. The earliest possible hour for a personal call was nine o'clock, if the recipient of the call lived in a household with servants. If not, then nine-thirty or even ten was considered more courteous.

Elizabeth, having gulped a cup of coffee and half a piece of toast, was on the line to Mrs Hemingway at eight-seventeen by the hall clock. The maid who answered sounded scared.

'Good morning, Emily. It's Mrs Fairchild. Is Mrs Hemingway able to come to the telephone?'

'Oh, Mrs Fairchild! I thought it might be . . . um, yes, ma'am. I'll fetch her.'

Elizabeth chastised herself. A call at an unorthodox hour might be from Ernest, who was often in trouble of one kind or another and was as unconventional about phone calls as about everything else. Elizabeth couldn't remember where on the globe that restless man was at the moment, but if he'd left Paris and returned to the North American continent . . .

'Good morning, Elizabeth. Is something wrong?'

Everything, she wanted to say. 'Nothing new, and I'm sorry to call so early.'

'Doesn't matter. What can I do for you?'

She took a deep breath. 'I'm hoping you might be able to help Mr Briggs. He's still in jail, and Mr Sanders, his lawyer, thinks it's unlikely that he can get out on bail. Mrs Hemingway, he doesn't have a piano, or anything else to make music. He'll shrivel up in there!'

'Why can't he be bailed out? If it's a question of money—'

'No, that's not the problem. The thing is, his lawyer thinks the judge will be reluctant to set bail, because the murder is exciting so much community interest.'

'Hmph! Because he's afraid of the Klan, more likely. Which judge?'

'I don't know. Fred would know.'

'Find out. I've known them both since they were in diapers. They'll listen to me.'

Elizabeth breathed a sigh of relief. 'That would be wonderful! Thank you, thank you!'

Elizabeth could almost see the dismissive shrug. 'Right. Now, what else are you doing?'

Elizabeth sighed. 'I, myself, am doing very little. My family fears that I might be in danger. They don't want me to leave the house; that's why I'm telephoning.'

'They may be right about that, you know. That was a brave thing you did yesterday, but also foolhardy. Your mother . . .' She faded out.

'Yes, my mother is unhappy, but she has . . . she will not interfere with what I'm trying to do. You won't need to try to dissuade her.'

'You've made a deal.' Mrs Hemingway cackled.

Elizabeth was silent.

'Very well. Your father is helping? And Fred?'

'Fred is looking into the legal aspects, working with Mr Sanders, who talked with Mr Briggs late yesterday. Fred is going to check in with me today, to give me Mr Briggs's side of the story. And Dad plans to talk again with the Briggs family, to find out what they know about Mr Anthony's friends. And enemies.'

'And what is my assignment, once I've dealt with the question of bail?'

'Talk to people. Everyone you can think of. Your students, your friends, the people you see at the grocery. And get them talking to other people. I know you don't like spreading gossip' – *and God forgive me for that bare-faced lie!* – 'but if you could find a way to suggest to the conservatives that the Mob might be involved, and to the liberals that you've heard rumors about the Walosas—'

'So as to set them at each other's throats.'

'That, perhaps, but I hope it will make both factions eager to prove that the other was responsible, which could lead to some discoveries. Someone has seen something or knows something about the murder, or saw Mr Briggs in some place that afternoon and evening, a place that makes it impossible for him to have committed the crime. I'll be doing the same, but on the phone. At least for now.' She paused. 'You see, I think that once the whole village is talking about this, we'll all be safer. The murderer can't dispose of everyone who's asking questions.'

'And we'll collect a lot of information.' Mrs Hemingway sounded approving.

'You will, especially. People will talk to you.' Or else, she thought, but didn't add aloud. 'Of course, a lot of what we all hear won't be true, but we may be able to find a pattern somewhere. Oops, I have to go. And thank you, so much!'

TWELVE

Elizabeth managed to hang up the phone a second or two before her mother came into the hall.

'I thought I heard your voice. Were you calling someone?' Mother asked suspiciously.

Elizabeth, tempted to prevaricate, simply said, 'Yes. And I'm going to get a second cup of coffee. Can I get you one?'

'Thank you. Mary will bring me everything I need.' She turned on her heel and went into the dining room.

Elizabeth drew a deep breath and opened the door to the kitchen. That wasn't too bad. Not cordial, but no tirade, no demands. In her own way, Mother was keeping to her word.

It was tempting fate, though, to take her coffee into the dining room. There would either be a frosty silence or, if her father was there, a lame attempt at conversation, avoiding the only issue they wanted to talk about. She stayed in the kitchen.

There was no sign of the weekend chaos. Susannah was not one to allow a mess to remain one second longer than necessary. The extra help had stayed late on the Saturday evening, and all three of the live-in servants had given up part of their time off on Sunday afternoon to finish cleaning up, just as soon as they got back from their afternoon church service. The kitchen was gleaming, every dish and pot and comestible in its proper place. Susannah sat in her rocking chair and Zeke in a chair at the kitchen table, his coffee in front of him. Mary was the only one doing any work, putting together a tray of coffee things. 'I be back in a minute, Miss Elizabeth,' she said over her shoulder as she flew out the door.

'Don't hurry; I'll serve myself.' She did just that and sat down at the table next to Zeke, who nodded and smiled. 'Are you getting a little rest at last?'

'Shore am, Miss Elizabeth,' said Zeke contentedly.

'For a whipstitch or two.' Susannah left no doubt that the normal routine would be restored very soon. 'And I hear you're not doin' no restin' yourself.'

'You hear right. I'm trying to figure out who really killed Mr Anthony.' And as Susannah opened her mouth, Elizabeth held up a hand. 'I know what you're going to say. Everybody has said the same thing. It could be dangerous. Leave it to the police. But the police have arrested the wrong man, and aren't looking any further. I can't leave it at that.'

'Who do you reckon did it, then, if it wasn't that music teacher?' Susannah had moved to the table to be closer to the conversation. 'And how come you say it wasn't him?'

'He's a friend of Dad's.'

That settled it, as far as Elizabeth was concerned. Apparently that assurance was all Susannah and Zeke needed as well. They nodded, and so did Mary, who had returned. 'Miz Walker wants some bacon and eggs,' she said timidly. 'Miz Susannah, I'd burn them eggs sure as my name's Mary.'

Susannah rolled her eyes but pulled herself to her feet and went to the stove. 'I feel sorry for any man you ever marry, girl. He gonna live on store bread 'n' canned beans. Now, Miss Elizabeth, I'm not gonna shout across the room. Your mama might hear. But you wanna come back, after supper, Zeke and I can tell you what we heard at church yesterday.'

It was a clear command to get out of her hair, and Elizabeth obeyed.

It was early still, too early to call anyone else. Everyone she knew, except Mrs Hemingway, was extremely conventional and would be shocked. Not the best way to seek cooperation. She could talk to Dad, though, if he wasn't stuck in the dining room with Mother. She slipped around to his study and sure enough, he was there, peacefully drinking a cup of coffee and reading the *Tribune*.

'Is school over for the summer?' she asked, sitting on the arm of his chair.

'Almost. Exams this afternoon, and after I've turned in grades I'm a free man. I'll get bored after about a week, but the first few days of being my own master are pure bliss.' He turned his head to look at her closely. 'However, you've found a way to occupy my freedom, haven't you?'

'I'm sorry, Dad. If it weren't so important . . .'

'But it is. Literally, it's a matter of life and death. I'm just waiting for a more seemly hour to visit Briggs's family. Have you heard any more about the possibility of bail? Or what transpired yesterday with his lawyer?'

'Mrs Hemingway is getting ready to twist a few arms as soon as I find out which judge she needs to talk to. I phoned her quite early. Oh, and I felt bad about it, Dad; Emily was in a panic because she thought it might be Ernest calling at such an hour.'

'Grace Hemingway has a good many trials to deal with in her family. Ernest is brilliant, but as unstable as a firecracker. He'll end by breaking her heart. And Dr Hemingway is far from well, I fear. However, Grace is a strong and determined woman. She'll twist those arms to some effect. I'd bet on Paul Briggs being home by this afternoon.'

'Much as I love her, I admit she intimidates me at times.'

'And you are not easily intimidated, my child! Now, what are your plans for the rest of the day?'

'I'll be on the phone, calling everyone I can. There are quite a few I need to talk to who may not have telephones, though.'

'Ask the ones who do have to spread the word to the others. I'd rather you didn't go out until it seems safe.'

'But that will be soon, Dad, as soon as everyone is talking about hunting for the murderer. Whoever it is, he won't be able to track the campaign down to a single source.'

'And even if he could, the genie can't be put back in the bottle. Will you be in touch with Fred?'

'Right away. That's the very next thing. We have to know what Mr Briggs told his lawyer. That might give us some ideas.'

'Right. Onward and upward!'

The telephone being where it was, Elizabeth had to wait until her mother had finished breakfast, over which she was dawdling in an unaccustomed way. Well, it's her vacation too, thought Elizabeth, trying to be charitable. The party is over, and she did work very hard at it. True, most of the nervous energy she expended was useless, but it was strenuous for her, all the same.

Really, of course, Mother was hoping to eavesdrop on any phone calls her daughter might make. For the five-hundredth time Elizabeth gritted her teeth at the idiotic location of the instrument. Mother had insisted it be put there so the servants couldn't make personal calls unobserved. Neither could anyone else.

She lurked outside the dining room for what seemed like hours. At last she heard her mother's chair scraped back. She ducked around the corner so as not to be seen when Mother came out.

But she didn't come out. The next thing Elizabeth heard was the sound of the phone being dialed.

So that was how she was going to play it! Tie up the phone talking to her friends. In her fury, Elizabeth also had to admit to a grudging admiration for her mother's cleverness. But now what was she going to do?

She almost ran to her father's study. He wasn't there.

The car! She ran out to the garage and sighed with relief. Her father was just closing the garage door, ready to get back in the car and drive off. She didn't dare shout, but ran up to him, panting.

'Something's wrong!' he said in alarm.

'No – wait!' She paused to catch her breath. 'It's nothing dreadful. But Mother has hit on a way to keep me from calling anyone. She's using the telephone herself, and I'm quite sure she's going to go down the whole list of her friends, and talk, and talk, and talk. You're going to have to take me somewhere else to phone. Or else I'll have to take my car and visit everyone in person, and we agreed that might not be a good idea.'

'No.' He thought for a moment. 'Get in the car. I'll go find Zeke and tell him to tell Susannah you've gone with me. We'll decide where we're going when we've started.'

By the time he had driven around the corner Elizabeth had thought it out. 'We'll go to Fred's house. He may already be at the office, but his aunt will be there. Fred says she approves of me, so I think she'll let me use the phone.'

Her father frowned. 'I can't let you stay if he's there alone, you know. Your mother would never forgive me.'

'I know. Not that it wouldn't be perfectly proper, but Mother cares a lot about what people think, whether it's true or not. But he won't be there alone, not at this time of day.'

'Mmm.'

Poor old Dad. He stood out as a liberal in ultra-conservative Oak Park, but he still had a few Victorian ideas about chaperones and that sort of thing.

Elizabeth was being lucky that day. Fred was just walking down the porch steps when the car drove up. 'Elizabeth! I was just trying to phone you, but the line's been busy for ages. Can you come in for a minute? Aunt Lucy just made a pan of muffins.' He waved at Mr Walker and said, 'I'll make sure she gets home safely, sir.'

'I mustn't keep you,' she said when she had been fussed over by Aunt Lucy and installed at the breakfast table with coffee and cinnamon muffins. 'You're off to work.'

'Yes, but I have to tell you what Sanders found out. I haven't time to go over everything, unfortunately. I've been trying to call you forever.'

'My mother is using the phone. All day, I'm guessing. Go ahead.'

'Well, the main thing is that Briggs has no idea who killed Antonelli.'

'Call him Anthony. I'll always think of him that way.'

'Anthony, then. He gave Sanders the names of a few of their mutual friends, mostly people from church. But he said he couldn't think of a single person who could be called an enemy. He was very popular in the church, and the community as a whole, he said. He had many friends among his customers.'

'Yes.' She fought back tears. Good sense was needed now, not foolish emotion. 'That doesn't help us much.'

'Briggs thinks it must have been a robbery gone wrong. He had a lot of valuable stuff in that shop.'

'What was taken?'

'He doesn't know. No one will tell him. He says the police

searched his house trying to find some stolen loot, but of course they didn't. That didn't slow them down at all. They just kept asking him what he'd done with it.'

'The most valuable thing was the highboy. What's happened to that?'

'He doesn't know. The cops didn't ask him about that.'

'Maybe they didn't know about it. It had just been delivered that day.' She sighed. 'I hope Sanders is going to keep pressure on the police to look further for any missing merchandise. I'm sure Mr Anthony must have kept a proper inventory. He was a careful businessman.'

Fred made a note. 'I'm sure he's following that up, for whatever good it'll do.'

'Oh, and you need to ask him which judge might be deciding the question of bail. Mrs Hemingway is going to try to persuade him. Could you call her when you find out?'

Another note. 'Poor man. She can be formidable. I'll have Sanders call her. Now I'd better escort you home.'

'I'm not going home. That is, if you don't mind. I have a lot of phone calls to make, and Mother is determined to prevent me. I'm hoping you'll let me use your phone.'

'Of course. Lucy!' he called. 'Elizabeth needs to use the phone. You'll be here, won't you?'

She came to the kitchen door and nodded. 'All day. I've got baking to do. The church rummage sale is Saturday, and I promised half a dozen cakes and as many pies as I can turn out. I'll be busy, but I'm sure you're welcome to the phone, honey.'

'You make the best pies in the county, Aunt. I can't wait. Elizabeth, give the phone a rest now and then so I can call you if I learn anything interesting. And don't go home alone! I'll come and get you whenever you want.' He hurried out the door, briefcase in hand, but stuck his head back in to call, 'And Aunt Lucy, keep the doors locked and don't let anyone in. Anyone!'

They heard the click of the lock.

THIRTEEN

L ucy took a long look at Elizabeth and then sat down beside
her. 'Now, honey, something's mighty wrong. You don't need
to tell me if you don't want to, but if it'd help to talk, I'm
a good listener.'

Elizabeth hesitated, only because she scarcely knew where to
begin. Lucy pushed back her chair and started to rise.

'No, don't go! I'd like to tell you, but it's a long story. And you
have your baking to do.'

Lucy settled back down. 'Don't be silly, child. I've got all week
to bake. Come to that, cooking doesn't stop me listening.'

Elizabeth took a deep breath. 'Well, it began with Mr Anthony's
murder.'

'Oh, yes, I know all about that, and you telling everybody that
they've arrested the wrong man. That's all over town, you know.'

'Yes. It was a foolish thing to do, and now my parents and Fred
and . . . well, everybody, really, is afraid that I've made myself a
target for the real murderer, that he needs to stop me before I can
find out anything.'

Lucy nodded thoughtfully. 'That's why you're not to go
anywhere alone. I see. And Katie-bar-the-door.'

'I think that's excessive caution, but Fred and my father feel
otherwise, so I suppose . . .'

Lucy nodded again. 'Can't be too careful. I doubt anyone knows
you're here, any murderous men, I mean, but anyone who
knows anything about you might guess. We'll just keep the house
tight and cozy, and you make all the phone calls you want. I suppose
you're looking for ideas about who it might have been, really?'

It was a pleasure to talk to someone who could read between
the lines and wasn't going off on a tangent about the danger of
what she was doing. 'Exactly. That and spread the word as fast
as possible.'

'So the murderer will give up the idea of shutting you up.
Clever.' She stood, creaking a little. 'Phone's in the kitchen. Hope
you don't mind. I can't help but hear.'

'There's nothing private about what I'll say. I honestly do regret imposing on you like this, but—'

'But your mother would throw a conniption fit. We all know what she's like, honey. A good woman but inclined to be managing. Well, this isn't getting a cake in the oven. Come with me.'

The kitchen was a compact place, cozy, but not at the expense of convenience. A modern gas range in green and cream enamel stood next to a splendid oak Hoosier cabinet. Gleaming white cabinets lined one wall above a long, enameled work surface. The dark green linoleum and the green gingham curtains were spotlessly clean. A small table and a couple of chairs made the space a little cramped, but not impossibly so. It was the kitchen of a house-proud woman who loved to cook.

Lucy pointed Elizabeth to the small corner cupboard that served as a desk. The 'candlestick' telephone covered almost the whole surface of the bottom shelf. 'Phone listing's in that little drawer underneath, but I expect you know your friends' numbers.'

'Not all of them. Thank you.' Elizabeth was reluctant to admit that she called her friends so seldom, she knew hardly any of their numbers. For that matter, she had few close friends. Mrs Hemingway. Fred. A couple of women in the choir. Almost no one of her own generation.

She sat for a moment listening to the comfortable sounds of Lucy's effort. Pulling out bowls and utensils. Sifting flour. Opening the door of the big green icebox, probably for the milk. Humming tunelessly all the while.

This was the sort of life she had never known. Mother, so far as Elizabeth was aware, had never in her life made a cake, or done anything else in a kitchen except harangue the servants. Nor, she had to admit, had she, herself. As a child she'd tried to 'help' Susannah cut out cookies, but she made such a mess and dropped so many bits of dough on the floor that she was allowed only to watch, and of course sample the end results.

She thought about the scene at the Antonelli home, the warmth, the comfort even in a time of great grief. What a lot she had missed in her life, she thought. No wonder she'd turned into an ice maiden.

And that self-pity woke her up to what she was supposed to be doing. She opened the drawer and pulled out the directory.

There weren't all that many listings. Only the relatively well-to-do had telephones in their homes. Businesses had them, of course. Doctors, dentists, lawyers, even the corner grocery, where you could call in your order in the morning and have it delivered by an enterprising boy that afternoon. Several churches had them, the big, well-financed churches.

She ran her finger down the G listings and found Grace Episcopal Church. Was it too early? No, somehow it had gotten to be almost ten. She picked up the earpiece and dialed the number, and only when she heard it ring at the other end did she think about what she meant to say.

The ring tone went on for quite a while, and Elizabeth had just begun to hope that no one would answer when the ringing stopped and a brusque female voice said, 'May I help you?' The tone implied that the owner of the voice hoped she could not.

The near rudeness galvanized her. 'Yes. This is Mrs Fairchild. I wish to speak to Dr Edsall, please.'

'I'll see if he's available. What did you wish to ask him?'

'I'll discuss that with him.' Her own voice was turning colder by the moment. She heard a barely suppressed 'Hmph!' and a clatter as the earpiece was evidently dropped on the desk.

An interval.

The gentle voice of the rector. 'Yes, Elizabeth, how good to hear from you. One moment, please.' He covered the receiver with his hand, but she could hear his muffled voice speaking, apparently to his secretary. 'Sorry to make you wait,' he said when he came back. 'I thought you might prefer privacy. What can I do for you, my dear?'

'First, I'm sorry I haven't been able to get those collection containers to you. My family feel I might be in danger and are keeping me close to home.'

'I think they are quite right. You have displayed your colors quite blatantly, haven't you?'

'Yes, and I suppose it was foolish, but I'm not a bit sorry. The real reason I called is that I'm starting a campaign. I'm asking everyone I know to spread the word that the police have arrested the wrong man. Just that, no more. But if people start talking about it, some facts will come to light. I'm sure of it.'

'And you will, at the same time, muddy the trail leading to you. Very good, Elizabeth. Now, how can I help?'

'If you are willing, I wish you'd talk to other clergy, the ones you know would be receptive. And perhaps don't be too discreet about it?'

'It is a great pity that you never went into administrative work, you know. You are gifted at organization.'

'And, I suppose, at telling people what to do. I never thought I was much like my mother, but I guess heredity holds true.'

'And speaking of your mother, how is she coping with all this?'

'I'm afraid she's upset. I did offer to move to an apartment of my own, so as not to embarrass her, but she said that wasn't necessary.'

She could have sworn she heard him chuckle. 'Yes, indeed, I understand. I will be happy to spread the word, and perhaps ask a question or two if I get the opportunity. You will be careful, won't you?'

'I'll try.'

'And I, of course, will pray for you and your quest. Ah, thank you, Mrs Barnes.' He had been interrupted by his secretary. 'That's just what I needed. Goodbye, Elizabeth. Call if you need me.'

She heard another disgruntled noise from the secretary as Dr Edsall hung the earpiece back on its hook.

Well, that was a start, and it hadn't been so bad. Who was next?

She didn't want to bother Mrs Hemingway, who was probably going about her arm-twisting, if Fred had given her the information. Nor did she want to call Fred just now to find out. He had his own work to do, more than usual since he was filling in for Mr Sanders. Besides, she didn't want him to think . . . anyway, she wouldn't call him.

Well, there was Leslie. She'd been her bridesmaid all those years ago, at the quickly-organized wedding before Will shipped out. Mother had been bitterly disapproving of the haste and the informality of it all. She'd wanted the full extravaganza, white satin and lace, six bridesmaids at least, an elaborate reception. 'People will think this is some sort of shotgun wedding!' Leslie had been a real support then, helping Elizabeth chose a pretty hat to go with a tea gown she already had, keeping Mother busy and out from underfoot, helping the newlyweds get away for their all-too-brief honeymoon.

They'd been close, she and Leslie, all through those wartime months. They had spent a lot of time reading the reports in the *Tribune* and keeping up each other's morale. Leslie had a beau in France, too. He'd joined up in 1917 and her parents had strictly forbidden her to marry so young. Both girls cried when the news was bad, cheered up when it was good, and began to be hopeful as summer turned to autumn and the horror seemed to be almost over. Elizabeth had begun to be uncomfortable in the lingering summer heat, with the baby she was carrying, but eagerly sewed tiny clothes for the new arrival, with Leslie at her side.

And then the war was over and Leslie's beau came home and Will didn't. That, with the loss of the baby, tore the friendship apart. Elizabeth couldn't bear to see the happiness in Leslie's eyes, couldn't help with the plans for her wedding. She sent a gift – but Leslie had wanted her in the wedding party. The newlyweds were understanding and tactful, but things would never be the same.

They saw each other now and then, at teas and church bazaars and charity events. Leslie had not asked Elizabeth to serve as godmother to either of the boys, and Elizabeth had not come to their christenings, though she meticulously asked about them when the two women met.

Elizabeth brushed away the tears that had come with the memories, memories of a friendship she had thrown away. 'I'll call her,' she muttered to herself. 'I won't ask her to do a thing. I'll just tell her I've been thinking about her and I'd like to see her. I've been a pig!'

Aunt Lucy, silently observing while she measured and mixed, wondered if she should try to offer some comfort. No, better not. The poor girl would deal with it.

She had to look up the number, after struggling for a moment to remember Leslie's last name. Adams, that was it. Mrs David Adams. She took a deep breath and dialed.

A woman answered the phone, an unfamiliar voice. Elizabeth swallowed. 'Hello, this is Elizabeth Fairchild, and I'm not sure I have the right number. I was trying to reach Leslie Adams.'

'Yes, this is her mother. Is this . . . could it be Elizabeth Walker?'

'That was my maiden name, yes. Mrs Blake, I know Leslie might not want to talk to me. I know I haven't been very friendly to her. But I'd like to make amends. Could you ask her to call me?' She gave her own phone number. 'I'm not at home right now, but I will be there this afternoon. I'd be very grateful if you'd give her the message.'

After a pause, Mrs Blake said, 'Actually, she just came in. I've been minding the children while she did some shopping. I'll ask if she has time to talk to you.'

Elizabeth couldn't hear the conversation between mother and daughter. It was probably just as well. She understood the mother's hostility, but it chilled her anyway.

However, after an interval, Leslie's voice came on the line. 'Elizabeth, is it really you?'

'I know you're surprised. Leslie, I've treated you very badly. I called to apologize and ask if we could try to forget the past few years and repair our friendship.'

'What's wrong? You sound . . . different.'

'I am different. That's what I'm trying to say. I've changed. My father says the ice has thawed.'

'Something has happened.'

'Yes, and it's too complicated to explain over the phone. I know it's asking a lot, but could you come and see me? I'm not home right now; I'm at Fred Wilkins's house, and that's complicated, too.' She took a deep breath. 'His aunt Lucy lives with him, and I'm sure she wouldn't mind if you brought the boys, too.'

'Wait a minute.'

Again there were muffled sounds from the other end. Leslie was probably consulting with her mother. Lucy whispered, 'Tell her to come for lunch. There's plenty, even if the children come.'

Then Leslie's voice. 'Mother says she can stay with them for a little longer.'

'Wonderful!' Elizabeth hoped her voice didn't express her profound relief. She wasn't ready to face someone else's sweet babies quite yet. 'Lucy says, stay for lunch if you can.'

'I . . . all right. What's the address?'

FOURTEEN

Elizabeth was shaking when she hung up the phone. Lucy came over and patted her shoulder with a floury hand.

'That was a very brave thing you just did, honey, inviting the children and all. I'm proud of you.'

'I . . . they're not coming. They'll stay with Leslie's mother. But how did you know . . .?'

'Land sakes, child, this is Oak Park! Everyone knows about

you losing your husband and then your poor little baby, and how hard it was for you. And people have noticed how you never get involved with children's charities, though you help with all the others. You may have changed, like you told her, but I know the hurt hasn't gone away.' She dusted the flour off Elizabeth's shoulder with her apron and bustled away. 'And if I don't get busy, there won't be lunch for anybody. I'm making a nice chicken salad, and some biscuits. And pie, of course.'

Elizabeth wiped away the tears that had come, unbidden. 'I'm not much use in the kitchen, but I'd like to help, if I won't be in your way.'

'You can cut up the celery, if you want. And cut the biscuits when the dough is ready.' She reached into a drawer. 'Here's an apron. I've dusted you with flour already, no need to collect more.'

Lucy patiently showed Elizabeth how to wash the celery, handed her the cutting board and the knife, and showed her the way to cut the size pieces she wanted. 'And careful with that knife! I keep it real sharp, so mind your fingers.'

Somewhat to her surprise, Elizabeth managed the simple chore fairly well. The knife came close enough once to nick a fingernail, and the celery slices were somewhat uneven, but on the whole the job went well. And she dropped only one biscuit on the floor when moving them to the cookie sheet, but managed not to step on it.

They had just gone in the oven when Fred came home and sank down in a kitchen chair. 'Whew! What a morning! Elizabeth, I'll take you home in a minute, but is it okay if I relax for a while first?'

'Nobody's going anyplace till we've all had some lunch,' said Lucy briskly. 'And Elizabeth's friend's going to eat with us. So if you wouldn't mind setting four places in the dining room, dear. Use the blue willow plates.'

'I'll come and help you, Fred,' said Elizabeth. 'Or you show me where everything is and I'll do it.' She did at least know how to set a table; Susannah had sometimes let her do that.

'I wanted to tell you,' she said quietly once they were in the small adjoining room. 'Leslie Blake is coming over. Well, it's Adams now, but I think of her as she was when she was my bridesmaid, all those years ago. We've sort of lost touch over the years, and I haven't been very nice to her, so I called to try and make amends, and Lucy invited her to lunch. I'm sorry if it's an annoyance.'

'No. Just a surprise. I didn't know you had any close girlfriends.' He was doling out plates. 'Do I need soup bowls or anything?'

'No, we're having chicken salad and biscuits. I suppose bread-and-butter plates. And you're right. I don't have any close girlfriends. I just realized that. That's why I want to get back together with Leslie. Where are the napkins?'

'In that drawer. I suppose you'll grill her about the murder and who might have done it and all that.'

'Not today. Today I just want . . . I don't know what I want.'

'A friend. Some support in a nasty time. Someone you can talk to. Seems reasonable to me. And about time, if you don't mind my saying so. But you'd better be careful. The Ice Princess is thawing fast, and you might end up standing in a large puddle.'

She was trying to come up with an answer to that when the doorbell rescued her. Lucy bustled from the kitchen to receive the guest and then left the three to deal with the rather awkward situation.

Introductions took only a minute or two. Fred showed them into the parlor, which Lucy had maintained in the fussy Victorian manner, complete with a small parlor organ. Leslie commented politely about one or two of the ornaments.

A silence fell.

Fred and Elizabeth spoke at once. Each deferred to the other. Finally Fred prevailed.

'I understand this is a real occasion, the first meeting in a long time of two old friends. I'm honored to be a part of the reunion. Mrs Blake, tell me something about yourself.'

'Oh, call me Leslie, please. But I don't know where to start.'

'How about at the beginning? Have you always lived in Oak Park?'

'Almost always. I was born in a little town in Indiana that you've never heard of, but my parents moved here when I was two. My father is an architect, and he wanted to work with Frank Lloyd Wright. He was very tired of the fussy styles of the past and wanted to do something new.'

'And did he work for Wright?' asked Fred, pretty sure that he knew the answer.

'No, he never did. I think Mother was glad, considering how Wright turned out.'

'That scandal died down, though, didn't it?' asked Fred. 'His mistress died quite a while back in that horrible fire at Taliesin, and his wife eventually gave him a divorce. Just a few years ago, wasn't it?'

'Yes, but you know nothing is ever forgotten in Oak Park, and he's still viewed as a pariah around here, for all his fame. No, Father never worked with him, but he did work with firms that were dedicated to the Prairie style. Still does, and that's made him happy again with his work.'

'Mother says she wouldn't be caught dead in one of his houses,' said Elizabeth with a sigh. 'I don't know if that's because of the scandal or because of the pared-down style. Myself, I rather like them.'

'All right, that's your father,' Fred persisted. 'We left you at the age of two. Bring me up to date.'

'Oh, it's just the usual. Went to school—'

'That's where we met,' Elizabeth interjected. 'Holmes School. We sat next to each other in first grade. I was so jealous of your curls! My hair has always been straight as a stick.'

'Oh, I'd forgotten those curls!' exclaimed Leslie with the first genuine smile she'd displayed. 'They disappeared, never to return, when I was expecting little Davie. I never knew you were jealous. I thought you were the prettiest girl in the class, and you always had the most beautiful clothes.'

Elizabeth made a face. 'Mother dressed me up like a doll. I think she wanted to show everyone that we could afford expensive clothes that I'd outgrow in a few months. I hated all those frills. As soon as she let me, I insisted on simpler dresses.'

'Oh, yes, there was the great dancing school battle, wasn't there? I seem to remember your father stood up for you in that one.'

'He's always been there when I really needed him.' Elizabeth paused. 'And so have you.'

At that both women broke into tears and hugged each other, talking at once. Fred decided his presence was redundant and went to the kitchen to tell Aunt Lucy that lunch might be delayed.

He stayed away until he could hear no more sobs, waited another minute or two, then went upstairs to his room to find a couple of clean handkerchiefs. Returning to the parlor, he found the women sitting next to each other on the couch, red-eyed but smiling, and talking a mile a minute. 'Here you are, ladies,' he said, proffering the handkerchiefs. 'Never known a woman to have a decent hand-kerchief when she needed one.'

They laughed at that, mopped their faces, blew their noses, and started to laugh at the sorry sight they both presented.

'There, now,' said Lucy, coming into the room. 'I'm sure that's done you both a lot of good. Go upstairs and wash your faces, and then come down to lunch. Those biscuits won't stay hot forever.'

Elizabeth would have said, an hour ago, that she couldn't eat a bite. She devoured everything that was set before her, including three biscuits and a large piece of cherry pie, all the while chattering with Leslie and laughing over 'do you remember'.

Leslie apologized at one point to Aunt Lucy. 'I'm sorry we're talking so much. It's just that we have a lot to catch up on.'

'And a lot of shared memories,' said Lucy with a broad smile. 'Never mind. I like to see young people enjoying themselves.'

Fred pushed back his chair. 'I'm afraid I need to get back to the office. Lots of work to do. Elizabeth, I can come back at about five, if that will suit you.'

Leslie looked up with a question on her face.

'I'll explain later,' said Elizabeth. 'That'll be just right. Could you let my mother know . . . give her some explanation?'

'I'll think of something. I'm a good lawyer, remember?'

That left Leslie more confused than ever.

Elizabeth laughed. 'I'll tell you what's going on as soon as I've helped Lucy clear the table and clean up the kitchen.'

'You will not,' Lucy said firmly. 'You'll get yourself a fresh glass of iced tea and take it to the parlor and talk all you want. I need the kitchen to myself – those cakes, remember? Scoot.'

'Aunt Lucy is a sweetie-pie, isn't she?' Leslie was curled up on the couch, shoes kicked off.

'She's the best. The berries!'

They both laughed at her unexpected use of slang.

'I only met her today, and she treats me like one of the family. It's amazing.'

'Oh. Did she just move in?'

'No. Fred's parents lived here, but they died when he was ten. He was away at a private school, but Lucy moved in to look after Fred until he went back to school, and when he came home on holidays. She never married, and never left. I think he's the son she never had. And before you ask, I hadn't met her before because this is the first time I've been in Fred's house.'

'But . . . I thought you were—'

'Fred would like it to be that way. I haven't known him long, at least not well. What with law school and all, he hasn't lived here full time until the last few years. Up until now, all I wanted was a friend who loved music as much as I do. He takes me to the symphony, and Ravinia, and sometimes local concerts.' She bit her lip. 'I was afraid of a close relationship. I was never going to be hurt again, you see.'

'So that's why you dropped me.'

'Ouch! I never thought of it that way, you see. Never said to myself that Leslie was becoming a bore and I wasn't going to bother. Please believe me! I didn't go to your wedding because my loss was too new, too raw. I couldn't bear to see you so happy, selfish pig that I was. I had curled up inside my shell like a snail. Then later, when you began to have babies, I kept remembering my baby that never was, and the pain—'

'Oh, Beth, don't! I do understand, I really do. And if you go on you'll make me cry again!'

'Me, too. No one's called me Beth for years!'

The two women dabbed at their eyes with the voluminous hankies Fred had given them and laughed at themselves.

'Okay, so why did you decide today to drop in on Fred?'

'I'll try to summarize, but it's complicated, as I said before. It has to do with the murder.'

She didn't need to go into detail about that.

'Oh, yes,' said Leslie, 'poor Mr Anthony. And everyone in town knows by now your determination to play detective and unmask the villain. Honestly, Beth! Who do you think you are, Sherlock Holmes or somebody?'

'I know it sounds ridiculous. Even I can see that. But did you know the police have arrested someone who didn't do it? Arrested him on false evidence provided by the Walosas?' Her voice was getting higher, moved by her indignation. 'The police aren't going to do a thing. And because both the victim and the accused are Italians, the Mob could very well get involved, and it could get even uglier than it is now. Am I supposed to just sit around and watch it happen?'

'Beth, you're shouting! Have some tea and calm down.'

'Oh, I suppose I got carried away. But you can see, can't you, why I can't leave it alone? Somebody has to do something, and I'm not easily frightened. Not by other people, anyway. As for why I came here, my mother—'

Leslie groaned. 'I get it. She hasn't changed, then, has she? Still trying to run your life and maintain her image?'

'If anything, she's even more so. I admit I more or less forced her into letting me do what I want to do. I told her I'd be happy to move to an apartment so as not to embarrass her.'

Leslie giggled. 'And of course she couldn't have it said that she drove her own daughter away.'

'Right. But she knew I wanted to talk to quite a few people, and everyone, even Fred and Dad, have told me I mustn't leave the house alone – they think I'll be in danger. So she sat down to make phone calls, all day if necessary, to thwart me. And the only place I could think of where I could use the phone in peace was here. Dad brought me and made Fred promise to take me home.'

'So here you are. And it has nothing to do with the fact that you knew Fred would be sympathetic and helpful.'

'Well, of course I . . . but don't get the wrong idea!'

'I wouldn't dream of it, my dear.' Her voice was smooth as cream, and her eyes widened with innocence.

'You always were so . . . so . . .' Elizabeth said in exasperation.

'And I still am. But I'm not going to pick a fight today. Though it's good to be able to quarrel with you again! You've been so terrifyingly polite for so long. Now, what do you want me to do?'

FIFTEEN

'Just talk to people, that's all. I can't remember – did you ever take piano lessons from Mr Briggs? Or any music classes?'

'Piano lessons for one semester. I was dire! He was so patient, but I have a tin ear, and I block when I try to read music. You were always the musical one; I specialized in art. Anyway, what about Mr Briggs?'

'He's the man the police have decided is the murderer.'

Leslie choked on her tea. 'No! Not Mr Briggs! He's the sweetest, kindest—'

'Exactly! That's what I want you to tell everybody. The thing is, Mr Briggs is Italian. I didn't know that, you didn't know it, but somehow the Walosas found out and decided that therefore he killed his friend and fellow Italian Catholic, Mr Anthony. It would be ridiculous if it weren't so terrifying. The only way we're going to find out who really did this is if everyone in the village is up in arms about it.'

Leslie tried to mop up the tea she had splattered down the front of her dress. 'Hmm. It's an idea, but there are some you'll never convince. A lot of people think all Catholics are in league with the devil, the Italians the worst of all.'

'You mean Italians like Mr Anthony, friend to everyone. Like Mr Briggs, who taught music to almost everyone.'

'Ah, but no one knew they were Italian. That's the point, isn't it?' Leslie affected a censorious, matronly tone. 'They fooled everybody into thinking they were fine people. That's deception. How dare they masquerade like that? They did it on purpose, to take us all in. Probably plotting to corrupt our youth.' She dropped the persona. 'Or whatever they think Catholics do. That's what they'll say, you know, the Walosas and their friends. And they're a dangerous bunch to cross. Actually, I think your parents are quite right to be worried about your safety. You've got a tiger by the tail.'

'Yes, but you see, there's another tiger lurking out there, an even bigger, fiercer one. How long do you think the Boss is going to ignore the murder of one of his countrymen, and the false arrest of another one?'

Leslie let out a low whistle. 'Oh, good grief, you really have started a war! Do you even realize how bad this could be? The Mob aren't the kind to ask questions or try to prove who's wrong. They just start shooting!'

'You're right. They shoot when they think they can gain an advantage by killing someone, mostly in a battle over who controls the liquor distribution in a given area. But what have they got to gain by starting a war in Oak Park? Oh, of course I know a few people drink here. I suppose they get the stuff from Chicago. But it's a small trickle. There are no taverns here, no speakeasys, no bootleggers. No big business for Al Capone or any of his rivals.'

Leslie thought about that. 'You may be right. But all the same, it's a powder keg we're sitting on. You're assuming all the gangsters are under Capone's control. Lots of them aren't. They're trigger-happy and unpredictable.'

'But I don't think they're stupid. They know which side their bread is buttered on, and they know breaking with their gang is dangerous, whether that gang is Capone's Outfit or the North Side Gang or whoever. So as I see it, they'll step carefully until they know more about what's going on.' Elizabeth leaned forward to emphasize her point. 'And the one thing they're sure is going on is the agitation caused by the Klan.'

'You think they know about that?'

'If they don't now, they will by the time I get a few people talking. You know how gossip spreads in this town. So it's really important that you start urging it along.'

'In other words, get out of here and get busy.' Leslie stood.

'You know I'm not trying to get rid of you, not after we've just become friends again. It's just that—'

The doorbell rang. Once, twice, a third time.

The two women froze.

'All right, all right,' Aunt Lucy muttered, moving from the kitchen. 'Hold your horses.'

'Don't answer!' whispered Elizabeth urgently. 'Don't let them see you!'

Lucy's footsteps stopped. 'But I saw them,' she whispered back. 'It's the police. I have to answer!'

Elizabeth peeked out through a chink in the draperies. 'It's the Chicago police, not ours! Don't let them in!'

Lucy tiptoed into the parlor. 'What should I do?' She was trembling.

'Sit down. It's all right. Just sit tight and they'll go away. Leslie, stay with her. I'm going to call Fred!'

The doorbell was still ringing. A heavy fist began pounding on the door. 'Police! Open up!'

Elizabeth couldn't remember the number of the law office. She dialed the operator and tried to keep her voice steady as she asked to be connected.

'I can't hear you. Speak up, please.'

'I can't. This is an emergency. Connect me to Carter, Sanders and Smith immediately!'

'I'll ring the police.'

'NO! The law office. Now!'

The pounding and shouting grew louder. The few seconds it took to get connected seemed like forever, and of course it was the secretary who answered in her calm, professional voice.

Elizabeth wanted to shout, but she didn't dare. She turned up her whisper to top volume. 'This is Elizabeth Fairchild. I need to speak to Fred Wilkins urgently. Please interrupt him, no matter what he's doing. This is an emergency.'

A brief pause while the woman assessed the situation, then she said, 'Certainly, Mrs Fairchild. One moment.'

Fred answered promptly, sounding agitated. 'Elizabeth, what is it? What's wrong?'

'The Chicago police are at the door, hammering to get in. Fred, I'm scared! You know how corrupt they are. What do they want?'

'I'm on my way. Lock yourselves in the bathroom in case they break down the door.'

He hung up. Elizabeth crept to the parlor and beckoned Lucy and Leslie to come with her. 'Are there back stairs?' she whispered. 'Fred says to go up to the bathroom, but the front stairs—'

The front stairs were in full view of the front door. 'No back stairs,' said Lucy, 'but we can go down to the cellar. Hurry!'

The hallway was dark and shadowy. Elizabeth had barely noticed the clouds gathering, but now a loud rumble of thunder shook the air, drowning out for an instant the assault on the door. Another summer storm was coming.

Good. A torrential rain might drive away those nasty cops at the door.

It didn't come quite soon enough. The three women had just reached the stairs down to the cellar when there was a distinct tinkle of breaking glass.

Lucy gasped. 'They're breaking in!' She fumbled for the light switch as she pulled the door shut behind her.

A single bulb dangled from a cord at the bottom of the stairs, which were steep and narrow. Lucy led them down as fast as she dared, but there was danger in haste. At one point Leslie slid, in her fashionable shoes, down a step, but Elizabeth managed to catch her. 'Is there any place to hide?' she asked, looking frantically around the dimness.

'The fruit closet!' said Lucy breathlessly. 'It'll be a tight squeeze for the three of us, but the door opens in. We can easily keep those awful men out.'

Elizabeth wasn't so sure about that. From the single glance she'd had, she thought the men were more than a match for three women. But there was no option. They ran up the stone steps in the corner, opened the sturdy wooden door, and crowded in among the jars and jars of tomatoes and green beans and jams of all sorts. By squeezing together almost to suffocation, they managed to get the door shut behind them.

Pitch-black.

'Now girls,' said Lucy, who had recovered her composure, 'I can't move at all. But if you'll feel around with your foot, whoever's closest to the door, you should find a wedge. If you can wedge it under the door, good and tight, we're safe as houses.'

As long as we can breathe, thought Elizabeth. She didn't speak the thought.

'Do you think they'll find us?' asked Leslie nervously. 'I can't hear what they're doing at all.'

'No, you wouldn't,' said Lucy. 'That door is very sturdy, and close-fitting, because of rats. And the walls are stone. This was meant to be a root cellar, but my brother – Fred's father, you know – wanted a place to store canned fruit and vegetables, so he had the shelves put in. His wife was a wonderful cook.'

'I'd have thought he'd have put a light in.' Elizabeth shivered a little. She wasn't cold. In fact it was growing very warm in the closet. But she didn't care for dark, enclosed spaces.

'Oh, no, he hadn't had the house wired for electricity before he died. It was Fred who did that. I was quite happy with lamps, but he thought they were too much work for me, so when Oak Park began to provide electric power, he insisted on having the whole house wired. I admit I was a bit uneasy about it at first. You hear so many stories—'

'What was that!' cried Leslie.

There had certainly been a noise, audible even in their stifling cavern.

'It sounded like a door closing, didn't it?' Elizabeth barely breathed the question. She felt Lucy's nod.

Then footsteps came up the three stone steps. A hand on the latch, a push. Another push.

The wedge held.

There were no voices. Elizabeth couldn't understand why the noisy cops were noisy no longer.

Then there was another noise, as of someone knocking over something heavy and metallic, and a few words. 'Blast the infernal thing!'

'Fred!' cried Lucy and Elizabeth together. 'Leslie, can you get the wedge out? Fred, we're in the fruit closet. We'll be out in a minute!'

Working in the dark and in close quarters, it cost Leslie some panicky minutes and a torn fingernail, but she eventually got the wedge loose enough to open the door a crack. Good cool air rushed in, and the faint light from the single bulb seemed as bright as the sun.

With a little help from Fred, Leslie managed to slither out through the narrow opening, and the other two followed.

And of course they all talked at once.

'Couldn't go upstairs, so we . . .'

'And I was afraid we'd run out of air . . .'

'They broke the window in the door! Are they allowed . . .'

'So I came as soon as I could, but . . .'

'Where . . .?'

'What . . .?'

'All right,' Fred finally said loudly. He picked up the coal scuttle he had stumbled over. 'Why don't we all go upstairs and have a nice cup of coffee, or tea or something, and get the whole story. But first, are you all okay?'

'Berries,' said Elizabeth with a shaky grin.

'Bees knees,' agreed Leslie.

'Cat's pajamas,' claimed Lucy loudly, reducing them all to helpless laughter.

SIXTEEN

Lucy made a big pot of tea and got the cookie jar out of the pantry, and they sat down comfortably in the parlor, gradually returning to calm.

'First we want to hear your story,' Lucy demanded of Fred. 'We couldn't hear anything down where we were.'

'Yes, but why were you there? You'd have been perfectly safe locked in the bathroom, and a lot more comfortable.'

'I told you,' said Lucy. 'We couldn't get there.'

'Yes, but why?'

'Fred, think!' Elizabeth was growing impatient. 'Where are the stairs?'

He smacked his head. 'Of course! They'd have seen you. And as long as they didn't—'

'We could pretend nobody was home. Besides, they'd have followed us as soon as they got in, and I don't think a locked bathroom door would have stopped them for long. But you haven't told us anything! I want to know how you got them to go away.'

'Oh, that was easy. I borrowed Sanders's car. He drives a big Buick, very impressive. So I drove up, walked up to them, put on my most intimidating manner and asked what they thought they were doing to my house. They started to bluster, and I informed them that I was an attorney-at-law and that they had no jurisdiction in Oak Park, and further that they were wasting their time pounding on the door when no one was home. Then I demanded to see their search warrant.'

'And they didn't have one,' said Lucy with satisfaction.

'They had nothing except bravado. Like most bullies, they were obviously cowards at heart. When I asked for their names and their identification, they couldn't get out of there fast enough. I did manage to write down a couple of badge numbers, though. Someone's going to pay for the damage to the front door!'

'Well, I think you were terribly brave,' proclaimed Leslie, raising her teacup in a toast. 'We were terrified, or at least I was.'

The other two nodded. 'They were so loud,' said Elizabeth, a small tremor still in her voice. 'But what I can't understand is what they were doing here.'

'Plainly they were sent by the Mob,' said Fred quietly. 'I think, my dear, that you were followed here.'

Leslie gasped. Elizabeth said nothing, but she stiffened and licked her lips. Lucy reached over and took her hand.

'What did they want with me, do you think?' said Elizabeth when she had taken a sip of tea to soothe her suddenly dry mouth.

'Probably just meant to frighten you. Which they did.'

'Yes.' Another sip of tea. 'But not enough to make me give up and crawl into a hole somewhere.'

'I think you're crazy,' Leslie pronounced. 'Dopey, nutty, cuckoo. But if you're determined to go through with this idiotic scheme, count me in. I don't much care for the idea of innocent people being bullied by the police.'

'Bravo!' Lucy clapped her little plump hands. 'Tell us what we can do to help.'

Fred raised a hand. 'The sentiments are admirable, the sense somewhat less so. You've had a little taste, Elizabeth, of what sort of strength is ranged against you. If you're still determined to go ahead with this—'

'And I am.'

'—then I suggest some elementary precautions, if Aunt Lucy agrees. For a start, I'd like you to remain here for a day or two.'

A half-smile appeared. 'Mother—' she began.

'Fred and I can deal with your mother,' said Lucy firmly.

Lucy plainly had hidden depths. Elizabeth thought perhaps she could, in fact, defuse her mother. 'Dad will be a bit worried, too, but for him it has to do with the propriety of me staying here with a man.'

'We'll set his mind at rest about that, too,' said Fred with a smile. 'I'll move out if necessary.'

'No, you won't,' said Lucy. 'I'm an adequate chaperone, and anyway, we need your stalwart presence. Now, what other suggestions do you have?'

'A wider publicity campaign. Your idea, Elizabeth, of word-of-mouth dissemination is a good one, but there are more efficient means of spreading the word.' He looked at his wristwatch. '*Oak Leaves* is the best way, but it won't be out till Saturday. Meanwhile, most people in town also read the *Tribune*, and it's a morning daily. If I hurry I can catch the next train to the city.'

'But will they run a story about the murder of a man of no importance, as they would think?'

'Not a story, my dear, but an advertisement. A big splashy one. No newspaper in the history of the world has ever turned down revenue. And maybe I can get someone in their art department to come up with a sketch to make it more interesting.'

'I can do that,' said Leslie. 'What would you like? A picture of Mr Anthony, or of his shop, or what?'

Fred turned to her, doubt written on his face. 'You could do Anthony's face? But it has to be in a hurry, you know.'

'Yes. Someone get me a sheet of paper. Stationery will do if you don't have anything bigger. And a soft pencil.'

They watched as, with a few quick lines and a little shading, she brought a dead man to life on paper.

Elizabeth was astonished. 'But it's him! How do you *do* that?'

Leslie shrugged. 'I could always draw. Your special talent is music. With me, it's art. Will this do, Fred?'

'It's perfect! If you'll all trust me to write the ad, I need to be off right this minute. Keep the doors locked, and put something over that broken pane!' he shouted as he grabbed his briefcase and ran out the back door.

'He's leaving the Buick behind,' said Lucy, the practical one. 'Poor Mr Sanders.'

'It's an easy walk from the office. He can come get it if he wants.'

'If Fred left the key in it.' Leslie sounded dubious.

'Not our problem, girls.' Lucy rose. 'Now, the first thing I need to do, Elizabeth, is to call your parents. It would be better if I could go and see them, but that would leave you alone, which I'm not about to do. What's your number?'

She bustled off to the kitchen, and the two women looked at each other. 'Your mother is a pretty tough nut to crack,' said Leslie with the freedom of an old friend. 'What are her chances?'

Elizabeth shrugged. 'Fifty-fifty, I'd say. If she talks to Dad first and convinces him, he'll stand up for me against Mother. He always does when it's really important. But in a sense it doesn't matter. They can't drag me out of here, after all. I'd prefer not to defy them, but I will if I have to.'

'Right. What's your next move?'

'When Fred gets back I need to ask him about the bail issue. Then I should probably call Mrs Hemingway. She's been waging her own campaign.'

'And I should get started on mine. But what I meant was what are you going to do when all the publicity has made you feel relatively safe?'

'I don't honestly know, to tell the truth. I'll start to follow up on any hints I get from the rumor mill. Someone's bound to know something! When I get enough ideas, I'll take them to the police. They'll almost have to cooperate, if public feeling is against them.'

'You keep forgetting the Klan, Beth!' Leslie sounded exasperated. 'They'll be doing all they can to undermine your campaign.'

'Yes, I know. But they'll also be fighting the Outfit, and the other gangs, who very much want to find out who killed one of their own.'

'You're not saying poor Mr Anthony was a gangster! I don't believe it!'

Elizabeth made a face. 'Heavens, no! I just meant he was an Italian Catholic. And so is Mr Briggs. These gangsters fight among themselves, but they unite against the outside world. They won't let Mr Briggs be railroaded. And formidable as the Walosas and their husbands are, I'd back Capone and his buddies to win, any time.'

Leslie shuddered and opened her mouth, but stopped when Lucy came back into the room.

'That's all settled, then, girls. Your father was at school—'

'Oh, of course! I forgot about exams. So you had to talk to Mother?'

'No, my dear, your maid or housekeeper or whoever answered the phone, and she said she'd tell your parents. I take it she's dependable?'

'As the rock of Gibraltar,' said Elizabeth firmly.

'I got that impression. She wanted to bring you some nightclothes and so on, but I told her I'd be happy to lend you anything you need. Of course anything I own would go around you twice, but I thought it would be better if she didn't come here. It's just possible, isn't it, that your house is being watched, and we want to keep them thinking that you're there and have been all the time. They couldn't have known for certain that you were here this afternoon; they never saw you. Oh, and I found a piece of an old orange crate to block the broken pane in the door. It's only wedged in, but it'll do until Fred can nail it down.'

'Aunt Lucy, you're wasted as a cook-housekeeper. You could be the star of the FBI!' Elizabeth walked over and gave her a hug.

'Nonsense! I'm just using the wits the good Lord gave me. Now, Leslie, we need to work out a way to get you home safely, and I think I've got an idea. Come to the back door, dear. Now look out. Disgraceful, isn't it? Fred manages to get the lawn mowed, but I'm afraid he hasn't had time to trim the bushes.'

The hedges were certainly out of control. A big quince by the back door was in full bloom, and though it was beautiful, it so blocked the door as to make it almost impossible to get out. A little farther down the path, on the other side, a big lilac was drooping fragrant heads of blossom. The rain had loaded them down, so no one could walk there without getting very wet. And on the perimeter of the back yard, privet hedges on either side of a gate rose to at least seven feet. 'Those have needed attention for years, but by now it would take two men on ladders to tame them, and I actually enjoy the privacy. So you see, you can easily get out of the house unseen, go down the back alley and through the neighbor's yard, and come out on the next street. You might stop and wave goodbye to a window in the nearest house, making it look more like you just left there. I think you'll be fine.'

Leslie hugged both women. 'You're both terrific! Aunt Lucy, give me your phone number before I leave, so I can stay in touch. And Beth, I'll start calling friends the minute I get home!'

'After you kiss your kids and tell your mother how grateful I am for her help. And thank you, Leslie – for everything.'

'I'd better leave before we get maudlin. You don't have to come with me.' This to Lucy as she started out the back door. 'I can figure it out.'

'Yes, dear, I'm just checking to see that no one's around. Then later, when Fred gets home, I'm going to leave and come back, too. Leave the back way and come in the front, to show anyone who might be watching that I've been away for some time.'

'Like I said, Aunt Lucy, you should get a job in espionage. You're a natural!' Elizabeth looked out the door for Leslie, who had already disappeared in the shrubbery, and firmly closed and locked it.

'And now, while we wait, let's go in the kitchen. I still have another pie or two to make today, and you can help me.'

'I don't know a thing about making pies,' Elizabeth protested.

'Then it's time you learned. Someday you'll need to know. You'll probably have a cook, but she'll need supervising, at least at first. And it's better than just sitting there worrying. Come along, dear!'

Elizabeth mused, as she put an apron back on, how astounding it was that after only a few hours in this house, she already felt completely at home.

SEVENTEEN

The afternoon wore on. Elizabeth fetched and carried, peeled and sliced apples, cleaned rhubarb and cut it into pieces. She was not entrusted with the delicate, skilled job of making piecrust, but she observed while Lucy explained the fine points. The kitchen began to fill with mouthwatering aromas, and also with stifling heat. The respite brought by the storm had been brief; heat and humidity were building again. Through the open windows they could hear the faint sound of trains from Chicago arriving and departing again. With every train whistle, Elizabeth's nerves tightened, and then sagged again as the sounds diminished into the distance.

Lucy was beginning to assemble the makings of a light supper when they heard the sound of the front door being unlocked. Elizabeth only then realized how tense she'd been.

The tension returned and mounted high when he came into the kitchen.

'Fred!' both woman cried.

His tie was askew, his jacket sleeve torn. One cheek was swollen and purple, and his nose looked like it had been bleeding. He sat down heavily.

'Fred, what *happened*?' Lucy had taken a small block of ice from the icebox and was breaking it up. 'Did you get in a fight? Did someone hurt you?'

'No, and yes. It wasn't a fight, but I do hurt. Ouch!'

Lucy had carefully wrapped the ice in a towel and applied it to his cheek. 'It'll feel better soon, I promise. Would you like some coffee?'

'Not right now. Hey, you're right. It's feeling better. Maybe some water? And an aspirin?'

When these remedies had been administered, Elizabeth said, 'Fred. Tell us.'

'It wasn't anything, really. I was coming back from Tribune Tower, just minding my own business, when I ran into a melee just outside the train station. There must have been fifteen or twenty men having at it with fists and broken bottles and I don't know what all. It was too confusing to see much.'

'Guns? Was there shooting?'

'No shooting that I heard, and I didn't see any guns. But I wasn't looking. I just wanted to get out of there, fast. I went around the block to come at the station from the other way, but there was a gang of toughs coming down the street there, too. It looked like turning into a full-scale riot, so I just tried to skirt the crowd and keep my head down. It didn't work too well.'

'I should say not!' said Lucy indignantly. 'Why did they start in on you?'

'They didn't, really. I was just in the way. At one point I got shoved into the wall of the station – that's where the bruise came from – and I fell once. That was the worst part. I thought they would trample on me. But I managed to roll away, into the door of the station, and that was that. I'm sorry I'm such a sight. There wasn't time to wash up before the next train left, and I just wanted to get home.'

'But who were these people? What was it all about?'

'I have no idea. Doubtless we can read all about it in the *Trib* tomorrow. Which reminds me. I did manage to accomplish my mission. Where did I put my briefcase?'

Lucy handed it to him, and he pulled out a piece of paper. 'They pulled a proof for me. Careful. The ink might not be quite dry.'

The piece of newsprint he pulled out of his bag was a full page. At the top, in large capital letters, the headline read: WHO KILLED THIS MAN?

Then the sketch of Mr Anthony, enlarged from Leslie's drawing. Below the picture ran the text:

Mr Enrico Antonelli, professionally known as Mr Anthony, was foully murdered sometime in the late afternoon of Thursday, June 4. His body was found behind his antique shop, Anthony's Emporium, on Marion Street in Oak Park. The initial suspect in the crime is almost certainly not the murderer, and has been released from police custody. If you have any information about this crime, REPORT IT AT ONCE TO THE OAK PARK POLICE DEPARTMENT, 651 LAKE STREET, PHONE EUCLID 2487, OR TO FREDERICK WILKINS, ATTORNEY-AT-LAW, AT CARTER, SANDERS

AND SMITH, 253 N. MARION STREET, PHONE VILLAGE
6982. A SUBSTANTIAL REWARD WILL BE PAID FOR
INFORMATION LEADING TO THE ARREST AND
CONVICTION OF THE CRIMINAL!

Elizabeth whistled. 'Fred, it's wonderful! It certainly ought to
attract attention. It will run tomorrow?'

'And for the next week. They agreed to change the position in
the paper every day, so those who read only one or another section
will see it. I'd planned to stop at the *Oak Leaves* office, but decided
I looked too disreputable. There's plenty of time before their
deadline for Saturday. I'll tell them to run it again the following
week, though I hope by then we won't need it.'

'We can hope. It's going to cost a lot, I expect. Did you have
to pay in advance?'

'No. A lawyer is assumed to be reliable, I suppose. They're
going to bill me.'

'And of course I'll foot the bill. Worth every penny, if it turns
up any information. This was a brilliant idea, Fred, and I'm grateful.'

Lucy asserted her authority. 'Fred, you go upstairs and have a
nice bath, with Epsom salts. Take your time; supper is cold and
we can eat it any time. Now I'm going to come home myself.'

She whisked off her apron, gathered up her handbag, and went
out the back door while Elizabeth explained the stratagem.

Fred chuckled. 'She's a lot more than just a sweet, fluffy, old
lady.'

'I told her she could have had a great career as a spy. Go get
into that bath.'

Only when he was gone did she let herself think about what
might have happened.

Lucy returned before Fred came downstairs, looking much less
like a gangster, and they all sat down to supper. By tacit consent
they left their problems out of table conversation, and only
when they had settled in the parlor with coffee did Elizabeth say,
'The ad said Mr Briggs was no longer in custody. Does that mean
he got bail?'

'It does. There wasn't time to tell you before. Mrs Hemingway
evidently twisted arms to some effect. Bail was set at two thousand
dollars, fairly low because they think there's little risk of him
trying to escape. And you don't have to worry about the cost; a

bail bondsman was quite willing to take it on. So he's home with his family, and everyone is much happier.'

'And what were you, or Mr Sanders, able to learn from Mr Briggs? Or from anyone else?'

'Quite a lot, though little of any immediate interest. He was able to give us a list of Mr Anthony's closest friends. You're on that list, by the way. Apparently several of his customers felt very close to him.'

'He was a lot more than just a shopkeeper. He was a friend.' She took a sip of coffee to hide her face for a moment.

'A friend to a bunch of people, it seems, from rich to poor, doctors and lawyers to laborers. Briggs said Anthony didn't make a lot of money, but enough to be comfortable and to give a hand to anyone in need. Father Cole thought very highly of him, I was told.'

'All this is just what I'd have expected,' said Lucy. 'He had an excellent reputation as an honest man who knew his business and treated his customers well. But as you say, that isn't very helpful now. The point is, who were his enemies?'

'And that's the problem. So far as the Briggs family are aware, he had no enemies. Just a kind, gentle man who loved beautiful things.'

There was a depressed silence. It was Aunt Lucy who broke it. 'Then we're back to the Klan. They hated him just because he was a foreigner and a Catholic.'

'But they hate all foreigners and Catholics,' Elizabeth objected. 'Why pick on him, in particular? And it isn't their sort of murder, anyway. They go for big, flashy demonstrations. Cross-burning, lynching, that sort of thing. To "teach them a lesson". I've never heard of them stabbing someone in the back.'

'The front,' corrected Fred with a shudder. 'He was stabbed in his chest, just below the ribs. Straight to the heart, they tell me. At least he died instantly.'

Lucy set down her coffee cup with a trembling hand. 'I wish you hadn't told us that, dear.' Her face was pale.

Elizabeth had to take several deep breaths before she could speak. 'Well, if not the Walosas or their henchmen, then was it in fact a robbery gone wrong? A chance victim, not killed because of who he was but simply because he was there?'

Fred looked at her with sympathy. 'That's hard to take, isn't it? But it's one possible answer. Except nothing seems to have been stolen. Sanders has managed to persuade the police to organize an inventory, and so far everything seems to tally, even the highboy, sitting there in the back room pristine as ever.'

'So it comes down to person or persons unknown,' said Elizabeth bitterly.

'Unknown, yes, but not unguessed at.' There was an odd tone in Fred's voice.

'What do you know that you haven't told us?' Elizabeth demanded.

'I don't actually know any more, but there are hints in the air. Lucy, is there any more coffee?'

'I can make some. But you'll never sleep if you have more at this time of night.'

'It isn't late, and after my experience in Chicago, nothing could keep me awake. But don't get up; I'll make it.'

'No, you won't. The last time you tried, I could have used it to clean the drains. Don't you say a word until I get back.'

'Fred, you're so lucky,' said Elizabeth when they were alone. 'I don't mean just in Chicago today.' She shuddered. 'I don't even want to think about that. No, I mean Lucy. She's the nicest person I've ever met. Here I descend upon her without warning, tie up the phone, create a terrible situation just by being here when those awful cops came – and she not only treats me like a long-lost daughter, but knows just what to do in a pinch. I've never met anyone like her.'

'There aren't many like her. I don't remember my parents very well; I was too young when they died. But every now and then something she'll say, or a tone of voice, will remind me of my father. I think he was probably a very good man.'

'Like mine. But he can't – you see, my mother—'

'Your mother is a deeply insecure woman. She values her wealth and social position, but she's always uneasy lest she lose them. She would like you to bow to her will, so she could show you off to her fine friends, but she doesn't understand that you are not a person who can be forced. Nor is your father. He seldom defies his wife, steers a middle course to keep the peace, but I've noticed he always supports you when it really matters. Ah! Here's our coffee.'

It was a good thing, because Elizabeth was nearly in tears again. She had cried more today, she thought, than she had since Will and the baby died. This time it was Fred's precise analysis of her family life. She had no idea her mother was so transparent to those outside the family. For a moment she felt a deep pang of pity for her.

And then Lucy handed her a cup of coffee with a cookie on the saucer, and said, 'All right. Carry on, Fred. "Hints in the air", you said.'

'Yes, and I mean just that. Hints. Nothing you can put a finger on. But you need to understand, both of you, that our police here in Oak Park aren't stupid. Nor are they corrupt, which is remarkable, considering the example set by our neighbor to the east. They are a small force, and they seldom have to deal with anything more serious than lost dogs and petty thievery and the occasional domestic disturbance. This is, by and large, a law-abiding community.

'But our police are, I repeat, not stupid. They know what a burglary looks like. And they know what a gangland execution looks like, even if they may never have dealt with one.' He held up a hand as Lucy was about to speak. 'I know, I know. They favor tommy guns. But that's when they want to set an example, to strike fear into someone's heart. See what happens when someone damages us, defies us? There are occasions, though, when the goons prefer a nice quiet murder. And for those occasions, they're expert with knives.'

'So you think—' began Elizabeth.

'I don't think anything, yet. As I said, there are just hints floating around, a vague suggestion that all is not as it seems.'

'But it just *might* be the work of one of the gangs, though that seems impossible, given what we know about Mr Anthony.' Elizabeth frowned and finished her coffee.

'That, at any rate, would explain why those Chicago cops were sent here,' commented Lucy, pouring another cup and pushing over the plate of cookies. 'Some gang doesn't want Elizabeth poking her nose into their affairs.'

'But it's absurd!' Elizabeth stood and began to pace around the room, finding her way gingerly between armchairs, ottomans, and occasional tables. 'Mr Anthony was just not that sort of man. He would no more get involved in a gang deal than my mother would!'

The others chuckled at that, but Fred sobered quickly. 'Sometimes a businessman is given no choice,' he said gently. 'I'm sure you know about protection rackets.'

'Of course! I'm not stupid either, Fred Wilkins! Nor am I uninformed. Gangs demand payment from other gangs to "protect" them. In other words, we won't shoot at you if you pay us enough, or let our bootleggers alone, or whatever. But not in Oak Park, where we don't *have* taverns or bootleggers or gangs.'

'We have gangsters, though. You know that. Individuals, to be sure, not organized locally, but not averse to a little unearned cash. And victims of the racket aren't always other gangs. That lucrative business has branched out. Let's say you own a shop selling, oh, antiques, perhaps. You have a good deal of valuable inventory, some of it displayed in a shop window. A breakable glass shop window. A customer walks in, someone you've never seen in the place before. He wants to buy something. You haggle a bit and finally sell it to him. He mentions that you have a lot of nice things. Be a shame if something happened to them, wouldn't it? One rock through that window . . . He leaves you with that thought and comes back again. And again, until you finally give in and agree to pay the minimal sum he asks. But it keeps increasing until at last you protest and say you can't afford it anymore, and anyway the police can protect you. It's not long before someone comes around to administer a little discipline.'

'I see.' Elizabeth had turned even paler than usual. She sat down abruptly in the nearest chair. 'And maybe the discipline went a little too far this time.'

'It's possible.' Fred spread his hands. 'Of course there's not a shadow of proof.'

'But there might be. A customer like that did come into the shop, the day before Mr Anthony was killed!'

She told the story of the man who bought the watch, the man Mr Anthony didn't much like. 'He didn't want to sell it to him, but he said he was "very persuasive". I took that to mean threatening. That's the way it sounded, anyway. Oh, and Mr Anthony quoted a really ridiculous price, hoping the man would go away, but he bought it anyway.'

'What was the price?' asked Fred sharply.

'I don't know. I didn't ask. But even a reasonable price would be pretty high, I'd think. The watch was gold, and very attractive. I'd wanted it for my father, and poor Mr Anthony was devastated that he didn't have it anymore. Why? What does the price matter?'

'Because your nasty customer might not have had that much cash with him, and might have had to write a check. Which just *might* still be in the cash drawer!'

'With his name on it!' Elizabeth's face brightened.

'Yes. But don't get too excited. We're dreaming up a scenario that might have no reality. It's your impression that the customer was a gangster, based entirely on your interpretation of what Mr Anthony said. That isn't even hearsay, but about six degrees removed. And even if he was, he might have paid cash. These bozos like to carry cash around. Makes them feel important. So it might lead us somewhere, but equally it might not.'

At that Lucy stood up and yawned. 'I've always loved your bright, optimistic outlook on life, dear, but I think I've had enough of it for tonight. Elizabeth, love, come up to your room and laugh at the nightclothes I've found for you. Fred, you'll make doubly sure everything is locked up tight, won't you?' She yawned again. 'Goodnight.'

EIGHTEEN

Elizabeth slept badly that night. She was in an unfamiliar bed, with a cotton nightgown that wound around her with every movement and eventually twisted itself into a straitjacket. She'd had too much coffee too late at night, and her mind was twisting as much as her gown, with much the same strangling effect on her thoughts. She finally crept out of bed, drank a little water from the jug Lucy had thoughtfully left for her, and removed the nightgown. The night was very warm, and she could sleep much more comfortably in her rayon chemise and bloomers.

But she couldn't divest herself as easily of her errant thoughts. Was it possible that Mr Anthony had somehow run afoul of a gang, and they had taken revenge? If that was the case, then she would still be in danger, and so might everyone who was helping her. As long as she thought the gangs were interested only in defending Mr Briggs, one of their own (in a way), then they could fight it out with the Walosas all they wanted, as far as she was concerned.

But what if it was in fact an execution? What if – oh, *no*! What if Mr Briggs were also involved, also in the clutches of the Mob? Could he have been forced to . . . no. That was the kind of nightmare idea that came at two o'clock on a stormy, unsettled night. Not possible. For the twentieth time she turned over, pounded her pillow, tried to find a comfortable position. It was too hot.

What had really happened in Chicago? Were those rioters gang members, or just ordinary street toughs? What if Fred had been . . . no. She wouldn't let herself even think about what might have happened. But if the men *were* gangsters . . .

She wished she had Ginger to pet, or even Charlie, though he was a little too active to be a satisfactory cuddle-cat, even in the middle of the night. And either of them would be hot.

She got up again, found a handkerchief in a drawer, moistened it from the jug, and ran it over her face and neck. She *had* to get some sleep! Hickory, dickory dock, the mouse ran up the clock. Baa, baa black sheep, have you any wool? Counting sheep was supposed to help, but her mind wouldn't conjure up pictures of sheep in any quantity. 'Sheep may safely graze . . .' The calming strain of music ran through her head and led to another. 'He shall feed his flock . . .' She fell asleep in the middle of 'Come unto me'.

She was awakened in the morning by a knock at her door. She sat up, remembered where she was, and – oh, dear! – that she was improperly clad. She clutched the sheet to her neck and croaked out, 'Yes?'

The door opened the merest crack. 'I'm sorry to wake you, dear, but Mrs Hemingway has called twice, and she's most insistent that she needs to talk to you.'

Elizabeth's head cleared slightly. 'How did she know I was here?'

'I expect she called your home and got someone to tell her.'

'Oh, I suppose. She can be very . . . persuasive. Well, I'm sorry you had to deal with this, Lucy. I'll be right down.'

'Take your time. I'm sure you didn't sleep well. Grace Hemingway can wait for a bit.'

The door closed, and Elizabeth fell back against the pillows, then sighed resentfully and forced herself out of bed. She resumed the nightgown for a quick trip to the bathroom, washed sketchily, and got into yesterday's clothes, which looked as discouraged as she herself felt. The weather didn't help. It was gray and gloomy, and still oppressively hot, the threat of another storm weighting the air.

Lucy was just pouring coffee for her when she plodded into the kitchen. 'This should help, dear. You look, if you don't mind my saying so, like a rag doll left out in the rain.'

That brought a faint smile to her face. 'I pretty much feel like that. You're right. I didn't get much sleep. It was so hot, and I couldn't stop thinking about . . . everything.'

'And it's so awful putting on rumpled clothes, isn't it? Lowers your spirits even more.'

Elizabeth nodded.

'I wonder, dear . . . now that Mrs Hemingway knows where you are, it won't be long before everyone knows.'

Another smile. 'Yes, she's known for spreading the word. She's been a very great help to me over the years, but there's no denying she's a force to be reckoned with.'

'Well, then, it seems to me there's no reason why she shouldn't send someone to get some of your clothes. That is, if you plan to stay here for a while. And I hope you do!'

'Oh, there's nothing I'd like better! But I think Dad would be very hurt to think I preferred to be away from my own home.'

Lucy nodded thoughtfully. 'Yes, I can see that. Do you think he wouldn't understand?'

'No, he would understand. He knows exactly how strained my relationship with my mother is. I've just realized that the whole town knows!'

'It's a small town. Of course everyone knows. But they also know what a fine person you are, how much you do for charity, and what a lovely voice you have. And they know and love your father. If you want my opinion, I think your father would want you to have this time to relax and be pampered a little.'

She paused for thought. 'Tell you what. Suppose I call your father and talk to him about it, and then you can talk to him, too.'

Elizabeth considered that as she finished her coffee. 'You'll have to be a bit careful about what you say. The phone is in the hall outside the kitchen. There's no privacy at all.'

'Understood.'

The phone rang, sounding unusually loud and demanding.

'Oh, dear, that'll be Mrs Hemingway again.'

Elizabeth jumped up. 'I'll answer it. No reason for her to scold you.'

Once Elizabeth had explained why she was answering ('Miss Wilkins is busy in the kitchen') and apologized for being unavailable earlier, Mrs Hemingway got down to business.

'Well, never mind. The point is, I have some information for you. First of all, Mr Briggs is out of jail. Where he never should have been in the first place, and I told that judge so in no uncertain terms!'

Elizabeth, withholding the information that she already knew about that, expressed suitable gratitude.

'Yes, well, it was the least I could do for a fellow musician. But there's lots more to tell you, that I don't want to say over the phone. You never know who might be listening in. Could you come to see me this afternoon about three?'

That meant Elizabeth had to explain why staying in the house seemed like a more sensible idea. 'But you could certainly come to visit me here at Fred's house. I'd love to see you, and I know Miss Wilkins would be delighted. Do you know the address?'

'Of course. Three o'clock, then.' She hung up, and Elizabeth went to break the news to Lucy.

'I'm sorry,' she said. 'I should have asked first, but you know how impatient she is, and I'd already kept her waiting all morning, as she saw it. I hope it isn't inconvenient.'

'Of course not. My dear girl, I told you, this house is yours, for as long as you want to stay with me. I must see what I have to offer Her Majesty in the way of refreshments. But first I'll call your father.'

Elizabeth looked at her watch. 'Oh, dear, I think I forgot to wind it last night. What time is it?'

Lucy grinned. 'Nearly noon.'

'Oh, no! I've never slept that late in my life! What must you think of me! But it's not the best time to call Dad. He'll be home all day grading test papers, but in a minute or two he and Mother will be having lunch, and the dining room is very close to the phone.'

'Ah. Well then, how about a nice fruit salad for lunch? Fred said he won't be home; some meeting or other.'

That reminded Elizabeth to check the *Tribune* for news about yesterday's small riot, but she could find nothing. Good grief, was violence so common in Chicago now that street fights weren't even news? How long might it be before the lawlessness reached Oak Park?

It was another thought to be pushed to the back of her mind.

After lunch, they cleaned up the kitchen quickly, and then Lucy set out to make another pie or two and some fresh cookies in

honor of Mrs Hemingway, stopping work after the first pie to call
Mr Walker.

After only a few words, Lucy handed the receiver to Elizabeth,
but stayed close.

'Dad, I— What? Oh, no! No! What can I— Oh. Yes, I see, but
Dad, I can't—' This time the pause lasted for a little longer. 'Yes.
No, I'm fine. Yes.'

She handed the receiver back to Lucy and sank into the chair.

'Yes, I'll look after her. Of course. You'll let us know?'

Lucy hung up the phone. 'Your mother,' she said. It wasn't a
question.

'Yes. Did he tell you?'

'Only that there was an emergency.'

Elizabeth took a deep breath. 'Someone broke into the house
early this morning, or tried to. Dad wasn't very clear about it.
He's . . . a little upset.' She paused to regain her self-control.
'Mother heard suspicious sounds and tried to go down to see what
the noise was, and fell on the stairs. She's in the hospital, and he's
going back in a few minutes. They think she might have had a
stroke, or a seizure, or something, that made her fall. She's . . .
not doing very well, Dad says.'

'And you want to go home. Well, we can manage that. I'll call
Fred—'

'No. Of course I want to go home, to be with Dad, but he thinks
I'll be safer here. Lucy, what *is* happening? What have I done?'
She broke into sobs.

Lucy patted her on the shoulder and uttered those meaningless
soothing noises that mothers have used from time immemorial to
calm their children. When the storm had abated a little, she moved
away for a minute or two and came back with a cup of tea. 'Drink
this,' she commanded.

Elizabeth sipped obediently and looked up, startled.
'What . . .?'

'I've always kept a little brandy in the house for emergencies.
Drink it down, dear. There's only a spoonful in the tea, along with
plenty of sugar, and it's very good for shock.'

'I do feel better,' she said in surprise, when she'd finished the
tea. 'Is that why people drink? To feel better?'

'Among other reasons,' said Lucy drily. 'But don't forget that
while a little may make you feel better, a lot makes you feel much,

much worse. Now. Do you want to go and see your mother in the hospital?'

'No. Or yes, but Dad doesn't want me to. Lucy, I'm not going to have hysterics again, but I don't understand. Did someone break into my house because they thought I was there? Is someone trying to—to kill me?'

'It's beginning to seem likely, isn't it?' said Lucy calmly. 'What are you going to do about it? Run away? Stay in hiding?'

'Those are the sensible things to do, aren't they?'

'For some people, yes.'

Elizabeth shook her head as if to clear it. 'You are the most amazing person! First you ply me with liquor, which incidentally is illegal. Now you're encouraging me to – what?'

'To think things out. To use that excellent brain of yours and then do what you think is best. If it's to go out and fight the dragon, then do it. And don't let anyone make you change your mind. I think you have all the armor you need.

'But first, call your friend Leslie and ask her to go to your house and get your clothes. That's if you're staying here. Either way, you need to get into something attractive, to lift your spirits!'

'And not shock Mrs Hemingway,' she said with a tiny smile. 'Do you think it's safe for Leslie? Lately it seems that any place connected with me is dangerous.'

'The servants will be there, won't they?'

'Yes. They'd never leave my father. They adore him.'

'Then I'd call her. Meanwhile I'd best get on with those cookies, or I'll have nothing to offer Her Majesty, and she'll be here in about an hour.'

Leslie wasn't home. No one answered the phone. It wasn't a nice enough day for her to be out somewhere with the children, unless they were maybe visiting her mother, or – oh, what did it matter? She was unavailable.

Once again Elizabeth was reminded of how few close friends she had. Was there anyone else who could be asked to run an errand at short notice, or really no notice at all?

She quickly dialed another number, and was greatly relieved to hear the voice she'd hoped for. 'Susannah, it's Elizabeth.' She held the phone away from her ear while Susannah gave vent to her feelings about a young girl getting herself into such terrible trouble, and frightening her mother into fits, and so on, and on. When the housekeeper finally ran down, Elizabeth said, 'Yes, I know. And I'm terribly sorry, but you know I wasn't the one who started it. Now, Susannah, I have a favor to ask. I'm going to be staying here with Fred's aunt for a day or two. Would you, very quickly, pack up a few things for me, and send them over with Mary or Zeke? Just a nightgown, toothbrush, underthings, and a couple of dresses. Nothing fancy, but I might need to talk to some important people, and I'd like to look presentable.'

''Spect you're gonna see that Miz Hemin'way. She been callin' and callin', pesterin' everybody till that Mary finally told her where you were. I gave her what for! Knew you didn't want anybody to know.'

'Oh, it's all right. But yes, she's coming over here soon, and Miss Wilkins says I look like an old rag doll.'

'Mercy me! I'll get on it. Can't have you disgracin' us. You better give me the address. I know where Mr Fred lives, but Zeke maybe don't. Miss Elizabeth, when you comin' home? We need you round here.'

'Soon, Susannah, just as soon as it's safe. I need you, too.' Tears again. Drat, when would she stop being such a crybaby?

'Hope so. Zeke will be right along.'

Elizabeth told Lucy who would be coming, and what he looked like, and then went upstairs to bathe.

NINETEEN

S he was decently attired in a crisp middy blouse and a blue pleated skirt when the doorbell rang. 'I'll get it,' she called to Lucy, who was still busy in the kitchen.

Mrs Hemingway was more formally attired and looked hot. Elizabeth welcomed her, locked the door behind her, and led her to the parlor, just as Lucy bustled in with a pitcher of iced tea and a plate of lemon cookies. Elizabeth introduced them.

'So you look after Elizabeth's young man, do you?' The tone suggested doubts about Lucy's competence in the role.

Elizabeth looked the other way. She could feel her face growing hot.

'I do my best, Mrs Hemingway. And you look after your young man as well, I understand. Though I hear he's out on his own now. In Paris, I believe?'

'Yes.'

Lucy ignored the terse answer. 'I do hope he doesn't fall into bad company there. One hears stories about Paris, and Ernest hasn't always . . . well. I'm so happy to meet you, but I must get back to my pies. For the rummage sale at the Presbyterian Church on Saturday, you know. I do hope you'll come!'

And with a swirl of her apron, she left them.

Mrs Hemingway broke the silence just as it was about to become awkward. 'Rather a . . . forthright person, isn't she?'

'Yes, she is.' Elizabeth quickly changed the subject. 'And a lifesaver for me, these past couple of days. I suppose you know about what's been happening.'

'I heard a garbled story about an attack on this house.'

'More of a siege.' Elizabeth gave her the details.

'Dreadful! These dreadful people! We've none of us been safe since that Capone man took over. And the police do nothing!'

'The Chicago police are paid off by the Mob; everyone knows that. Our men here are honest, but they're a small force, pretty helpless against organized crime. But the incident here isn't the worst. Last night someone broke into my house, or tried to, and now my mother is in the hospital.' She resolutely kept her voice steady.

'They attacked a *woman*?'

'Not directly.' She explained what had happened. 'I still don't know what actually made her fall down the stairs. Dad thought it would be safer for me not to go to the hospital, so I haven't been able to talk to a doctor.'

'Oh, you poor girl! I know you don't get along with your mother, but it's terrible that you can't even go see her!'

Elizabeth said nothing.

Mrs Hemingway looked closely at her and changed the subject. 'Well, that's not what I wanted to tell you. Yesterday I spent a lot of time talking to people. I know quite a few people, and they were all happy to talk about the murder and your scandalous declaration!'

Elizabeth smiled a little at that.

'And of course there are two schools of thought. About half the people I talked to thought you were absolutely wrong, that it was obviously the work of the Mob, whether Mr Briggs or some other Italian. Well, I set them straight about Mr Briggs!'

I'll just bet you did, Elizabeth thought. Out loud she said, 'Good. Maybe some of them will take it to heart.'

'Of course some of that crowd are friends with some of the Walosas, and though they'd deny it, they've picked up some of their attitudes. Do you know any of those pernicious women?'

'Probably, though I couldn't give you any names. With all the committee work I do, in a town this size, I've met a good many women, but casually, not well enough to talk about that sort of thing. And . . . well, I'm not reticent about my liberal views, and I donate to a lot of charities, so women on the other side of the issues would hardly try to recruit me. They'd know I wouldn't listen anyway, since I'm so misguided as to tolerate foreigners and people of other religions. But no one's ever made an issue of it with me. They might lose my patronage!'

Mrs Hemingway barked a laugh. 'You've got that right! But as I was saying, those people were resistant. But the others were mostly my students. Promising musicians, some of them, though a few have tin ears, poor things. And they know Mr Briggs and are appalled at the injustice and will do anything they can to help clear him. And one of them . . .' She paused for effect. 'One of them can give Mr Briggs an ironclad alibi!'

'No! Who? What's the alibi?'

'A student of mine, Susan Ryan. I don't think you know her. She's several years older than you. She studied piano with me and then moved on to voice. She's a lovely contralto, sings in a lot of local productions. Oh, in fact you might have heard her at Ravinia last year; she sang Katisha when they did *Mikado*.'

'Oh, yes, I did! She was great, a wonderful voice and so funny!'

'Yes, well, she's getting ready to do a charity concert in Chicago, some operetta, some art songs, a nice repertoire. I sent her to Mr Briggs for coaching; he's better with that sort of music than I am. And on Thursday, the day Mr Anthony was killed, they were working hard from mid-afternoon until about five, and then Mr and Mrs Briggs invited her to stay for supper. She didn't go home until nearly eight, she says, and by that time—'

'By that time Mr Anthony's body had been found! Oh, it's marvelous!'

'Yes. I told her to go straight to Mr Sanders, and he'll go to the police, and the charges against Mr Briggs will be dismissed, although that will take a while. Legal things always do. But I'm going to make sure the story goes to *Oak Leaves*, so it's public knowledge that his name has been totally cleared.'

Elizabeth's jubilation faded. 'The trouble is, though—'

'Yes. We still have no idea who the killer really is. And that's dangerous for you, isn't it?'

'And apparently even for my family. But I can't stop now, can I? Even though Mr Briggs is no longer in trouble?'

'My dear girl, you couldn't stop now even if you wanted to. You've created a juggernaut, as unstoppable as a runaway elephant. It will have to run its course.'

'Trampling anyone who gets in its way.'

'Exactly. So the only thing to do is to try to keep *out* of its way while working hard to uncover the murderer. At least now the police will be helping.'

Elizabeth managed a wan smile. 'I think now they'll do their best. But it isn't their usual kind of thing, is it? And if the Mob is involved . . .'

'We'll just have to hope they're not. And don't plan to be! Have you planned your next step?'

'No. Things haven't gone the way I'd thought they would. I'd pictured the two sides fighting each other, with me and my friends neatly out of the middle. Instead, the Klan seems to have vanished from the scene, and the Mob is looming ever larger. To tell the truth, I'm sort of scared.'

Mrs Hemingway snorted. 'If you're only sort of scared, you're not as smart as I always thought you were. You should be terrified!'

'You're probably right, but I can't give in to that, don't you see? If I once let myself admit real fear, then I'll be paralyzed. I have to stop thinking about it and just . . . just forge ahead. I'll do my best to be careful, but I can't curl up in a ball and shiver and try to shut out the world.'

The older woman looked at her, an odd expression on her face. 'I see. I think, Elizabeth, that one day I will be proud to say I knew you back when. Now I'd better leave you to think out your next move. You know I'll help any way I can.'

'I'm going to need all the help I can get. Thank you. For everything. And you be careful, too.'

Elizabeth poured herself a glass of no-longer-iced tea and sat in thought. Her first motivation to investigate the murder had been the injustice done to Mr Briggs. That would shortly be remedied.

But what about the horrendous injustice done to Mr Anthony? To a gentle lover of beautiful things and a sympathetic friend. Could she let his murder be forgotten? The police would do their best, now that they knew they'd been given false information. But the fact remained that the community as a whole viewed Mr Anthony as one of 'them' rather than one of 'us', now that they knew he was Italian. Certainly there had been outrage when Mr Briggs was suspected. The community knew and loved him. He had taught many of their children. But now that he was exonerated, would the murder be swept under the rug?

And the possibility of a Mob connection made the whole mess much worse. Even those who had been genuinely fond of Mr Anthony would think twice before getting involved in such danger. Would think three times, ten times.

So, it came down to what Mrs Hemingway had said. The juggernaut would go rolling on. If she was the one who cared the most about justice, she had to do whatever she could to bring it about.

But how? Would the ad help at all? She had seen it in the *Trib* this morning, very prominent on page five. Would anyone respond with information, or would it merely frighten the murderer into new action?

She put that thought firmly aside, picked up the tray, and took it back to the kitchen, from which came the mouthwatering smell of the cherry pie that sat on the kitchen table. Every window was open, in defiance of security issues, and Lucy was sitting in front of one of them, trying to cool herself with a funeral-home fan. 'I swear,' she said, 'they always manage to hold the rummage sale the week of a heatwave. I wish they'd move it to January.'

'Then there'd be a blizzard and no one would be able to come. You go into the parlor, and I'll bring you some iced tea. Mrs Hemingway's gone, and it's a few degrees cooler in there. I need to talk to you.'

'I'm too hot to move.'

'No, you're not. Shoo!'

They settled in straight chairs dragged in from the breakfast room, as being cooler than overstuffed ones. Lucy, after a few grateful gulps of tea, said, 'All right. I'm listening.'

'I want you to tell me what skills and abilities I might bring to a murder investigation.'

Lucy put down her glass and looked Elizabeth straight in the eye. 'I've known you for a little over twenty-four hours.'

'After listening to Fred talk about me for some time, I imagine. And our time together has been . . . intense. I know you very well, and I think you know me.'

Lucy chuckled. 'Well, one of your skills is persistence, certainly. Allied with persuasiveness. Then there's courage, sometimes to the point of foolhardiness.'

'I admit it. I suppose all that could be summed up as "stubborn as a mule", as my mother often says.'

'Depends on the point of view, doesn't it? All those things, however you phrase them, will be a help to you. But your strongest asset is your intelligence. You think clearly and you have a logical mind. Two and two, for you, will always equal four, never five-and-a-half or three-and-three-quarters.'

Elizabeth blushed at that.

'Finally – and I'm guessing at this – you're very well-read, aren't you?'

She shrugged. 'I do read a lot, yes. But it's a hodge-podge of everything, history, biography, fiction, what have you.'

'Good. That means you have a broad understanding of human nature. Are you too intellectual to enjoy detective novels?'

'I've read a few. Agatha Christie, some of the Sherlock Holmes stories. Are you suggesting that I emulate the methods set forth in those works?' She almost laughed.

'Not Sherlock Holmes, no. You would, I think, be hopeless at crawling around looking for cigarette butts, and I'm sure you've never even seen a Trichinopoly cigar, much less identified its ashes. No, Agatha Christie's the author for you. She's brilliant about people, seems to turn them inside out. That, I think, is where you can do the most good in this case. You want to find out as much as you can about Mr Anthony, first of all. Not just what he did on the day of the murder, but what he was like. Did he have hobbies? Was he born here in America or in Italy? Where did he go to school? What about his family? You'll think of other questions, and all that information will help you form a rounded picture of him. *Then* you can start to have ideas about how he might have died.'

Elizabeth pondered that. 'Yes, and that's the sort of thing the police aren't going to get into. They want evidence, good solid "where were you at such-and-such time on such-and-such day?" and "doesn't this cufflink match one of yours?" and all that, not what he did in his spare time and who his pals were. I do think you're right about the approach. But how am I going to find out about the poor man? I can hardly go into a house of mourning and start asking questions about a man they loved!'

'Why don't you start with his priest? You've already met him. And when there's something he doesn't know, he'd know who you should ask.'

'Yes,' she said slowly. 'Yes, that's the place to start. But how, when no one wants me to set foot outside this house? I don't think I can impose on a busy priest and ask him to come here.'

'Probably not, but that one's so easy I don't know why you haven't figured it out. Ask to meet him at your own church. I'm sure your rector would agree to that, and Fred could take you. Unless you met at the police station, I can't think of any safer place for you!'

Elizabeth smacked herself on the head. 'Of course. I think my brain's turned to jelly. The obvious place! I'll call Fred right now and ask him—'

'Ask me what?' Fred stepped into the room. 'What *I'd* like to ask is why, with two able-bodied women in the house, there's no sign of supper being prepared!'

TWENTY

'It's all ready, in the icebox,' said Lucy, unperturbed. 'Ham, cheese, and a salad.'

Fred raised his head and sniffed. 'And cherry pie for dessert?'

'Of course. Come in and help, both of you.'

While Fred cut fat slices of ham and Elizabeth rather clumsily sliced the bread Lucy had somehow found time to make, they told Fred about the eventful day.

'I knew about the alibi for Mr Brooks,' he said. 'The singer involved phoned Sanders, and he's arranging for the dismissal of all charges. Trying to do it tactfully, so the police don't look too bad. But you were going to ask me something?'

'Yes, a favor. Lucy says that the way to uncovering a murderer is, first of all, to understand the victim. And since I can't in decency go to Mr Anthony's family and ask them a bunch of nosy questions, she suggested I talk to his priest.'

'Go to St Edmund's? I'm not sure—'

'No. Meet him at Grace. I've heard that Father Cole and Dr Edsall get along reasonably well, given the rather fraught history. I know I can arrange a meeting. And what could be a safer place than a big, solid church?'

Fred sighed. 'And you want me to drive you there.'

'You will, won't you? I'll be quite safe in a car.'

'I'll take you there, while registering my profound doubts about the wisdom of your continued involvement. And on one condition: I will stay there with you.'

Elizabeth opened her mouth to protest and shut it again. Fred had always been pliable, ready to go along with whatever she wanted. Now, she could see, she had reached the core of steel that made him such a good lawyer. Never, her father had once told her, try to argue with a lawyer. 'Okay. Thank you. What would be a good time for you?'

'Whenever both men are available.'

'The sooner the better, I think, don't you, dear?' said Lucy. 'This needs to be settled quickly.'

'If possible.' Fred was plainly dubious. 'And now we're not going to talk about it or think about it anymore. We'll eat our supper in peace, and then, Beth, let's have some music. The parlor organ is old, but it puts out good music. Do you know how to play one?'

The look she gave him would have suited Mrs Hemingway. 'Of course. Pass the butter, please.'

She hadn't even noticed his use of her nickname.

Elizabeth woke abruptly the next morning. Her heart was pounding and her brow slick with sweat. She no longer remembered the dream, only the feeling of sheer terror.

She'd forgotten to wind her watch again, but it was very early, she could tell from the light, and the slight breeze that came through her open window was cool. A better day, maybe.

There were no sounds of activity in the house. She must be the only one awake. But early as it was, she knew she'd never get back to sleep. She washed and dressed as quietly as she could and went down to make coffee. She had watched Lucy do it. Surely she could figure it out.

Half an hour later she sat down with a cup of tea. It wasn't very good, but she had given up on coffee. She realized she had no idea how much ground coffee should go in how much water, nor how long it should be boiled. It seemed so simple, but ground coffee was expensive – she'd once heard her mother complaining to Susanna about it – and she didn't want to waste it.

When Lucy came down a few minutes later, Elizabeth had cut a piece of bread and was trying to find a fork for toasting it over the gas flame.

Lucy looked at her cup, half-full of pale liquid. 'Tea this morning, dear?'

Elizabeth gave a shamefaced laugh. 'I couldn't figure out how to make coffee. Shameful, isn't it, at my age? And the tea isn't very good, either. It all looks so easy!'

'You don't know how because you've never had to learn. It *is* easy when you know how. First, the tea. Did you make sure the water was boiling?'

'It was hot.'

Lucy shook her head. 'Hot isn't good enough, not for tea. You want a good boil. Would you like to try again?'

'Actually, I'd much rather have coffee.'

'Ah, that's easy, too – but also easy to spoil. Fred does, about half the time, because his mind's on something else. Now, there are lots of ways to make coffee, but I like the good old fashioned way. It's the easiest, but you have to measure properly. All you do is put cold water in the coffee pot, up to an inch from the top. Bring it to a boil. As soon as it boils, add exactly this much coffee.' She held up a small glass, full of ground coffee almost to the top. 'Stir it, let the water come to the boil again, and then turn off the heat. That's very important! If you let it keep boiling, you'll get bitter mud like Fred's. Put the lid back on, let it sit a few minutes – no more than five – and you're done.'

'Won't there be lots of grounds floating around?'

'Not if you pour slowly, with a steady hand. They're all at the bottom, you see. But if you're uneasy about it, pour it through the strainer. Now you try it.'

It did look easy. First Elizabeth wound and reset her watch by the kitchen clock, and then took a deep breath and launched into coffee making, Lucy watching every move.

To her own astonishment, a few minutes later she was sitting at the table, drinking a perfect cup of coffee of her own brewing and smiling broadly. Lucy had showed her how to make toast using a long-handled grill held over the gas, and they were just buttering some when Fred came in.

He looked at their meager breakfast and frowned. 'No biscuits? No bacon and eggs?'

'What you are looking at,' said Elizabeth tartly, 'is a minor miracle. This is the very first time in my life I've ever done anything truly useful, and I'll ask you not to disparage it. I want you to know that *I* made this coffee and *I* made this toast. And they're very nice, thank you!'

Fred reacted admirably. 'Good for you! Though I'd argue that you've done a great many useful things in your life.'

'Charity stuff. Committees. Never, never anything practical. Do you realize, Fred, that I have never dusted a room, never washed a dish until I came to this house, never ironed a shirt? There have always been servants for all that.'

'You were married for a short time, weren't you, dear?' Lucy was obviously wondering how her poor husband had fared with a totally incompetent wife.

'For a week. That was all the time we had before Will left for France. We stayed in a hotel. Our honeymoon.'

Her voice was tight, and Lucy changed the subject. 'Well, if you're to get your business seen to this morning, you and Fred, you'd better start making a phone call or two, while I see to my demanding nephew. I can teach you about bacon and eggs another time. Scoot!'

Fred was devouring his breakfast when she came back and sat down. Lucy inclined her head to the stove and raised her eyebrows in question, but Elizabeth shook her head. 'I'm too full of nerves, or something, to be hungry. I wouldn't mind another cup of coffee, though, if there is any.'

'None of yours. That dratted nephew of mine drank it all! But I made some more.'

'So what's the plan?' Fred asked, swallowing the last forkful of egg.

'It isn't quite set yet. Dr Edsall's trying to get hold of Father Cole, who is apparently out on calls. As soon as he can set something up, he'll call.'

'Any idea when? I do need to call the office and let them know when I might be in.'

'I *do* wish you wouldn't do this! You can't afford to—'

'To lose my job? That won't happen. I'm allowed some time off the chain. And a bargain's a bargain, remember? After what happened to me yesterday, you are not to be anywhere alone. I give you a ride only if I stay with you.'

'You may as well give in, dear,' said Lucy placidly. 'You won't win this one. When he's made up his mind, he's the original immovable object. And there's the telephone. You might as well get it; nobody'd be calling me at this hour of the morning.'

She came back to the room almost at a run. 'Father Cole can see us in ten minutes, at Grace Church. Are you ready to go?'

'As soon as I call the office. Get your hat.'

Fred's Model T was one of the newer models with a self-starter, so they were at the church in a very few minutes, and went in the side door together. The day was already starting to get hot, but the building was pleasantly cool. Elizabeth showed her determined escort where the office was. Mrs Barnes wasn't at her desk so early in the morning, so they tapped on Dr Edsall's office door and went in. The two priests rose when Elizabeth came into the room. She introduced Fred, as briefly as possible, and he said quietly, 'I'll wait in the hall.'

'He insisted on coming with me,' she said apologetically. 'He seems to think I won't be safe out on my own.'

'And he's probably quite right,' said her pastor. 'Now, would you prefer to talk to Father Cole alone? I can easily—'

'No, it's fine. I only want to talk to him about poor Mr Anthony. I mean Antonelli. You see,' she said, turning to Father Cole, 'I don't know enough about him to have any idea who might have killed him. I know you can't tell me anything truly confidential, but I'm hoping you can give me an idea of who he was, how he lived. All I know is he was courteous and pleasant and had a good eye for antiques.'

'You're looking, I assume, for some reason for someone to wish him harm.'

'Yes, and I've had no luck coming up with anything. He was such a *nice* man.'

'He was that. A good family man, who worked hard at his business.'

'He truly loved the work. He cherished beautiful things. But was there anything to do with the business that was . . . I don't know how to put it. That was causing him distress?'

Father Cole thought about that for a moment. 'There was something, I think. He was not quite himself lately. Nothing I could put my finger on, just a little distracted, as if he was worrying about something. And I thought he looked as if he hadn't been sleeping well. But he never said anything specific to me, and when I asked if he was all right, he assured me he was.'

'Pardon me for interrupting,' said Dr Edsall, 'but I knew even less about him than Mrs Fairchild, and I can't help wondering if he was the sort of man who wouldn't admit to any problems.'

The other priest smiled. 'He was exactly that sort of man, but not for the reason you might think. Some men, of course, will refuse to admit even to themselves that anything in their life could possibly go wrong. They're too smart, too clever, too well-organized to fail in anything. It's a question of ego, of bravado. That wasn't Enrico Antonelli. He was a modest man. No, the reason he didn't talk about his troubles was that he didn't want to worry anyone with them. I believe he felt that any problems he might encounter were his to deal with. With the help of God, of course. He was a man of great faith.'

'Would he have shared his worries with his wife or a good friend?' I asked.

'Certainly not with his wife. He was an old fashioned sort of husband. His duty, as he saw it, was to protect Luisa from every trouble, to shelter her, to make her life as smooth and perfect as humanly possible.' He paused. 'I admit I sometimes wondered if he was wise to treat her with kid gloves. Luisa is not a fragile flower. She's an intelligent, capable woman, and I thought she'd be happier with more equally shared responsibility.'

'There are children?' asked Dr Edsall.

'Only one, a little girl about six. It was their great grief that they couldn't have the big family they'd planned. The two older children died in the influenza epidemic, and then something went wrong with little Angelica's birth. Luisa had to have an operation that meant she couldn't have any more. And to make matters worse, Angelica was in a bad accident early this spring. Tripped and fell into the path of a trolley and broke a lot of bones. They thought at first she wouldn't be able to walk, but she's coming along, after a long stay in the hospital. The family's been under a lot of strain, and now this.'

Elizabeth made the appropriate shocked noises and then asked, 'Was anyone else involved in the accident?'

She had tried to sound casual, but Father Cole was an astute man. 'Someone who was also injured, who might bear a grudge? No, Mrs Fairchild. I do realize you're trying to work out a motive for this terrible crime, but I believe there is no one in this village, indeed no one anywhere, who had any reason to hate Enrico Antonelli.'

'Yes, I see.' She sighed. 'I can't say I expected anything else, but it's frustrating. Everyone I talk to says that no one hated poor Mr Antonelli, that he was loved by all. The police say it's unlikely it was a matter of a robbery gone wrong, as nothing seems to be missing from the shop. He is certainly not known to be involved in anything criminal, or any gang activity, or anything like that.'

'No.' Father Cole looked uncomfortable. 'I'm afraid I'm not certain I can say the same about all my parishioners. Only a few are Italian, but some of those haven't lived here for very long. The ties to the Old Country are very strong, and of course the ties to family.'

'Are you saying you have suspicions of some of your flock?' Dr Edsall sounded shocked.

'Certainly not! If I had suspicions it would be my duty to go first to the person, or persons, involved. I would speak to them sternly, in both legal and spiritual terms. If I discovered that they were mixed up in something criminal, I would require them to confess first to me or another priest, and then to the police.'

'Would you inform the police yourself?' He still sounded shocked.

'Not if I had heard any details in the confessional. I could not, as I'm sure you know. But I would keep after them until I knew that they had done so. However, this is all academic. I have no such suspicions, simply a vague feeling that a few of the men are acting a little secretive around me. Of course most people have little secrets, even from their parish priests.'

'Sometimes especially from us.' Dr Edsall shook his head.

'Things they're ashamed of, but not ashamed enough to feel repentance. With my people, it's often their wealth. They know quite well they could do far more for the church and for charity, but they can convince themselves that it isn't necessary.'

Father Cole laughed. 'I think that's a problem for most parishes, though I will say some of my flock are extremely generous to the church. But most of their secrets are about peccadillos they'd rather no one knew about. If they'd confess and get them off their consciences they'd feel much better, but they don't because, often, they intend to keep right on doing whatever it is. And confess on their deathbed. Possibly!'

'And you think some of the "peccadillos" might include Mob connections?' Elizabeth leaned forward and rested her chin on her hands.

'No, I don't think any such thing. I told you, it's just an impression. If I had to spell it out, I suppose my idea is that some of them might be skating fairly close to something not quite legal, that's all. And' – he raised his hand to forestall comment – 'if indeed they are, it would be petty things like hiding a friend from the police. Or lying to protect someone.'

That triggered a thought. 'That reminds me,' said Elizabeth. 'My friend Fred Wilkins talked about the possibility that Mr Anthony was caught up in a protection racket.' She looked at both men with raised eyebrows. They both nodded understanding.

'Yes, that menace is growing in Chicago,' said Dr Edsall sadly. 'It hasn't hit here yet, or not to my knowledge. What have you heard, Father?'

'Again, nothing I can put my finger on. The business owners in my parish might be wealthy enough to be promising targets for that sort of crooked scheme, but I've heard no hints about it. Mr Antonelli was doing very well, but I think not quite in that tier. Not rich, you know, but comfortably able to support his wife and daughter. Now, of course . . .'

'Yes, and that reminds me. I said I wanted to help. You know I have money of my own. Would it be better for me to write a check to St Edmund's, so you could act as if it came from the church, or to Mrs Anthony – I mean Antonelli – personally?'

'To St Edmund's, please. There is already a fund to help the poor. I can simply say it has been augmented by an anonymous donor.'

Elizabeth had already written the check. She took it out of her purse, filled in the payee, signed it and handed it to Father Cole. He glanced at it, then looked up at her in amazement.

She waved off any thanks. 'As Scrooge said in a similar situation, a great many back payments are included in it.'

The clock on Dr Edsall's wall struck the hour. 'Oh, good heavens,' said Father Cole. 'I should have been back at St Edmund's fifteen minutes ago for a meeting with the acolytes. Was there anything else, Mrs Fairchild?'

'Only that I thank you, and I hope you'll let me know if you should learn anything that might help.'

'Of course I will. Sorry, but I have to run.'

Elizabeth had opened the office door. 'I'm sure Fred will take you back in his car, and save you a few minutes.'

Fred nodded. 'Of course. Elizabeth, you'll wait here for me.'

She sighed and nodded and went back into the rector's office.

TWENTY-ONE

'Are you getting anywhere?' the rector asked.

'I don't know. I do know that I don't yet have a thread to follow. Mr – I've got to start calling him Mr Antonelli – was worried about something. A lot of help that is! Could be anything. His daughter, maybe, if she had a setback. Something that was bothering his wife. Or a cousin in Italy, or . . . anything.'

He sat back in his chair. 'Elizabeth, I've been a pastor for a long time. Sitting at this desk, I've heard more troubles than you can imagine. Some were trivial, some serious, but all were important to the sufferers. In all the years, I've only had to try to deal with three kinds of trouble that could cause a man to lose sleep. One is unexpiated sin. A man would come to me to tell me of something he did long ago, something so terrible that he had never been able to tell anyone, never been able to make it right. That will eat a person away more surely, and more painfully, than the worst kind of cancer. Our Catholic friends have their sacrament of confession to deal with this sort of thing. Although we Episcopalians are allowed to use that practice, we almost never do, which may be a mistake. It falls to us fallible pastors to try to help that poor sinner. Sometimes I think I've succeeded. Sometimes I've failed, and those failures haunt me.

'The second trouble is with relationships, and that, by far, is the one that brings the most people to my office. A man is afraid he's losing his wife to someone else, or vice-versa. A parent is in despair over a child who is turning out badly, or who has become estranged. There are endless variations, and in every case there seems to be no way to heal the breach. Fortunately, most of the clergy have some training in ways to help, and even if the poor souls are never able to reconcile with the one who seemed to be faithless, I have usually been able to bring them to some kind of peace.

'The third trouble is financial. Most of our congregation are reasonably well-off. But even when a family has comfortable means, a sudden, unexpected disaster can bring near-ruin. I'm thinking of things like the failure of a business that provides income, or of a bank holding someone's life savings. Or criminal matters like theft, or relentless blackmail.'

Elizabeth nodded. 'My father had a friend who was wiped out when his investments turned out to be worthless. Someone had embezzled a great deal from the company he'd held shares in, and the whole financial structure collapsed.'

Dr Edsall nodded. 'I have known that to happen to several people. A real tragedy. Well, in short, that kind of thing can affect anyone. Their family helps, of course, their friends, the church. Our small Italian community here in Oak Park is very close-knit, Elizabeth, very protective of one another.'

'Except when they get involved with gangs and start killing each other.'

Dr Edsall shook his head sadly. 'Yes, that's the other side of the coin. Loyalty to one community, to one clan, so to speak, can so easily turn into hatred of another. And when large amounts of money are involved, and seriously criminal activities, then outright war can ensue. As it has a few miles to our east. I thank God every day for the wisdom of our founding fathers here in Oak Park in forbidding alcohol within our village. That has kept the gangs' interest away from us. I can only hope it stays that way.'

Elizabeth thought of Fred's nasty experience, and her worries about the violence spreading. 'But are we sure the gangs are leaving us alone? Are we sure Mr Antonelli's murderer wasn't one of the Mob?' Elizabeth's voice began to shake.

'That, my dear, is one reason the murderer must be discovered, and captured, as soon as possible.'

'And another reason is the matter of your safety.' Fred walked into the office. 'I was followed just now, when I took Father Cole to the church, and when I came back here.'

'Followed!' Elizabeth stood, alarmed. 'Did you see who it was?'

'They. Two of them, in a dark red Duesenberg the size of a locomotive.'

'Plainly they were not trying to be inconspicuous.' The rector's voice shook a bit, too.

'No. They wanted me to know they were there. But they didn't want to be identified. They had their collars turned up and their hats turned down. Elizabeth, it was meant as a clear warning. "We know where you are and we can get you any time."'

She was silent.

'My dear, it would be safest for you to give this up,' Dr Edsall said gently. 'Let the police handle it.'

'I know that,' she replied after a long pause. 'Do you think, Dr Edsall, that I should do that?'

Another pause. 'Are you asking me as an old friend, or as your pastor?'

'As my pastor.'

'Then I have to say that you must follow your conscience. You have felt that you must pursue this investigation, for reasons that seem good and sufficient to you. There are also many good reasons why you should not. If you persist in your determination, then I can only tell you that I will provide whatever help I can and will pray for your safety.'

'Thank you.'

They shook hands, and Elizabeth left the office with Fred.

She didn't turn to go out the side door but walked down the hall to the empty church. Or at least, thought Elizabeth, not quite empty. It was filled with light coming through the stained-glass windows, with the faint scent of old books, with the dust motes that floated in the rays of gold, blue, red.

It was filled with quietness and peace.

She stood for a few minutes looking at the altar, and then turned back to follow Fred.

'Feel better?' he asked when they were outside.

'Yes, and I know what I have to do.'

He didn't ask, but helped her into the car and quickly got in on the other side. 'You know,' he said as he drove off, 'you could easily hire a bodyguard.'

'I know. And I know that would make everybody happier about me. But I can't live that way, Fred. Fenced in, never being alone for a second. Oh, I don't mean you! You're doing this out of concern for me, not as a hired hand.'

'They're behind us again,' he said. 'No, don't look around.'

She drew a breath, and then said, 'Stop the car, please.'

'Are you out of your mind? They'll . . . I don't know what they'll do, but it won't be anything good.'

'I want to talk to them. Stop the car.'

'*Please*, Beth, be reasonable! These men want to kill you.'

'I don't think they do. They could have, easily, in the past few minutes. I have to find out what they do want. Please stop the car.'

She already had the door open. Fred had to stop the car or risk her jumping out of the moving vehicle. He didn't stop protesting, though.

She didn't even hear him, but walked over to the opulent Duesenberg, which had also stopped, only a few feet away. Fred was right behind her.

'Good morning, gentlemen,' she said in as calm a tone as she could manage. 'You've been following us. Is there something we can do for you?'

The man in the passenger seat got out of the car and stood looking at her. His hat was still pulled down, nearly covering his face. Fred grabbed Elizabeth's arm and held it tight.

'You've made a mistake, lady. Wasn't us following you.'

Fred tugged at her arm. She stood fast. 'Oh, come now. No one else could possibly have a car that beautiful. It really *is* a doozy!'

'Maybe you'd like to climb in and take a ride, huh?'

'Oh, thank you so much, that would be lovely, but I don't believe I have time just now.' Fred's grasp was so firm it was beginning to hurt. 'No, I just wanted to talk to you for a moment so I could understand what you want of me. Perhaps we could sit in the shade? You must be awfully hot in those coats and hats.'

'We'll talk to you.' The voice came from the back seat, a man they had not seen. 'Frankie, you stay in the car.'

'Run for it!' whispered Fred in her ear. She ignored him and walked toward the little park across the street, where spreading elms created at least the illusion of coolness. She sat down on one of the benches, Fred glued to her side, and watched as two men strolled toward them.

They had removed their coats, but not their hats. Their suits, expensive by the look of them, fit rather tightly, and Elizabeth could see no awkward bulges. Perhaps they had left their guns in the car, as well. They were both of medium height, well-groomed and clean-shaven. In fact, only their fedoras made them look at all like gangsters.

'Now, isn't this better?' she said with a smile. 'Much cooler and more pleasant. I do understand that you gentlemen prefer to remain anonymous, and of course you know who I am. Have you met my friend?'

'Your bodyguard, you mean?'

She laughed merrily. 'Oh, no, no, no. Just a dear friend who wonders, as I do, why you were tailing us. I believe that's the expression?'

'Yeah, we know who he is.' Both men fixed him with a look that was not at all friendly. The spokesman continued, 'What we don't know is what you two are up to. We'd kinda like to know.'

'Oh, is that all? I can tell you very easily. You see, I think the police haven't the slightest idea who killed Mr Antonelli. He was a friend of mine, and I'm very, very angry about his death. I don't believe the Mob had anything to do with it, though you gentlemen might know more about that than I do. I know for certain that the man who was arrested, Mr Briggs, is totally innocent. And since everyone who knew him tells me Mr Antonelli had no enemies, I talked this morning to his priest to find out more about him. I hope that learning about his background, and about any problems he might have had, will lead to the truth.' She leaned forward for emphasis. 'And the answer must be absolutely proven, or the terribly conservative elements in the village will cling to their ill-conceived notions that the Italian community is somehow responsible.'

'Yeah. Them Walosas in it, are they?'

'I'm afraid so. They're very experienced in stirring up hatred.'

There. She had planted the seed. Now she could sit back and wait to see what fruit it bore.

The two men looked at each other and then back at Elizabeth. 'Thank you, ma'am. Glad we had this little talk,' said the spokesman. Then, turning to Fred, he said, 'The lady won't be bothered any more. You can stop worrying.' He doffed his hat and elbowed his companion, who had still spoken no word, to do the same.

With that they strode back to the car and drove off.

Elizabeth heaved a great sigh. 'I think maybe that did the trick.'

'I—you—you could have been killed, you know! Both of us could have been killed!'

'They weren't carrying guns. Can you think of any other way I could have delivered my message? They thought I'd be scared to death of them. When I wasn't, it took them off guard enough that they listened.'

'Why *weren't* you scared?' demanded Fred. 'I was terrified. I thought I'd pass out.'

'Me, too, but I've had a lot of years practicing the ice maiden persona. I just dropped into it and pretended I was in charge of things. Apparently they believed it. And now, Fred, I badly need a cup of Aunt Lucy's coffee!'

TWENTY-TWO

They had their coffee and a sandwich, and gave Lucy all the details. She received them with her usual calm. 'That was very brave of you, my dear.'

'Foolhardy,' said Fred. 'I thought I'd have a heart attack.'

'But it accomplished what I intended it to,' Elizabeth argued. 'The Mob is called off, and the Walosas had better watch out. And soon, I hope, we'll begin to see some results from that ad. It's run for two days now. Surely somebody has responded.'

'I'll find out when I go back to work. Probably a lot of crackpots wanting to make themselves important.'

Lucy patted his shoulder. 'You'll know what to do with them, dear. Don't worry too much.'

He responded to that with a grunt and went on his way.

'He's cross with you, my dear. You ignored his wishes and got away with it. That annoys even the best of men.'

Elizabeth laughed. 'They hate to be proven wrong, don't they? Even my father, who is so even-tempered. And speaking of my father – Lucy, much as I hate to do it, I'm going back home. I don't need protection anymore, and I can't impose on you forever.'

Lucy nodded. 'I was afraid of that. You're not imposing in the least. I don't want you to go, but I understand your need for independence. But have you thought this through? You're probably right in believing you're safe enough from the Mob. They've realized you're not a threat to them, and now they'll turn their attention to the Walosas. But what about your danger from *them*? As we both know, some of them are not very nice people.'

Elizabeth laughed. 'Like the Kaiser wasn't a very nice man! I know they might try to cause trouble, but now that the Mob is on my side, so to speak, I think I can handle a few narrow-minded women – and their husbands!

'Look, Lucy, I know I'll still run into problems. After all, someone out there is a murderer, and though I don't know who, I do know he won't be happy about any investigation. And I don't want to leave here! You've made me feel like family, more than . . . well, but it *is* my home, and I know Daddy is missing me, especially with Mother ill.'

'I'm sure he is. He's a dear man. Well, I won't try to keep you. But you must promise to let us know how your mother is. And come and see us if you ever feel there might still be danger. Or even just because you'd like another cooking lesson!'

They hugged, tears on both faces. 'I'll call Fred to come take you home.'

'I don't want to take him away from work. He's done too much for me anyway. I can walk, and I'll send someone to get my clothes.'

'Honey, he could never do too much for you! If you don't know that, you're not nearly as smart as I thought. Now, are you sure you'll be safe on the street?'

'I'm sure. We've heard that word spreads quickly in the Mob. And it will feel so good to walk again!'

More hugs and waves, and Elizabeth was on her way home.

It was a longish walk on a hot day, but she didn't mind. She was free! She couldn't help looking around nervously when she heard footsteps behind her, or someone approached from a side street, but it was always a mother pushing her baby in its carriage, or a shopper, or equally harmless people interested only in their own business. No one paid her any more attention than a brief smile and greeting.

She thought about Lucy's parting words. It was true that she could no longer pretend to believe that Fred was no more than a friend. She had pushed away the knowledge, but now she had to admit it. Fred was in love with her. And what was she going to do about it?

Nothing, she said fiercely to herself. I didn't ask him to love me. I don't want him to love me. Love hurts.

Her essential honesty rejected that notion. Pretending Fred's love didn't exist was a lie, and the one who would be worst hurt by that was Fred.

But it would hurt her, too. She liked Fred a lot. She enjoyed going to concerts with him and conversing with someone as intelligent as he was. Aunt Lucy, in a couple of days, had become like a mother to her. It would be painful to cut those ties, as she must if she rejected Fred.

The other voice began arguing again. *Look what happened when you let yourself become too fond of Mr Antonelli. His death has led you into all kinds of dangerous situations.*

Dishonesty again. It was her own sense of justice that pushed her into the fray. She would have felt the same about the murder of any innocent man.

Oh, really?

Her attention to the problem was distracted by a growing sound of people shouting. Women shouting. Screaming? Holding on to her courage by sheer force of will, she pressed against the wall of an apartment building and peered around the next corner.

Something was happening on Oak Park Avenue. A group of women, walking north in the street, were now running to get away from three big cars heading in the opposite direction. The cars – oh, dear heaven, one of them was the dark red Duesenberg, the same one from her earlier encounter. The one used by the gangsters.

She stepped a little farther away from her sheltering wall. The women had their backs to her, most of them, facing north toward – oh, good grief, toward St Edmund's church a few blocks away.

And the cars, two abreast with the third following close behind, were being driven slowly but inexorably toward the crowd.

Herding them away from the church?

She could hear some of the cries now. 'Heretics! Satan worshippers! Murderers!' The shrieks came from the women. The men in the cars said not a word but proceeded down the street.

Some of the women ran up on the sidewalks, but were faced with a phalanx of men, arm in arm, coming toward them. Men with collars turned up, on the hot day, and hats pulled down. They said nothing. They made no menacing gestures. They brandished no weapons. They were simply there, solid, as impregnable as a fortress. And they moved on, closer and closer, keeping exactly to the speed of the cars.

The women were moving away now. Their shrieks turned to mutters. The crowd broke up into groups of two and three, headed south or turning off onto side streets. Elizabeth dived into the nearest recessed doorway and tried to become invisible, turning her face aside as the strange parade passed.

The red Duesenberg was the last car. She ventured to look up as it passed, and saw, from the back seat, a tip of a fedora and a faint smile.

After a while her knees stopped shaking and she was able to walk on home, thinking about what she had put in motion. The gangsters hadn't been after her. And there had been no violence. But if that sample of sheer intimidation didn't scare the devil out of the Walosas, they had no imagination. She thought about the expression and decided it was a literal truth. Anyone who could hate as those women did was surely possessed of the devil, and if a good strong fright could exorcise it, good!

But what if it didn't stop with intimidation? What if one of the renegade gangs decided on more forceful action? What if the juggernaut could not, in fact, be stopped?

She was still wrestling with the problem when she reached home. The door, of course, was locked. Another result of her headstrong insistence on having her own way. Rather than use her key and startle everyone, she rang the bell.

Susannah came to the door, opened it a crack, and then practically pulled Elizabeth inside. 'What you doin', girl?' she scolded. 'Don't you got no sense? Gangsters all over the place lookin' to shoot you an' all of us, an' your daddy frettin' hisself into fits worryin' about you and your mama, an' you come waltzin' in here all by yourself, not even by the back way—'

'Susannah!' She had to shout it twice to stop the flow. 'It's all right. I'm not in danger anymore, just hot and tired and very thirsty. Is there any iced tea? And is Dad home?'

'Your daddy, he still at the hospital, been there all day.'

'How's Mother doing?'

''Bout the same, far as I can tell. They don't think she had no stroke, though. Prob'ly just stumbled and fell. But she hurt her head pretty bad, and she ain't come to yet.'

Susannah's grammar was usually much better than that. The lapse was an indication of her stress.

'Will they let me go and see her?'

'No point, your daddy says, till she wake up. Honey, she wouldn' know you was there, even. Anyway, you *sure* you okay out there by yourself?'

'I'll come out to the kitchen with you and get some of that tea and tell you all about it.'

Of course she didn't tell Susannah *all* about it. The housekeeper would have been horrified by the full story of her darling's confrontation of a trio of hoodlums, not to mention the encounter she'd just witnessed. But she did manage to convince Susannah that no one in the household was in any further danger from gangsters. 'They'll leave us alone, and they'll make sure everyone else does, too.' Elizabeth was far from certain about that part, but she could be very convincing, and Susannah needed reassurance.

Refreshed by the tea, Elizabeth sat down in the parlor and tried to decide what to do next.

The house had an odd feel to it. Of course it was hot and airless; the windows were shut tight. She got up and remedied that in the parlor, opening them to their fullest extent. But there was almost no breeze, so the room remained stuffy.

That wasn't the real reason for her unease, though. It was the absence of Mother. She was nearly always there. She was nearly always an irritant. And though Dad was away for hours every school day, his calm, peaceable influence balanced Mother's tantrums, even when he wasn't physically present. An equilibrium was maintained, and the sense of it kept the house alive, not static, but stable.

Now there was none of the tension of opposing forces. To her astonishment, Elizabeth found herself missing it, in fact missing her mother. Could it be that she somehow enjoyed their battles? Enjoyed her feeling of superiority, of being unquestionably right about the issue and her mother absolutely wrong?

Could that smugness over the years have made matters worse? For everyone?

The familiar feeling of shame crept over her. What odious sort of person was she, anyway?

She heard the phone ring, and in a moment Susannah hurried into the room. 'Miss Elizabeth, your daddy's on the phone, honey. He sounds a mite happier than the last time.'

She sprinted to the phone. 'Daddy! How's Mother?'

'Much better. She regained consciousness for a few minutes this morning, and apart from a truly awful headache and a broken leg, there seems to be little damage. She's gone back to sleep, but it *is* sleep, not a coma, and the nurses say it's the best thing for her, and I should go home and get some rest myself. But Daughter, why are you there? I thought—'

'We all thought, but things have changed, Dad. It's too complicated to tell you over the phone. When are you coming home?'

'As soon as I can get a ride. One of my friends brought me this morning.'

'Dad, I can—'

'No! I don't want you on the road! I'll catch the trolley.'

He hung up before she could protest that her safety was no longer in jeopardy. Well, at least not much. At least not from the Mob.

She hurried through the house opening windows and doors to try to cool things a bit. She had reached her father's study when he walked in and was enveloped in a bear hug.

'I suppose you spoke to Susannah when you came in,' she said when she released him.

'For a moment. She said you weren't afraid anymore. She also said she thought maybe you'd lost your mind.'

'I'll bet she worded it a bit differently!' Elizabeth chuckled as she raised the last window to its widest extent. Her father watched, his head cocked to one side.

'Am I to assume that Susannah is correct?' he asked mildly.

'No. And I haven't decided to commit suicide. What's happened is I've tamed the Mob.'

He raised his eyebrows and waited.

She sat down and explained, an unexpurgated version this time. 'Fred says he nearly had a heart attack,' she finished, 'but it all worked out. You taught me long ago how to stand up to bullies, even when I was scared, and you were absolutely right. They won't bother us again.'

'*They* probably won't. What about other gangs?'

'The gangs know how to stick together when it's a question of protecting everyone. They have turf wars, and they fight betrayal, but it's in the interest of the whole Italian community to get this crime solved.'

'Perhaps. And have you forgotten about the Klan?'

She sighed. 'No. But something happened this afternoon that gave me some hope.' She told him the story of the confrontation she had witnessed. 'I didn't tell Susannah that part. She'd have thrown forty fits. The thing is, I'm hoping that threats like that from the Mob will keep the Walosas and their husbands from trying anything violent, but they're not very predictable, nothing like as well-organized as the mobsters, or as uniform in goals and beliefs. Virtually the only thing that unites them, as far as I can see, is fear and hatred of the "other", meaning anyone who is different from them, in any way. Race, religion, nationality, social practices, anything. I know they're dangerous, but I think they may be too afraid of the power of Capone and his kind to fight against them.'

'You think.'

'I hope.' Time to change the subject. 'But tell me about Mother. Is she really going to be all right?'

'She's in a good deal of pain, what with the head and the leg, along with terrible bruises, but the doctors say she'll heal completely. It will be several days before she can come home, and longer than that before she'll be able to walk.'

'No—no brain damage?'

'They say not. She got a concussion, but they think it's a mild one. Certainly she was entirely coherent when she became conscious, and remembered what had happened.'

'What *did* happen? You said someone broke into the house.'

'Actually, it appears they only attempted a break-in. They – or he, we don't know whether it was one thug or several – tried to open one of the windows in the kitchen, but Zeke had fixed them to open only two inches. The next attempt was at the back door, which as you know is quite solid. The noise woke your mother, who's been sleeping very lightly of late.'

Because she sleeps most of the day, thought Elizabeth. Then she waved the thought away. It was just that kind of thing . . .

'So she put on a robe and slippers and started downstairs to see what was happening—'

'She didn't wake you?'

'She says she thought it was just the cats getting into some sort of mischief. She was going to put them out. She didn't bother to turn on the lights. And about halfway down the stairs one of her slippers came off and she stumbled and started to fall. And that is all she remembers. You must understand this came out slowly, in bits and pieces, and I may have misunderstood some of it. Her voice isn't working too well yet.'

Elizabeth shivered in spite of the heat. 'What a good thing she didn't fall down the whole flight! That tile floor . . .'

'And what a good thing she *did* fall. If she hadn't, she might have opened the back door and let in . . .'

The silence that fell was not comfortable. Along with the sounds and scents of summer – children at play, freshly cut grass, the occasional harsh squawk of a crow or the hammer of a woodpecker – something else crept into the room: doubt and unease and uncertainty.

'What are your plans?' her father finally asked.

'I don't know yet. Daddy, I'm too tired to think. It's been . . . an interesting week.'

'And you had a long, hot walk to get home. Unless Fred brought you?'

'No.'

That brought a speculative look to her father's eye, but he said only, 'And not much sleep lately, I'd guess. Go take a nap, Daughter, and I'll do the same. I'll wake you if something comes up.'

TWENTY-THREE

Elizabeth woke to the sound of masculine voices. For a moment she was gripped by panic, and then her head cleared and she recognized the speakers as her father – and Fred. Fred! What was he doing here? Had something happened?

She slipped quickly into her shoes and ran downstairs. The two men were standing in the hall.

'Hello, Sleeping Beauty!' said her father. 'Feel rested?'

From his smile, and the way he spoke, it was apparent that there was no new crisis. She looked from him to Fred.

'I brought your bag,' he said. 'No reason to trouble your household. Aunt Lucy said she'd phone later, after you'd had a chance to get settled.'

'I . . . thank you.' There was an awkward silence. Elizabeth could find nothing to say.

'You sound like you haven't quite waked up yet,' said Fred, grinning. 'I suppose we were talking too loud. Didn't mean to disturb you.'

'No, no. I just . . . maybe I'm *not* quite awake. I think I must have had a nightmare, and when I heard you talking, I was really frightened, for a moment.'

'Small wonder. Your life of late has been sort of demoralizing, shall we say? At least your mother is doing better. Your dad was just telling me about it.'

'Yes, it's such a relief to know she isn't as badly hurt as we thought.'

'But as I said, she won't be coming home for a while,' said Dad, 'so our table is going to look kind of lonely. I'm hoping you might be able to stay with us for dinner tonight.'

'Actually, I only stopped by to bring Elizabeth's things back. It's very kind of you to offer, but—'

'We really could use the company.'

Elizabeth exchanged glances with her father. What was this about?

Fred caught the exchange, smiled and said, 'Mr Walker, it's

very good of you, and I accept gladly. I'll need to call my aunt, though, to let her know I won't be home.'

'I'd better go tell Susannah,' Elizabeth said. 'Fred, the phone's this way.'

She got back to the parlor before Fred had finished his phone call. 'Daddy, are you up to something?' she asked.

'Not at all,' he said, perfectly straight-faced. 'We'll both miss your mother at table. Fred will help fill the gap, for one night at least.'

He's decided that Fred will do for me, she thought.

They all sat in the parlor until Susannah called them to dinner, and what could have been an awkward silence was instead a pleasant interlude. Fred took over the conversation, steering away from recent horrors and turning the focus on Mr Walker and his work as a teacher. 'I'm sure you must have been busy with end-of-semester duties at the high school,' he said. 'I've heard a great deal about the respect your pupils have for you, sir.' Mr Walker made a deprecatory gesture. 'I believe Ernest Hemingway was one of your pupils, wasn't he? I wonder what he was like at that age.'

'He showed great promise at school, but he was erratic. Went in for writing, even then, and he wasn't too bad. Edited the school newspaper.'

'But he was more interested in sports,' put in Elizabeth. 'And he always had a swelled head. I never liked him.'

That, of course, led to a lively discussion of the man's obvious talents and equally obvious character flaws, and they were all surprised when Susannah appeared to announce that dinner was ready.

Susannah had made an extra effort, considering the short notice she'd been given of a guest, and produced a wonderful meal. It was all in honor of Fred, of course, and when they had finished the strawberry shortcake and Mary came in to remove the dessert plates, he asked her to tell Susannah how much he'd enjoyed it. That, of course, sealed his place in Susannah's heart forever.

The evening had cooled enough for them to drink their coffee hot. The cats knew that meant cream on the table, and came slinking into the room to seize the moment in case the pitcher was left unguarded.

Fred saw them at once. 'Oho,' he said, 'come to do a little begging, have you? Beth, what are their names?'

'Ginger and Charlie. Easy enough to tell which is which.'

'Indeed. Ginger, you are a beautiful cat. Of course you know that.' He held his hand down for the cat to sniff, and stroked his head when it appeared that was acceptable.

Then Charlie came over to demand his share of attention, and got it, and they both got a little of the cream that Fred poured into a saucer he set on the floor.

'That's enough, Fred,' said Elizabeth, laughing. 'They know perfectly well they're not supposed to beg at the table.'

'But they do, don't they? And you give in to them.'

'I'm afraid I do. They're going to get terribly fat.'

'They deserve it. They're very fine cats, both of them.'

Charlie continued to twine around Fred's ankles after all the cream was gone. Ginger was wiser. Experience had taught him that a dignified withdrawal, followed later by another appeal, complete with pleading eyes and a pitiful cry or two, was more likely to produce the desired result, at least with the human he knew best. This one was a newcomer, but he showed promise.

The humans finished their coffee and withdrew to the parlor. All the windows were open, and a fresh breeze brought the scent of the roses, blooming anew, and the sweetest smell of all, the lilies of the valley that bloomed in profusion close to the house.

'They're late this year,' said Elizabeth, taking a deep sniff. 'It was so cold earlier. And now it's gotten so hot, they won't last long.'

'Beautiful while they do, though,' said Dad. 'Sometimes late bloomers are the sweetest.'

Elizabeth hoped he was still talking about flowers. She was trying to think of a tactful way to end the evening when Fred stood.

'I'm sorry to leave such agreeable company,' he said, 'but I have to be in court early tomorrow, so I'd better be off. Thank you so much for having me, Mr Walker. Goodnight, Beth.'

'I'll walk you to the door.'

When they were alone, he smiled at her and said, 'That was very pleasant. Your father is a charming man.'

'And you were charming in return.' It wasn't exactly a compliment.

'I'm a good trial lawyer, you know. Grace under pressure.'

'I suppose all this means I'm forgiven.'

'Until next time.'

She grimaced and said, 'Were there any ad responses at the office?'

'None worth bothering about. Crackpots, as I predicted. Sanders called the police station; same situation there. People are afraid, I imagine. Tomorrow may be different. I'll be in touch about the investigation. Night, my dear.' And he leaned down, gave her a light kiss on the cheek before she could turn away, and was gone.

Well! She was furious with him.

Wasn't she?

Ginger came up just then, annoyed that his new servant had left without offering a second helping of cream. He voiced his disapproval in feline words as plain as English, and sat staring at Elizabeth.

'You,' she told him, 'are a spoiled brat.'

He replied with a feline, *So?*

Elizabeth gave in, as Ginger knew she would, and went to the kitchen. Of course Charlie followed. Now that Ginger had done the groundwork, he was quite happy to reap the benefits as well.

That little diversion had taken her mind off Fred for a moment, but the problem returned as soon as she sat down in the parlor again.

What was she going to do about Fred?

He was a nice man. She liked him a lot. He'd been stalwart in protecting her the past few days, and he didn't hold a grudge.

But she didn't want to be protected! She was an intelligent and capable woman, and she could take care of herself.

Not always, replied the insidious inner voice.

'Bets, you're climbing back into your shell,' said her father. 'Why don't you play me something? A little Chopin, perhaps?'

She welcomed the suggestion and smiled her thanks as she moved to the piano and played an arpeggio. 'Ouch!' she said. 'Needs tuning. This hot, humid weather hasn't been kind to it.'

'Yes, we'd planned to have the tuner in a couple of days ago but had to call him off. Can you manage?'

'Probably.'

She played a couple of her father's favorite Chopin nocturnes, and then launched into a noisy Rachmaninoff prelude to relieve her feelings. Finally she very gently played 'Claire de Lune', and closed the lid over the keys. 'I think the Rachmaninoff scared some of the strings back into tune,' she said. 'It sounds a little better now. And if you'll excuse me, it's been a very long day and I'm going up to bed. Goodnight.'

TWENTY-FOUR

Ginger woke her in the morning. She had slept so soundly she hadn't even known he was there, but his favorite spot by her side was warm, even though he had moved to the pillow and was staring at her.

'Were you here all night, you little beggar?'

He responded with a pat on the cheek and his loudest purr.

'And now you want your breakfast. Your second breakfast, right? I know Susannah already fed you.'

He denied it with a plaintive mew.

'Little liar.'

There was a tap on the door and Mary poked her head in. 'You awake, Miss Elizabeth? Miz Susannah sent up your coffee and said to tell you Mr Fred wants you to call him. Not till you're down to breakfast, though.'

And there was her problem back in her lap. She sighed. 'Thank you, Mary. You can put the coffee over there on the table and tell Susannah I'll be down in about half an hour.'

The gentle breeze was still cool, but it was early yet, not even seven when Elizabeth came down. Her father was up, though, reading the *Tribune* as usual. Elizabeth poured herself some orange juice and another cup of coffee and sat down.

'Anything more about Mr Antonelli?'

'No. Apparently Chicago no longer finds it news. No more raids or gang killings, either. A slow news day.'

'The best kind. Have you heard from Mother?'

'No, but I'm sure no news is good news. Are you hungry? Susannah's made something new with bacon, a bread of some sort. It's very good.'

'Bacon muffins, Miss Elizabeth,' said Susannah, coming in with a fresh basket of them. 'Just out of the oven, and don't you let 'em get cold, now. And I baked some o' last fall's apples to go with 'em.' Mary followed with a steaming dish of apples stuffed with brown sugar and raisins and smelling like heaven.

'Susannah, you're not going to be happy until you've made me as fat as Mr Taft.'

Susannah snorted. 'You got a ways to go for that, child. You just have a good breakfast now, so you can go out and gallivant around some more. Mary, we got work to do!' She shooed her back to the kitchen, and Elizabeth tasted and approved a muffin.

'And what are your plans for gallivanting today?' asked Dad, folding his paper.

'First I have to call Fred. He called early this morning, but he didn't tell Susannah it was urgent. I don't know what he wants.'

Mother would have told her, with emphasis. Dad just said, 'I expect you'll find out. Just don't go and do anything stupid.'

'I'll try not. What are your plans for the day?'

'First a haircut. It's needed it for a week, at least, and I can't go visit your mother looking like a tramp.'

'You had a good excuse, since you couldn't leave the house. Thanks to me.'

He ignored that. 'And then I'm going to go to the hospital, but I won't stay long. I don't want to tire her. After that I plan to see the Briggs family again, see how they're getting along.'

'Oh, can I come, too? To the hospital first, of course, but I do want to talk to Mr Briggs, to the whole family really, to find out more about Mr Antonelli. Do you think they'll mind?'

'Mind! They're probably planning to put up a statue of you in St Edmund's and light candles in front of it. They know who's spearheading the campaign to exonerate Paul, and there's nothing they wouldn't do for you.'

Elizabeth grimaced. 'I just hope I can live up to their hopes. I'm no Sherlock Holmes.'

'I'm certainly glad to hear it. He was addicted to cocaine, and I suspect he played the violin badly. I'm off.'

With some reluctance, Elizabeth went to phone Fred.

She intended to be businesslike on the phone with him, if not positively frosty. When he answered, she said, 'Good morning, Fred. I was told you had called. What can I do for you?'

'Good morning. I apologize for calling so early, but I wanted you to know as soon as possible. There has been an incident. Nothing truly critical, or I would have told Susannah. But I thought bad news can always wait.'

'Bad news? But you said not urgent? Fred, what *happened*?' Gone was her cool manner.

'The Klan showed up last night and burned a cross on our lawn. Aunt Lucy is quite upset. It scorched her favorite lilies.'

'Oh, Fred! This is awful! Was anyone hurt? Why did they attack *you*?'

'They probably know I've been helping defend Briggs. More likely, though, it was meant for you. Their information may be a little dated. They probably thought you were here.'

She sank down in the chair beside the phone. 'Then it's all because of me!'

'I thought you'd say that. It is not. It is the fault of the person who started this horrible chain of events by killing Mr Antonelli. If anyone should have a cross burned in his yard, he's the one. But in fact no one should. And you know that quite well, when you're thinking properly. Meanwhile we have called the police, who are trying to pin down just who did this.'

'And even if they succeed, the real villain is still at large. Fred, I was planning to talk to the Briggs family this morning. Do you think I should come over there instead? For Lucy?'

'She would like that very much, but I believe she's all right. She's tough, you know.'

'I do know, but all the same, this must have been very disturbing for her. I'll walk over right now, and she can make me coffee and fuss over me.'

Fred chuckled. 'The sort of thing she loves more than anything. You're right. That will do her a lot of good. But what about the Briggs family?'

'Dad's going there, after he sees Mother. I asked him to take me with him, but he can just as easily pick me up at your house. I'll be there soon.'

She hung up, told Susannah her plans, and hurried away.

Fred was on his way out the door when she walked up the path. An ugly scorched place on the grass and a few singed maple leaves from the tree above were the only signs of last night's disturbance.

'She's in the kitchen stirring up a batch of muffins for you.

Best therapy in the world. I have to be off; I'm late as it is. Good luck with the Briggses. See you later.'

He left without a second glance, except at his watch. Elizabeth, who had been prepared to fend off some display of affection, was glad he hadn't tried it.

Extremely glad.

She went into the house feeling a little blank.

Lucy bustled out of the kitchen, from which good smells were coming. 'I never heard of cherry muffins, but I decided to try it. Blueberries won't be in for almost another month. Come in the kitchen, dear, and have a cup of coffee while the muffins bake. And there's only today and tomorrow to bake for the rummage sale, so don't mind if I whip up a cake while we talk. Always could do three things at once, my mother used to tell me.'

She was talking too much, too fast. Elizabeth followed her into the kitchen and pulled a chair up to the table. 'Lucy, sit. I'll pour our coffee and the cake can wait another few minutes. Or all day, for that matter. One cake more or less at the sale won't matter, even if yours will be the best ones there. What on earth are you doing with all of them, by the way? You started making them on Monday, and they surely wouldn't stay fresh for almost a week.'

'Fred's been taking them to Petersen's for me. They have extra space in their ice cream freezers, so they do it for me every year.'

'What a good idea! They'll be good as new. Now take a break, or you're going to wear yourself to a frazzle, and then what will become of Fred?'

Oh, dear. She shouldn't have put it quite that way. Lucy might have a suggestion about who could look after Fred.

But Lucy had other things on her mind. She sat, rather to Elizabeth's surprise. She actually slumped. 'I am a little tired, I guess. Last night wasn't exactly restful.'

'Tell me all about it. Fred just said the Klan came and burned a cross.'

'Oh, my dear, that was the least of it. We'd gone to bed early, both of us.'

'Me, too. We'd all had quite a day.'

'And Fred had wanted to tell me all about dinner at your house, of course. But we were in bed by ten, I guess. And I don't know about Fred, but I was asleep the minute my head hit the pillow.

And then in the middle of the night I woke up to the most awful noise. Screaming and shouting and I don't know what all.

'I didn't know what to think. First I thought maybe a neighbor's house was on fire, but I looked out my window and couldn't see any flames or smoke or anything. Well, then of course I got a little scared, what with all that's been happening. But you and Fred had both said the danger was over and it was all going to be all right, so when I remembered that I was just plain mad. Nobody had any right to make such a racket and wake up decent folks. So I was about to go and give them a piece of mind when I saw the flames start up. Right in my front yard!'

'Your doors were locked, I hope!'

'Yes, we've always locked them at night. The first thing Fred did, though, was to go around and check them all. Then he told me to go back to bed and put my fingers in my ears, that he'd handle it. Well, by that time I'd made out a word or two of what they were saying, so I could see his point. Such language you never heard! Cursing us all up, down and sideways, and calling us names – well, you can probably imagine.'

Elizabeth had heard a good many things during her time at Northwestern. She nodded grimly. 'So did you go back to bed?'

'Of course not. I had to keep an eye on what was happening. Fred told me later that the first thing he did was call the police, and they got there almost before he got off the phone. I think the neighbors had called them, too. So then he went out to the front porch and told them he was a lawyer, and that they were disturbing the peace, and he'd see to it that they were charged with that and other crimes. Then the police began going around and trying to take names, only they all had on those silly white robes and hoods, and I don't think they got many. Anyway, most of them had left by that time.'

'Cowards.'

'Oh, yes, bullies are always cowards. So are people who hide their faces. They'd claim it was to frighten and intimidate, but it's really just foolishness. Makes them feel important.'

'So they left. Then what happened?'

'We started to clean up the mess. They'd left signs and burnt matches all over the place, and an empty bottle that smelled of gasoline. Oh, and Elizabeth, they'd trampled all over my roses and burned most of my lilies and even part of the maple tree. I'm just so mad I could spit!'

'Good! It's so much better to be mad than scared. But you said they left signs. You mean, signs that they'd been there? You already knew that.'

Lucy finished her coffee, cold by now, and jumped out of her chair. 'My muffins!'

They were a little too brown, but they smelled wonderful, even after Susannah's breakfast less than an hour ago. Elizabeth turned out the muffins onto the plate Lucy handed her.

Lucy bustled about. 'Oh, dear, I really do need to start on that cake. It's a complicated one, three layers, and it's hard to make them all come out even—'

For the second time Elizabeth interrupted her. 'Lucy. There's something you're not telling me. I'm not the sort who hides from the truth.'

'I know you're not. But it isn't easy to tell a friend that she's . . . she's hated.'

'The signs.'

'Yes. Oh, my dear, they called you the most horrible names, that I won't even repeat.'

'The "Whore of Babylon", I imagine. It would be typical of the bigots who interpret the Bible to serve their own hatreds.'

'Well, yes, that was the worst one. And there were threats.'

'Lucy, I can't possibly say how sorry I am I brought this upon you. I should never—'

Lucy set the plate of muffins on the table with such force that two of them bounced onto the floor. Lucy ignored them. 'That's what Fred said you'd say, and it's nonsense! This hullabaloo all began when someone killed that poor man, and then these yahoos in the Klan decided to blame it on someone who had nothing to do with it. All the trouble stems from that, not from anything you've done.'

'But I shouldn't have involved you—'

'Of course you should! You're trying to right a wrong, and you need help, and what are friends for? Now I'll pour us some more coffee, and we'll have some muffins, and you'll tell me what your next moves are.'

Elizabeth had begun to tell her when the doorbell rang. Lucy went to the door and saw Mr Walker, who said, 'You must be Fred's Aunt Lucy. I've heard a great deal about you! I'm Kenneth Walker, and I've come to pick up my daughter, if this isn't a bad time.'

'Happy to meet you, Mr Walker. I've heard many good things about you, too. Won't you come in for some coffee and a muffin?'

'I'd love to, but I'm on . . . I suppose you'd call it an errand of mercy. I'm hoping to find out what, if anything, I can do to help the Briggs family.'

'Well, then, take some muffins with you. Wait a minute.' She came back with a paper bagful. 'Here. You can give some to those poor people, with my love.'

As he and Elizabeth walked down the porch steps, she said, 'See what I mean?'

'I do, indeed.' And if his tone was full of speculation, he was smart enough to say nothing of what he might have been thinking.

TWENTY-FIVE

'Aren't we going to the hospital first?' she asked when they were under way.

'No. I called and they said she was sleeping peacefully, and then the doctor needed to see her, and it would be better if we came around two.'

'But she's getting better?'

'They say so.'

'Dad, I haven't always been very nice to Mother.'

'No.'

'I've just begun to understood that. I had thought it was all on her side.'

'She can be irritating. I know that, Daughter. But you could try to respond with a little less antagonism.'

'I almost never actually talk back to her.'

'No. But your face shows exactly what you're thinking. Your mother isn't as well-educated as you, but she is not stupid. You've showed her that you think she is, and of course she resents that.'

Elizabeth looked down at her hands.

'It's not a tragedy, Bets. Don't blame yourself too much. You'll make more effort from now on, I'm sure. And here we are.'

Dad had been right about the Briggs family. They all but genu-flected before Elizabeth. They accepted the gift of Lucy's muffins with profuse thanks – in Italian, mostly, but the meaning was obvious. They showed her to the best chair, loaded it with so many cushions that there was almost no room to sit, pressed cookies and confections on her, and even tentatively offered a small glass of wine. She was afraid they would be offended when she refused, but they understood, just shook their heads and exchanged what sounded like good-natured comments in Italian.

She knew Mr Briggs, of course, and wanted to greet him, but before she could get to his side of the room she was surrounded by what seemed like several dozen people, some speaking English, some Italian, but all wanting to hug her and thank her effusively. She was once more overwhelmed by the warmth of Italian family life.

When he could get through, Mr Briggs came to rescue her. 'Please forgive my family,' he said with a smile. 'They want you to know that from now on, you are a daughter, a niece, a cousin – one of the family.'

She tried hard not to cry. 'It's an honor, sir. Your family is wonderful. And even though I can't understand their words, I understand their kindness. Will you tell them that for me?'

There was widespread laughter. 'Most of them understand English, even if they may find it a difficult language to speak. They know how you feel. Now, I think you both want to speak to me alone. I'm not sure there's any clear space here in the house. Let's go outside.'

There were a couple of wooden chairs in the small back yard. Mr Briggs brought another from the kitchen, and they all sat down. Elizabeth and her father exchanged glances. He nodded, and she began.

'First of all, Mr Briggs, I need to bring you up to date on what's been happening. I'm sorry, but most of it isn't very good.'

She began with her intemperate speech at church on Sunday. 'Good heavens, that's only four days ago! It feels like a month.' With occasional prompts from Mr Walker, she went through her stay at Fred's house, the police attack there, the attempted break-in at her house and her mother's injuries.

'Don't forget the brawl in Chicago,' Dad reminded her.

She complied, finishing: 'That might not have had anything to do with Mr Anthony, but it's a sign of how bad things are in Chicago.'

'But Mr Wilkins was not badly injured?' asked Mr Briggs anxiously.

'A few bruises and a bloody nose,' answered Elizabeth. 'He was in the wrong place at the wrong time, that's all. It could have been much worse. But there's been more. I won't tell you the whole long story, but I had an opportunity to talk to two of the gangsters yesterday and explain a few things. They won't bother us anymore.'

'But that's wonderful!'

'Yes, but there's still more. The KKK is on the move. Yesterday the Walosas were marching to St Edmund's as I was walking home. I don't know what they intended, but nothing good, I'm sure. But the gangsters intervened! No violence, praise the Lord, but silent intimidation.' She described the incident. 'And then, very early this morning, the KKK burned a cross in front of Mr Wilkins's house. So we do still have to worry about them.'

'Which isn't going to stop her.' Dad's voice was resigned.

Elizabeth ignored him. 'Well, at any rate I wasn't getting anywhere with finding out who the real criminal was, so I went to talk with Father Cole. I wanted to find out more about Mr Anth— Antonelli, what he was like, who his friends were, if he had enemies.'

'And you learned that he had many, many friends and no enemies. It's all true.' Mr Briggs was emphatic.

'Yes. And then I asked if anything seemed to be worrying him. Father Cole said there was certainly something on his mind, but he – the priest, I mean – didn't know what it was. Mr Antonelli hadn't confided in him.'

She let that comment lie there.

'He didn't confide very much to me, either. But yes, he was worried about something.'

'Do you have any idea what his problem might have been?'

'No. But I wasn't his closest friend. There's one man he might have talked to – his brother-in-law. They were close from the time they were children, back in Italy. The families moved to America and came here to Oak Park because both fathers could get jobs nearby, and the two boys wanted to stay together, insisted they *had* to stay together. That's how he got to know Luisa. Of course he didn't notice her when they were children. She was just an annoying little sister. But as she grew up and became so beautiful, her own attractions merged with Enrico's love of her brother, and they married and were very happy together. Of course the death of their two older children was a great grief. You would know about that, Elizabeth,' he said gently. 'But they weathered it together and it made the bond stronger. Then Angelica's accident took its toll. But nothing and no one ever came between them.'

That took care of one of Dr Edsall's categories. No relationship problems. As for his suggestion of unexpiated sin, it seemed very unlikely in Mr Antonelli's case, but she had to explore the possibility. 'This seems intrusive, Mr Briggs, but I have to ask. Had anything gone amiss with his faith? I mean, he still went to Mass regularly and so on?'

'Every Sunday, without fail, and often during the week as well. He was more faithful about Confession than I am, and often lectured me about it. He loved the Church if any man ever did. It isn't intrusive, Elizabeth. No question is, if it can help uncover the truth.'

'Then there's only one other sort of big worry that I can think of. Actually, it was my rector, Dr Edsall, who thought of it. He's been a pastor for many years, and he said the troubles people brought to him, the big ones, were either broken relationships, or terrible sins that were eating away at them, or money. So I'm asking. The doctor bills for Angelica must have been very large, and I'm sure the family isn't rich.'

'They were comfortable. No, not rich, but you know Enrico did well in his business. He knew his merchandise, he knew his customers, and he was a good, careful businessman. Yes, Angelica's injuries did mean serious bills, but it seemed he could always meet them. It wasn't until just recently, the past couple of weeks or so – before he died, I mean – that he suddenly began to look anxious about something. You could be right. But I don't know how that kind of trouble could come on without warning.'

Silence again as each of them tried to think of a simple answer. The phrase 'protection racket' rose in Elizabeth's mind.

Mrs Briggs looked out the back door. 'Paolo, your aunt Fran is ready to leave, but she wants to say goodbye first and give you a blessing.'

Elizabeth stood. 'I've taken up enough of your time. If you'll give me the name of Mr Antonelli's brother-in-law, and his address, I'd like to talk to him.'

*   *   *

Before anything else, though, they had to visit the hospital. Elizabeth was nervous about that. What was she going to say to the woman she had openly defied just four days ago? Should she apologize?

Her father understood. He almost always did. 'It'll be all right, Daughter. Don't force it.'

'Don't let me say something stupid, Dad.'

He chuckled. 'I'll try my best. Just think before you open your mouth.'

'Before I put my foot in it, you mean.'

The hospital was small and, like all hospitals, somewhat forbidding. Afternoon visiting hours had just begun. They were shown to Mrs Walker's room by a very young volunteer. 'Here's your mother, miss.' She indicated an almost-closed door. 'You'll be very quiet, won't you? She has a terrible headache.'

Elizabeth forced back the thought that she almost always did. This time it was probably real, and probably very painful indeed.

The aide opened the door, and Elizabeth and her father walked in, hand in hand.

She had to suppress a gasp. Never had she seen her mother look so utterly helpless. She lay in bed, looking very white and somehow very small. Her head was wrapped in bandages; bruises on her face were turning from purple to bilious yellow. Her right leg, in a cast, was suspended above the bed. Her eyes were closed, but they opened, slowly, as she heard footsteps approaching.

She tried to speak, but her voice cracked. The aide came to her side and offered a spoonful of cracked ice. She swallowed and tried again. 'Elizabeth,' she said.

'Yes, Mother.' Her voice cracked, too, but it was because of imminent tears. 'Can I do something for you?'

'Just . . . be here.'

At that the tears did come. Elizabeth started to turn her head away, but her father shook his head. 'Let her see,' he murmured.

'Kenneth.'

He went to the bedside and took her hand. 'Are you feeling any better, my dear?'

'A little. Pills.'

'They're giving you pain pills? Good. You'll heal better if you're not fighting pain all the time.'

'Make me groggy.'

'We'd better go away and let you rest.'

'No!' Her voice was still strained, but emphatic. 'Stay a little. Good to see you both.'

'Mother, we'll stay as long as you want us to. Or as long as the nurses will let us.'

That brought a feeble laugh. 'Like to see them stop you. I never could.' She started to cough. After the aide gave her a little more ice, she lay back on her pillows and closed her eyes.

The aide gestured at them to leave, but Mr Walker shook his head and mouthed, 'Not till she's fully asleep.'

It was only a few minutes before a soft snore began and they very quietly left the room.

'Well done, Bets,' her father said when they were out of the building. 'You cried, which showed her you cared about her, and you made her laugh.'

'Oh, but Daddy, I didn't know she'd look so—so—'

'I think "diminished" is the word you're looking for. No one looks or feels her best swathed in bandages. For the first time in years she's in a situation she can't control. She's accustomed to dominating, and she can't.'

'She really liked it that we came to see her, didn't she? I thought she might – I don't know – tell me this was all my fault and I should go away.'

'She needs us, sweetheart. She forgets that from time to time, but this has made her remember. My darling daughter, you think your mother doesn't love you. She does, I promise you. She shows it in a way you don't understand, by trying to make you into the kind of woman she thinks you ought to be. She thinks that will make you happy. You know it won't, but don't underestimate her good intentions.'

'I've told her often enough I don't want the life she has planned out for me.'

'Yes, but she just thinks you're too inexperienced to know what's best for you. Perhaps when she comes home you can sit down for a talk and explain – gently – what you do want for yourself.' He paused while he negotiated a busy intersection. 'Of course, before you do that, you'll have to work out for yourself how you see your future.'

She was silent all the way home.

TWENTY-SIX

M r Walker brought the car to a stop before the garage. 'Do you want to get your car out, Bets? How far away does this friend of Mr Antonelli's live?'

'Too far to walk,' she said, looking at the address Mr Briggs had given her. 'I'd better drive.'

'Are you up to it? That hospital visit wasn't easy.'

'No. It wasn't. But driving will give me some time to think about it. And maybe Mr' – she looked at the paper – 'Mr Corelli will give me some ideas about a direction for me to follow next. Would you mind cranking the car for me?'

Her car, though also a Model T like Fred's, was a smaller, cheaper model without a self-starter. Her father obligingly operated the crank, and she set out.

The Corelli house was very much like those of the other Italian families she had visited lately. Small, well-kept, with flowers wherever they could be planted. Unlike her own gardens, these were not designed but simply planted, in exuberant colors that ought to have clashed badly, but somehow didn't. She parked the car on the narrow street, hoping she'd left room for another car to pass, and walked up the path to the front door.

There was no bell, and only the screen door was closed. As she lifted her hand to knock on its wooden frame, she was suddenly struck with several thoughts, things she should have considered earlier. This was a weekday. She didn't know what Mr Corelli did for a living, but almost certainly he was out doing it in mid-afternoon on a Thursday. Unless he was home for lunch, but it was very late for that. If he *was* eating, it was a most inappropriate time to call. Her mother would be horrified at her breach of manners. And what if no one in the house spoke English?

Too late. A woman came to the door. '*Sì? Posso aiutarti?*'

Oh, dear. 'I'm sorry, I don't speak Italian. My name is Elizabeth Fairchild. Do you speak English?'

A man came up. He had a napkin in his hand. 'I speak English a little. Can I help you?'

'You are Mr Corelli?'

'Yes.' He looked puzzled.

'My name is Elizabeth Fairchild,' she repeated, 'I wanted to talk to you about Mr Antonelli, but I see that I have come at a bad time, while you are having your lunch.'

He shook his head and opened the screen door wide. 'No, no, no, no, no. You are lady who wants to do the right thing for my friend. No bad time. Come in, come in!'

His wife spoke to him in agitated Italian.

Elizabeth heard the word *tardi* repeated several times and thought she understood. 'Mr Corelli, is your wife afraid you will be late back to work? I can save you a few minutes if I drive you there. And we could talk on the way – I mean, while we are driving. In the car.' She struggled for simple terms he would understand, and finally he smiled, nodded, and spoke to his wife, who nodded and smiled, too, and saw both of them out the door with the greatest goodwill.

He insisted on cranking the car for her. 'I know how. I work with cars. I am good with them,' he added, pointing to himself and laughing. 'I have car, but I drove customer home. Very late for lunch, and long walk to go back. I show you where.'

Elizabeth tried to frame her questions in the simplest possible English, mixing in the few Italian words she knew. 'Signor Corelli, you were a friend to Signor Antonelli, yes?'

'Friend, yes. Good, good friend.'

'He was worried about something.' That brought a puzzled frown. 'He had trouble. Problem. Difficulty.' Ah, that did it.

'Yes, bad difficulty. Bad, bad. Very unhappy.'

'Why, Signor Corelli? What was the difficulty?'

'Money. No money to pay – I do not know the English. *Debito.*'

'Debt?'

'Yes, that is the word! Debt. Big, big debt.'

They had arrived at the garage where Mr Corelli worked, way east on Madison. It would indeed have been a long walk. Elizabeth tried one last question. 'Big debt to a bank?'

'No. Not bank. I not know. Enrico, he not tell.' Someone inside the garage called to him. 'I go now. *Grazie*, signora!'

'And thank *you*, signor.'

But, she thought as she drove home, one question answered left another, perhaps the most important one. To whom had Mr Antonelli owed money?

It was time to talk to Fred again.

But first, home to her lonely father. She pulled her car into the garage so Dad wouldn't have to put it away, and walked in the house to find him napping in his study. Poor Dad! He'd been having a harrowing time so far this summer, when he was supposed to be enjoying some leisure. And it was her fault. If she hadn't . . .

Stop that, scolded her inner voice. You're trying to fix the problem. Start being positive about it.

She had headed for the kitchen. As she walked in, Susannah looked up from the bread dough she was kneading. ''Bout time you started bein' sensible, 'stead o' blamin' yourself for ever' bad thing that happens.'

'Oh, dear. Was I thinking out loud?'

Susannah's reply to that was a snort. 'I s'pose you didn't have no lunch, just like your pa. You go to the fridge right this minute and get yourself some ham while I finish this bread. *And* some cheese. You so thin, your clothes gonna fall off you.'

Elizabeth obeyed. One did, in Susannah's domain. She even cut some of yesterday's bread and made herself a sandwich, and sat down at the kitchen table to eat it.

'Hmph. You been learnin' how to do in a kitchen, have you?' Thump, thump as the dough was pounded and slammed down on the board.

'Lucy's taught me a little. I can make coffee and toast. That's about all.'

'Better than nothin'. I 'spect you wondering why I never taught you cookin'.'

'Because you didn't want me getting in your way!'

'Nope. 'Cause your mama didn' want me to. She wants you to be a fine lady, never needin' to get your hands dirty.'

'But that's not the kind of person I want to be.'

'She thinks you don' know what's good for you.'

'That's what Dad said when we were driving to the hospital, that she wanted what was best for me, and was always sure she knew that better than I.'

'He right about that.' Thump, thump. 'How is your mama? The mister, he was so tired when he come home I didn' even ask, jus' gave him some food, which he didn' even eat afore he fell asleep.'

'She's doing pretty well, they say. She woke up and talked to us for a little while, even laughed once. But she looks terrible! All bruised and bandaged, and pale as milk where she isn't purple and yellow.' The tears came to her eyes. She brushed them away with the back of her hand.

'Your mama' – thump, thump – 'she love you, you know. Her and me, we don't hardly ever agree 'bout most things, but she not a bad woman, jus' confused. Don't know what's important. 'Spect your daddy told you, you got to learn to treat her nicer.' Thump, thump. 'She the aggravatin'est lady I ever did know, but you don't make things any better between you, the way you act.'

'I know. And I really will try. But Susannah, when you get that bread in the oven, would you teach me how to make coffee your way? Lucy has a different kind of coffee pot.'

Susannah gave the dough a final thump, formed it into a smooth round ball, rubbed it with butter, and put it in a huge bowl with a towel over it. 'Now see, you really don't know nothin' 'bout a kitchen. The dough gotta rise afore it goes in the bread pans, an' agin after. Won't go in the oven for another couple hours. Takes time, bread does.'

She went to the sink and washed her hands, and then sat down with a sigh next to Elizabeth. 'We'll make coffee another day. Too hot for it now. In a minute I'll get up and get us some lemonade.'

'You're tired. Where's Mary? She ought to be helping.'

'I give her the day off. Her mama not feelin' so good, and with just you and your daddy to do for, I can manage.'

'Well, no wonder you're tired out. I can see that bread-making takes not just time, but a lot of work.' Elizabeth did at least know where the glasses were kept, and the lemonade was of course in the refrigerator. She poured some for each of them and then sat and looked around the kitchen.

'You know, I never thought much about kitchens, how different they could be. We have everything new and up to date, and you cook the most wonderful food here. Lucy's kitchen is much more old fashioned and inconvenient. She has an old icebox, not a very big one, and none of the handy gadgets you have. I don't even know what most of them are for, but they're clean and shiny, so I know you use them all. And I don't think Lucy has a big budget for food. Fred does all right, but he's not rich. And yet she's a great cook, too.'

Susannah laughed her big rolling laugh. 'Honey-chile, I was cookin' on a wood stove in a kitchen jus' big enough for me to turn around in when I married my Billie. An' talk about budget! We didn' have none atall. I cooked whatever we could grow an' whatever Billie could catch or shoot, an' we et good. Billie, he made a little money as a farm hand, an' if there was some left over at the end of the month, I'd buy a sack of flour an' one of cornmeal. It's the cook makes the difference, honey, not the kitchen. I'm right pleased to have a fine place to work, and it's nice bein' able to get what I want to cook in it, but sometimes I miss the old days. A potato you just dug – you wouldn' believe how much better it taste than a old one from the store.'

Elizabeth laughed. 'The store ones taste great to me, when you cook them.'

'Nothin' to cookin' a potato. The easiest thing they is, 'cept maybe a boiled egg! Tomorrow, if your mama don't come home, I start teachin' you some o' the easy things.' She paused. 'Lessen you gonna be off gallivantin' agin.'

'I don't know what I'll be doing, Susannah. I know I'd rather be here in your kitchen learning to cook, but I'm committed to doing what I can about Mr Antonelli's murder. I've found out a little. I talked to his best friend today. Sort of. His English isn't terribly good, and of course I don't know Italian at all, but I did manage to understand that he – Mr A., I mean – had money problems that were worrying him. A big debt, his friend said, but he didn't know who the lender was. Not a bank, he was sure, but Mr A. didn't tell him any more than that.'

'I mebbe know who it was. Leastways, I know somethin'.'

Elizabeth was too startled to speak. Here in her own home was a source of information she had never even considered. She stared, open-mouthed.

Susannah nodded. 'You 'member I was gonna tell you bout what we heard at church last Sunday, 'n' then things got complicated and we all forgot.' She reached a long arm and lifted the cookie jar over. 'Snickerdoodles. Baked 'em this mornin'. Have some.' She took two herself and continued. 'So Zeke 'n' me, we goes to Mount Carmel Baptist, like most of us colored folks around here. It's a real friendly place, and we all stands around and talks for a little after the service, till we gots to get back to work. Well, a course ever'body was talkin' about the murder. Reverend Neely, he weren't too pleased about that. Said it weren't no fit thing to talk about at a church. But we was outside, and most of 'em paid him no mind, and Zeke 'n' me, we listened real hard, on account o' you bein' smack dab in the middle of it.' She took a few bites of cookie.

'So they was all talkin' 'bout Mr Anthony, like we thought his name was, an' sayin' what a nice man he was. He mostly did business with white folks, 'cause the stuff he sold cost a lot, but ever' now and then one of us'd see some little somethin' in his window that'd make a nice present, an' he'd treat us jus' like he did ever'body else. So we was all sorry he was gone, and tryin' to figger out why somebody'd kill a man like that. An' that's when somebody spoke up an' said he didn' know why, but he knew who.'

'Susannah!'

'Don't get all excited. He said he didn' know the man's name, but he saw him plain, an' he'd know him again. See, he – the man at church, well, he's no more than a boy really, his name's Joshua Jones – anyway, he was cleanin' up where he works, the fillin' station down the street from Mr Anthony's shop, an' he saw this man come high-tailin' down the alley toward the fillin' station. Saw him plain as plain. So Joshua thought somethin' was wrong, an' he was about to step up and see if he could help, when he saw what the man was carryin'.'

Elizabeth held her breath.

'Joshua said it was a big ole knife, an' it was drippin' blood.'

Elizabeth pushed away the cookies. 'Dear heaven! Did— Oh, please say the man didn't see Joshua!'

'The folks at church asked the same thing. Joshua said not. It was afternoon, 'member, an' the sun was shinin' towards the man with the knife. Joshua was inside the garage, in the shadows. An' Joshua, he real dark complected, an' he was wearing dark clothes for workin' round grease an' that. So you get a colored man in dark clothes, in shadow, an' a man comin' toward him with the sun in his eyes. No, Joshua think he safe.'

'What did he do?'

'Jus' froze there. Didn' move, didn' make no noise, scared to kingdom come. Waited till the man was good 'n' gone, an' then he locked up the place an' high-tailed it home. Wasn't till next day he heard about the murder, but he say he'll swear on a stack o' Bibles he saw the murderer.'

'Did he go to the police?'

Susannah looked at her pityingly. 'Honey, you's smart an' all, but you got a lot to learn if you think a colored man gonna go to the po-lice an' tell 'em they done arrested the wrong man. 'Specially when all he know about the right man is what he look like an' what he wearin'. An' Joshua, he still pretty young, like I say, an' kinda shy.'

Elizabeth shook her head despairingly. 'I wasn't thinking. Joshua was right to be wary. Well, so what *did* the man look like?'

'I didn' hear Joshua say. Zeke an' me had to get back quick so's I could get breakfast started afore your mama came downstairs. An' speakin' o' food, I got to get movin', or nobody won't have no supper.'

Elizabeth glanced at her watch. 'Oh, no, it can't be supper time already! Susannah, do you think it's too late to find Joshua at his job?'

Susannah considered, looking at the kitchen clock. 'Not all that late. They's open till six, an' Joshua, he always the last one to leave, 'cause he locks up. You can make it if you take that car of yours.'

'Don't wait supper for me. I'm not hungry.' And she was out the door.

TWENTY-SEVEN

She couldn't find Zeke immediately, and she wasn't confident about starting her car without him, so she set off on foot, nearly running. There was only one filling station downtown, but it was a fair ways away.

The day was too hot for running. She was sweaty and breathless by the time she saw the gas pump, and a young colored man just walking away from it. Toward her, fortunately. She tried to catch her breath. 'Excuse me, but is your name Joshua Jones?'

He looked wary. 'Yes, ma'am.'

'Susannah told me I might find you here. Susannah Lewis. She works for my parents, and she's a good friend of mine.'

The wariness diminished. A little. 'You Miz Fairchild?'

'Yes. Look, I expect you're on your way home, and I don't want to delay you, but I do want to talk to you. Can I walk with you for a little way?'

The wariness returned.

'You a rich white lady. Why you want to talk to a no-account colored boy?'

She couldn't let that pass. 'That's not who you are. You don't really think so, and neither do I. You may not have a lot of money, but you work hard at your job, and your employer trusts you, or he wouldn't have given you keys to the station. And that's not who I am, either. Yes, I have a lot of money, but I try to spend it in ways that help people. Right now I'm trying to help a good man who was killed.'

'He dead. Nothin' gonna help him now.'

'Justice will help him, and his family. Whoever murdered him must be found, and punished.'

'Nothin' to do with me.' He had started walking with her, but now she moved in front of him and stopped.

'Mr Jones, that isn't true and you know it! You saw the man who killed him. Everyone at your church knows it. How long will it be before everyone in the village knows it? The murderer will know it! And you will be in very serious danger!'

'Not if I keeps my mouth shut.' He moved around her and kept on walking.

'No! Think! When the murderer finds out you can identify him, he's going to want to keep your mouth shut permanently. If you tell the police what you know, it will be too late for the murderer. If you even tell me, and I tell the authorities, you'll be safe. Oh, can't you see? Look, Mr Jones, we are going to sit down right here on this nice shaded bench, and you're going to tell me everything you can remember about that man you saw.'

'No! Not here! Ever'body'll hear me! Then we both gonna be in bad trouble!'

His voice had risen in his panic. A policeman walking the beat strolled over. 'Is this person bothering you, ma'am?'

'No. Not at all. In fact, he's helping me a great deal. He has some important information, and I'd like you to hear it, too. Why don't you sit down with us?'

Elizabeth Fairchild was not her mother's daughter for nothing. She could be forceful when necessary. The policeman sat gingerly on the very edge of the bench. Next to Joshua.

'Now, Mr Jones, you can tell your story to me and to the police at the same time. Save us all some time and trouble.' She addressed the policeman. 'I'm sorry, sir, but I don't know your name.'

'Sergeant Daniels, Mrs Fairchild.'

'Delighted to meet you. Sergeant, this is Mr Joshua Jones. On the day Mr Antonelli was killed, Mr Jones saw a man we presume to be Mr Antonelli's murderer just leaving the scene. He was understandably stunned and alarmed by the encounter, but he managed to get a good look at the man and can describe him. We both think that may be a big help to the police. Mr Jones?'

He wasn't at all happy about it, but he was beginning to see the logic of her argument. And Susannah Lewis was not a woman to cross. If she heard he'd been contrary with Miz Fairchild . . . He looked up. 'I don't know his name.'

'No, we understand that. Was he a big man?'

'Not so big. Taller'n me, but not fat. Just ordinary. He had black hair, kinda long. He looked scared.'

'I'm sure he did! What was he wearing?'

'That was kinda funny. He was wearin' a suit. On that hot day. It was kinda tight and a sorta tan color. Only—'

'Only what?' asked the policeman gruffly.

'There was something odd about the suit?' asked Elizabeth gently.

'It—it had somethin' red all down the front. Mebbe paint, but I think . . .' Again he ran down.

They waited, sure of what he would say, but not wanting to prompt him.

He gulped. 'It was blood. Fresh, too. I lived on a farm once.'

He didn't have to explain further. The policeman nodded. 'Me, too. I never could forget the first time I saw an animal slaughtered. Saw, and smelled.' He looked at Joshua with a certain amount of sympathy.

'Mr Jones, you said the man was carrying something.' Surely that much of a prompt was all right, thought Elizabeth.

He shuddered. 'He had a knife. Big huntin' knife. It was all bloody, too.'

'Fresh?' asked the policeman.

'Still drippin' a little.'

'Sergeant, I'm sure you agree this is important information.'

'I sure do. Mr Jones, if you'll come with me down to the station, we can—'

Joshua stood and looked around wildly. 'No, sir! I didn' do nothin', I swear! Don' take me away—'

'It's all right, Joshua,' Elizabeth soothed. 'They're not going to do anything to you. They just want to take down what you've told us, and maybe ask you a few more questions about the man you saw.'

'No, ma'am! Please, don' let 'im take me away! Please!' He was trembling. Tears came to his eyes.

'Sergeant, you can understand how he feels. Is it really necessary that he go to the station?' She thought for a moment. 'I have an idea. I have a friend who is a lawyer. Couldn't Mr Jones tell him all he's told us, and swear to it? A deposition, I think it's called. Then you'd have your evidence, and I believe it could even be used in—in formal proceedings.' She didn't want to mention court in front of Joshua. He was panicky enough already.

Sergeant Daniels considered. It wasn't a usual procedure, but he knew it was sometimes used when a witness was too ill to testify in court or would be away on unavoidable business. 'Would that be better for you, Mr Jones?' he asked, trying hard to sound unmenacing.

Joshua was still shaking. 'You'll come with me, Miz Fairchild?'

'Of course. It's nothing to worry about, I promise.'

'I guess I got to.' Joshua dropped his hands in unwilling surrender.

'Good. Now we've kept you from your supper long enough. Your family will be wondering where you've been.'

'Don't got no fambly, ma'am. Just my dog.'

'Well, then, you need to get home to him. Are you working at the garage tomorrow?'

'Ever' day 'cept Sunday, ma'am.'

'Then I'll talk to my friend, and tomorrow sometime we'll come to see you.'

'Cain't talk much when I'm workin'.'

'I thought we'd come near your quitting time.' She put out her hand. 'It's been a pleasure talking to you.'

'Uh . . . yes, ma'am.' He wiped his hand on his dungarees and took hers for a very brief moment before hurrying away.

'Poor guy,' said the sergeant. 'Scared to death.'

'Of course. Police have always meant trouble to him.'

'And his kind have always meant trouble to me. But he's different. I think he was telling the truth.'

Maybe it's your thinking that's different, she thought, but all she said was, 'I'm sure he was. Now if you'll tell me what other questions you wanted to ask him, I'll be sure they get answered in his deposition.'

'Just a few details. An exact time when he saw the guy, as near as he can come. And whether he saw which way he was headed when he left. Oh, and any more details he can give about his appearance – his face, I mean.'

Elizabeth frowned. 'Not many people are very good at describing faces. I can see a friend's face in my mind, but when it comes to describing her, I can't find the words. Oh!'

The sergeant waited.

'I just thought of something. I know someone who can draw portraits of people. Well, she's the one who drew Mr Anthony's face for that ad, if you've seen it.'

'Oh, Lord! Sorry, ma'am, but it's tacked up on the wall at the station, and every time the phone rings it's somebody else with some useless hint. I have to agree it's a good likeness.'

'Well, I'm wondering if she could try to draw a man from Joshua's description. She could try out different shapes for noses and eyes and all, and maybe she'd come up with something not too far off.'

'Worth a try,' he said with a shrug that clearly showed his opinion of the idea. 'I got to get back to my beat, ma'am. You'll get that deposition to us as soon as you can? We're pretty anxious to get this guy. The village isn't happy with us right now.'

'They're not happy with me, either. But between us, we'll track him down!'

'Just be careful, ma'am. The guy who did it wouldn't mind rubbing you out, too, you know. Like they say, you can't hang a man twice.'

'Sergeant, everyone I know has been telling me to be careful for the past week. My family wanted me to stay locked up in my house. I couldn't do that, and I can't be running away all the time,

either. I won't act recklessly, but quite frankly I'd rather help find
Mr Antonelli's killer than hide like a scared rabbit.'

She could see that the policeman disagreed with her, but her
social position kept his mouth shut. Most of the time she hated
that kind of unearned deference, but she had to admit it sometimes
saved trouble.

'Yes, ma'am. You'll be seeing about that deposition?'

'As soon as possible. I hope to deliver it to the station tomorrow.
Till then.'

She walked rapidly home.

TWENTY-EIGHT

Her father met her at the door. 'Susannah and I were beginning to wonder if you'd gone on a hunger strike. Supper's
been ready for almost an hour.'

'I'm sorry, Dad, but I've been doing something important. I did
tell Susannah not to make you wait.' She went with him to the
dining room and sat down.

'All Susannah told me was that you were trying to talk to
someone who saw the murderer, or says he did.'

'Oh, he did. No question about it. His description was too full
of details to be fabricated. I won't tell you all those details. Some
are not fit conversation for the dinner table. But he convinced me,
and the really important thing is, he convinced a policeman, too.'
She told him the story between bites of ham and coleslaw and
sweet potatoes. 'He was terrified, poor man, at facing the police.'

'An' no s'prise, neither,' said Susannah, coming in to refill their
iced tea. 'The po-lice don't like us colored folks much.'

'Well, one of them has changed his mind a little, I hope.'

Susannah snorted as she left the room.

Elizabeth sighed. 'I do have hopes. Sergeant Daniels started out
being very suspicious of Mr Jones, but ended by believing every
word he said, and feeling sorry about frightening him. It's only a
little wedge, but maybe it'll help. And tomorrow maybe Mr Jones
will learn not to be afraid of lawyers, or one lawyer, anyway.' She
explained about the deposition idea.

'Good grief, Daughter! You actually paid attention in civics class!'

She grinned. 'Not in high school. I thought it was the ultimate in boredom. At Northwestern, though, I took a class in government, and the teacher was so good I actually got interested, and even remembered some of it.'

'It's a good thing you did, for Mr Jones's sake.' Mr Walker sighed. 'It's a great pity the police inspire such fear in our colored neighbors. You and I know that they're citizens just like us, and most of them law-abiding, but old attitudes die hard.'

'Especially when you have people like the Walosas spreading their propaganda all over the village. Dad, why do they hate colored people so?'

'And Catholics, and foreigners, and anyone who's the least bit different from them. It's fear, my dear. I know you don't read many novels, but from them and from history you must surely have learned that most hatred is born of fear, much of it irrational.

'The people on the high steps of the ladder, the ones who have money or social position, or whatever else they prize, fear losing it. I think not consciously, not at first. There's just an uneasy feeling of "What are *they* doing in *my* town? What are *they* after?" Note the pronouns. The sense of ownership. The fear that *they* might take it away, whatever *it* is.

'Think about it, Daughter. What are the things about your life that you simply take for granted?'

'The things I've always known, I suppose. A place to live, food on the table.' She thought a little more deeply. 'The right to go wherever I want and do whatever I want, within reasonable limits.'

'And to worship as you wish, associate with whom you please. Now suppose someone new moved to town, and you heard rumors that even one of those privileges was threatened. The person planned to buy Grace Church, tear it down and build a gorgeous house on the property. Or, less ridiculously unlikely, planned to build a new church, practicing a very different sort of worship. What would your reaction be?'

'I wouldn't believe it! I never believe rumors.'

'Never? Not if you hear them from someone you trust? Suppose you heard from an absolutely reliable source that this person had applied for a building permit? Even if you knew none of the details about what and where this person planned to build?'

'Then . . . then I'd start to feel uneasy. All right, Dad, I get your point. Once I started having even a little fear, I'd also start resenting this person who was stirring things up. I might start making plans to stop him. And if my friends started agitating about it, too, my resentment would build on theirs. And yes, it could turn to hate. I'd like to think I'm a better person than that, but the crowd mentality . . .'

'And remember, all these reactions you think you might have are based on rumor and one incomplete piece of data. And you're a logical person who weighs the facts. Sadly, many people are ready to believe almost anything. And think about this, too. You are at present engaged on a manhunt.'

She made a protesting sound.

'Call it what you will. You believe that you are doing this for the sake of justice, and I won't dispute that. But you'd better make very sure you're not also seeking vengeance. There's a narrow line, and the difference can be found only in your heart.' He smiled at his daughter and picked up his fork. 'Here endeth the sermon. I wonder what Susannah made us for dessert.'

'I'll go see.' Elizabeth was glad to escape to the kitchen. She never liked her mother's habit of ringing her little bell for service. It seemed so pompous, so demeaning to Mary and Susannah.

Besides, her cheeks were burning, and she wanted to get away from Dad for a moment.

Susannah was resting her bulk for a moment, sitting at the kitchen table with a glass of iced tea. 'What you need, honey? I didn' hear no bell. An' you was talkin', so I didn' like to butt in.'

'I don't like that bell. Dad wondered what you had for dessert. Maybe something light?'

'How about a gelatin fruit mold? Made it this mornin'. Ought to be ready by now. You go set down, an I'll bring it to you. Coffee?'

'Not for me. Too hot.'

'You go back to your daddy. Shoo, chile!'

The fruit mold was good, and refreshing, and so was the iced coffee Susannah gave them.

'Daddy, I've been thinking about what you said, and I wonder how I would feel about Susannah if I hadn't known and loved her all my life. If she were just a colored woman I might pass on the street. And . . . and I wonder what she and Zeke and Mary think of us.'

'You know quite well what Susannah thinks of you. She loves you like a daughter, and treats you like one. And she and I are good friends. Your mother—'

'I've been learning these past few days what she thinks of Mother. She pities her, I think. She knows Mother can't really help the way she is, because she's never learned how to get along with people.' She swallowed. 'And she thinks I haven't tried hard enough to be nice to Mother. And she's right.'

'Yes, but I keep telling you not to beat yourself up about it, Bets. We both know she can be hard to deal with, but if you try to remember that she loves you, you may find it easier. Now, it's been a long day. I want you to play me something quiet and soothing, and then we're going to go to bed and forget about the troubles of the world for a while.'

Unfortunately, the troubles of the world don't automatically go away when the lights are turned out and the covers pulled up. Elizabeth was as tired as she ever remembered being, but sleep wouldn't come. Maybe it was the coffee, or the heat, or both.

Her father's words kept coming back. *Was* she pursuing Mr Antonelli's murder out of revenge? Revenge over a man she had loved, in her cool, remote way.

No. No, that wasn't the kind of love that sparked revenge. Revenge is hot-blooded. She was sure of that. So many opera plots – and operas were so often Italian. Italians are hot-blooded.

Or were they? Was that just another rumor spread about them, to make them seem even more different, even more dangerous?

Certainly they were more emotional than most of the people in Oak Park. Or at least their emotions were more open. Could one of them have gotten into a dreadful argument with Mr Antonelli and stabbed him in fury? Maybe not meaning to kill? And then fled in the horror of what he had done?

She tried to settle herself comfortably in bed, but there was no comfort to be found. An Italian. One of Mr Antonelli's family, or his friends. Those warm, delightful people.

There was money involved. Had Mr Antonelli borrowed money from a friend and then not been able to pay it back?

No. That didn't make sense. If Father Cole was right, his Italian parishioners, who comprised most of the Italians in Oak Park, had very little money to spare. A few dollars to meet an immediate need, perhaps, but no one would kill a friend over a few dollars.

Would they? What if the lender were in dire need himself? Elizabeth had never in her life been short of money to buy anything she needed or wanted. What if it were a question of medicine for the baby, or gas for the car that got you to work?

But Joshua hadn't said anything about the murderer looking Italian.

Would he know? Was he one of those colored people who thought all white folks looked alike? Or did they actually think that? Elizabeth knew there were lots of white people who claimed all colored people looked alike to them. Which was absurd.

She got up to go to the bathroom and wash her face. The bathroom window had no trees near it. She looked out and saw a bright star shining near a crescent moon. The whole sky was full of stars.

Tomorrow was going to be a beautiful day. And tomorrow she would start learning to cook, and would see Fred, and would maybe bring this nightmare close to an end.

Take no thought for the morrow . . . sufficient unto the day is the evil thereof . . .

The lines of scripture running through her head, she went to bed and almost immediately to sleep.

The morning did dawn beautifully, but Elizabeth didn't see it. She woke much later than usual, after her delayed sleep, and the sun was already high in the sky. And miracle of miracles, the air was clear and cool. A beautiful day, indeed.

Dressed and downstairs in less than fifteen minutes, she headed straight for the kitchen.

'So you still alive, Rip van Winkle,' was Susannah's greeting. 'Your daddy's already gone to the hospital to see your mama. He told me not to wake you up, reckoned you needed the sleep. Which you did. You been doin' too much an' sleepin' an' eatin' too little. You sit yourself down right here an' eat your breakfas'.'

She set a cup of steaming coffee before her. 'How you want your eggs?'

'I don't really . . .' she began, but the look in Susannah's eye cut her short. 'Uh. Scrambled, I guess.'

Susannah kept right on talking as she scrambled eggs, fried

bacon, made toast, and peeled an orange. 'The phone been ringin' off the hook. Lots o' ladies wantin' to know how come you missed this meetin' and that meetin'. An' Miz Hemin'way called. An' your friend Leslie. An' Fred.' She moved to the table to set toast and butter and jam in front of Elizabeth. 'An' they all want you to call 'em back right away. But you gonna eat your breakfas' first.'

Elizabeth wondered if she should salute, but instead she smiled and picked up a piece of toast. 'Why isn't Mary helping you? Or is her mother still sick?'

Susannah sighed. 'Her mama not gonna get well, from what I hear. She got the flu real bad all those years ago, an' never did get quite right again, an' now she can't stop coughin'. Spittin' up blood sometimes, I hear. They think it's that consumption.'

'Oh, no! But that's terribly dangerous! Mary could get it, along with the rest of the family.' She paused as Susannah shook her head.

'No family, honey. Her daddy worked on the railroad, an' got killed when a freight car broke loose an' run over him. Long time ago. There was a baby brother, but he was born puny an' jus' kinda pined away. So they's jus' Mary an' her mama now.'

'Susannah, is there anything we can do to help? Take them food, or anything?'

'Pray. 'Specially pray Mary don' get it. Can't do nothin' for her mama now, an' Mary, she got a good home here. An' you listen here! Not gonna help nobody if you don' eat up!' Susannah set a full plate before her. 'Your mama wouldn' like it if you wasted all that food, you know.'

There was no help for it. No matter how upset Elizabeth was about Mary and her mother, no matter how many phone calls had to be returned and how many things she had to do today, Susannah had laid down the law, and Susannah must be obeyed.

Actually, the food tasted good, and Elizabeth was surprised at how much she was able to eat. She surreptitiously fed the last few bits of bacon to the cats, who were never, never supposed to enter the kitchen, but of course did whenever they smelled anything they particularly liked. Susannah pretended not to see.

'That was really good, Susannah, but I honestly don't have room for another bite. Do you think Daddy will be home soon?'

'Visitors gotta leave at noon, so he won't be long.'

Elizabeth looked at the kitchen clock and gasped. 'Eleven-thirty! It's nearly lunchtime, and I just finished breakfast! I'm ashamed of myself.'

Susannah chuckled. 'You don' act like a lady of leisure very often, do you? No shame in lettin' yourself relax once in a while. But you better go make those phone calls afore they all start callin' again.'

Of course she called Fred first. He might have something important to tell her about the murder. At least that made a good excuse.

She tried his office first and was lucky. The secretary knew who she was by now and put her through immediately.

'Susannah said you called earlier. I'm sorry I didn't answer; I slept shamefully late this morning.'

'Good. You needed some rest, and I'm sorry I called so early, but I had an interesting visit from the police.'

'The police? Oh, about the cross-burning.'

'No, about the witness to the murder. A Sergeant Daniels seemed to think you'd told me all about it.'

'Oh, dear! I did mean to tell you, first thing this morning, but . . . anyway, the man didn't witness the murder, only the murderer running away a few minutes later.' She explained about the encounter and Joshua's fear of going to the police station. 'Fred, it's absolutely sickening how afraid he is. And he's done nothing wrong. But I don't think he'd ever have told his story if Susannah hadn't told me about it. So the point is, I explained to him about depositions, and Sergeant Daniels said it would be all right to take his testimony that way. So we're to meet him, you and I, a little after five, at the filling station. I'm so hoping you can be there!'

'Of course. I have an appointment at four, but I'll keep it short. Shall I pick you up on the way?'

'No, I'll walk. It's a beautiful day. I think I'll get there a little early, in case he loses his nerve and heads for home.'

'I'll bring my secretary, too. We'll need a written record of what he says, and she's a whiz at shorthand.'

'Will she intimidate him?'

'I can't imagine why. She's about fifty, with gray hair and a few wrinkles. Looks like everybody's grandmother.'

'Not like Joshua's, though. I'll tell you what. I'll see if I can get Susannah to come, too. Being a member of his church and all, she might make him feel more comfortable.'

'Or not. Talk about intimidating. I hear she can freeze even your mother. But she can probably get the poor guy to cooperate, just by looking like *his* grandmother. I'll see you then.'

He hung up, leaving Elizabeth with a lot more to say.

The phone rang again almost immediately. It was Mrs Hemingway, with a diatribe that ranged between concern for her welfare and irritation that she had not yet solved the murder. It went on and on and would, Elizabeth thought, have continued much longer if Mr Walker had not come home.

'You're absolutely right, Mrs Hemingway, and I'll try to do better. I must go now. My father just came home from the hospital, and he looks distraught.'

'I do?' he said after she had hung up.

'No. That was Mrs Hemingway. I had to think of some way to cut her off.'

'Ah. An excellent woman but inclined to some verbosity.'

Elizabeth laughed. 'To put it mildly. How's Mother?'

'Physically, doing very well. Her bruises are fading, her headache is much better, and her leg is healing properly, the doctor says, though of course it's still very painful. But she's fretful. She hates enforced idleness, hates the hospital.'

'Hates being bossed around by the nurses, I'll bet.'

'That, too. She'd like to see you. She wants to know what you've "been up to", as she puts it, and I wasn't quite sure how much you'd want her to know.'

She considered that. 'She's my mother. She deserves to know what I'm doing, but I'll have to tone it down considerably. She's not well. I don't want to make her worse.'

The phone rang. 'Oh, drat. That'll be for me, I expect. You go sit down at the table and Susannah will give you some lunch.'

'What about you?' he called as she sprinted for the phone.

'Later!'

For the next half hour she explained to various callers, with varying degrees of patience, that she had been occupied with emergencies that prevented her attendance at the guild/committee/planning/club meetings. Apologies, promises to do better. After the fifth call she quickly dialed Leslie's number.

'Where have you been? I was getting really nervous about you.

Nobody but Susannah was ever home, and then she said you were in bed. You never go to bed unless you're sick. And then I tried to call again, but the phone was busy for *hours*!'

'Leslie! Be quiet and listen! I'm fine. I've been out a lot and doing a lot, and then last night I didn't sleep well at all, which is why I got up really late.'

'Out doing what? Being nosy, I'll bet.'

Elizabeth laughed. 'That, and visiting Lucy after their awful night, and visiting the hospital.'

'Oh. How are Lucy and Fred, and how's your mother?'

'Mother's getting better. I'm going to see her this afternoon. And Lucy and Fred didn't really come to much harm. Lucy's furious about the damage to her favorite tree and her flower beds. Fred's furious about the whole thing. Look, Leslie, I want to tell you everything, but not on the phone. I'm busy the rest of the day, but would you like to go to Petersen's for ice cream tomorrow afternoon? Bring the kids.'

'They'd love that, but I won't bring them this time. I have a feeling the conversation might not be suitable for their ears.'

'Oh, right! I didn't think. Would three o'clock work for you?'

'Meet you there. And Beth – it's good to be friends again. Bye.'

TWENTY-NINE

Elizabeth sat for a little while with her father, Susannah having explained to him why his daughter wasn't interested in lunch. 'But Daddy, after I get home from the hospital this afternoon she's going to start teaching me how to cook. Lucy taught me to make coffee, but Susannah doesn't do it the same way, so I need to re-learn that. She says potatoes and boiled eggs are the easiest things, so I'll probably start with that.'

'Ah. I foresee potato salad for supper. Good thing it's summer. And then you're meeting Fred and the witness.'

'If he shows up. I'm not sure he will. Oh, and I'm going to try to talk Susannah into coming with me. If anybody can keep Joshua from running away in a panic, she can.'

'Good idea. Now, my dear, shall I drive you to the hospital?'

'No, I'll drive myself. Maybe you could stand by in case I have trouble cranking the car? I really have to learn how to do it myself.'

'It's time you got yourself a better car with a self-starter. But yes, I'll watch and advise.'

It took three tries, but she finally managed, and drove off with a triumphant wave.

She had dressed carefully for the visit, in a dress she was sure her mother would approve of and a new hat. She hated both of them, but that didn't matter. It was a small gesture toward reconciliation.

'So you finally came,' was the cordial greeting she received.

'Yes, and I brought you some flowers.' They had been an after-thought, plucked hastily and thrust into an old vase from the potting shed. She set them down where Mother could see them from her bed, and bent to kiss her cheek. 'Dad said you weren't feeling too good this morning.'

'I told them to stop those dratted pain pills. They made me feel dizzy and stupid. But now my leg is killing me, and my head's bad too.'

'You always have been a martyr to headaches. I hope they're still giving you aspirin.'

'Yes, but how can my head get better when I'm worried sick about you? Kenneth tells me you're still determined to carry on with that fool investigating thing. Can't you leave well enough alone? The police are the ones who are supposed to do that kind of thing. All my friends say you're likely to get yourself killed.'

She went on in that vein for quite some time. Elizabeth let her talk. When Mother finally paused, Elizabeth quickly stepped into the gap.

'Your friends are right about my determination. You know what I'm like, Mother. I'm too much like you to let a little trouble turn me aside from a goal. But I'm sure you'll be relieved to know that I've found a way to work with the police.'

Mother's eyebrows rose. 'Oh?' It was her best club-woman voice, indicating both doubt and disapproval.

'Yes, truly. I learned of a witness who actually saw the murderer, and described him to me, with a policeman standing by.'

'Who? And how did you find out about him?'

'No one I knew. No one you'd know, either. He was simply near Mr Anthony's shop and saw the man running away. This afternoon he's going to tell his story again and swear to it, with Fred and his secretary standing by to take notes. So that's really good news. The police will be sure to find the man, with such a good description. And that means the whole village will be able to breathe again.'

'You're sure this man is telling the truth? Who is he?'

'The police are quite sure, Mother. I really know very little about him, except that he seems pleasant and reliable. I do know that he's a regular churchgoer and has a responsible job. Now, I don't want to talk on and on and make your head worse. Would you like some water?'

'No. I need . . . Would you call the nurse for me?'

She was moving restlessly. Elizabeth guessed what her need might be and stood up. 'I'll get her on my way out. Try to rest now, Mother. I'll see you tomorrow.'

How would Lucy have acted if she was lying helpless and needed a bedpan? Elizabeth pictured her saying so quite frankly, and almost laughed as she walked out to her car.

The visit hadn't taken long. There was plenty of time when she got home to learn how to peel potatoes, cut them into the right size pieces, and put them in a pan of salted water. She cut herself only once, and it was minor, though Susannah grumbled about blood on the potato. Then she learned the shortcut of putting the eggs in the same water, and boiling them along with the potatoes.

'Should I get the egg timer?' she asked, reaching for the little hourglass on the shelf.

'No. That one's for soft-boiled eggs, three minutes. You just gotta watch the clock. But don't start checkin' till the water boils. For hard-boiled you want twelve minutes. And you gotta watch the pot, too, cause it'll want to boil over once the potatoes get to cookin'. An' when the eggs are done, you gotta fish 'em out an put 'em in a bowl of cold water, so's they don't go on cookin'. So get one ready. An' then you gotta check on the potatoes, cause they gonna be almost done.' She told her how to do that, with a fork

'I thought you said this was easy,' Elizabeth complained. 'Seems like you have to work like a one-armed paperhanger.'

Susannah chuckled. 'It's easier doin' the potatoes an' the eggs in different pots, but why wash two pots when you can do it in one?'

Elizabeth realized that the washing of the pots had never occurred to her.

There were a lot more steps to making the potato salad, of course. Elizabeth had learned from Lucy how to chop celery. Susannah always also used green onions, cut fine, and some of her own bread-and-butter pickles, chopped. Once Elizabeth had managed all the chopping, Susannah let her sit down. 'There's the eggs to be peeled, yet, once the potatoes are cool. I don' make my own mayonnaise any more. Mine's better, but it's tricky to make. I jus' get that from the store, and the mustard, too. Now, you think you know how to make the salad your own self next time?'

'I'll forget something, but I'd like to try. With you standing over me!'

'You go write it all down, so's you'll remember. You not so bad, for a beginner. Now scoot. You rest yourself a little while I cleans up.'

'Susannah, I—I have a favor to ask you.'

'What, honey? I'll do anythin' for you, you knows that. You need somethin' hemmed, or taken in, or buttons sewn on?'

'No, it's not clothes, it's . . . well, you know I'm going to be seeing Joshua this afternoon at the garage?'

'I heard you talking to your daddy 'bout it. Didn' understand why.'

'It's to take down his statement, with Fred there to make it all legal. And I think he's pretty scared, so I wondered if – well, only if it won't spoil any plans of yours—'

'You want me to come along, so's he won't run away.'

'That's it. It's a lot to ask, I know, but—'

'But you reckon if I'm there, along with all the white folks, he gonna feel better about it. How come you so scared to ask me?'

'I . . . you—'

'I'm not here to help you with your 'vestigatin'? Honey, I'm here to do anythin' you wants me to do, you or your mama or your daddy, 'lessen it agin my principles. Only I can't walk there. Too far for my old feet. Your daddy gonna drive us?'

'I can drive.' She cast a doubtful look at Susannah's bulk.

The housekeeper laughed. 'Honey, I wouldn' fit in that little car o' yours if you used a shoehorn. Best go in your daddy's car. When we need to leave?'

*   *   *

They bundled into Mr Walker's car a little after four-thirty, just to be on the safe side. It was a tight squeeze for Susannah, but she managed. She and Elizabeth got out just around the corner, not to startle Joshua into flight, and Susannah led the way.

And stopped so suddenly Elizabeth ran into her. There was a squeal of brakes.

'Can't you look where you're going?' shouted a furious female voice. 'You nearly ran me into that post!'

'You nearly ran her down!' responded Elizabeth just as furiously. 'Susannah, are you okay?'

'Jus' kinda shook up, is all. Leave it, chile. No harm done.'

'No harm! Scared both of us half to death! And that woman was driving much too fast. She must have been going at least twenty miles an hour, and in the middle of town, on a narrow alley. She should be arrested for reckless driving!'

The driver abandoned her car where it was, in the middle of the alley, and marched toward Elizabeth.

They recognized each other at the same moment.

'You! I might have known. You with your high-flown notions, trying to prove some decent God-fearing man killed that filthy foreigner, instead of one of his own kind. Your mother would die of shame if she saw you standing up for a nigger!'

'And I know you, too, though not by name. You are a member of the Walosas, aren't you? And the wife of the drunken man you had to sneak out of my mother's party before anyone saw. I believe the shame is on your side. My companion, Susannah Lewis, is an indispensable member of our household, and both my parents will be very upset when I tell them you insulted her.' She was barely holding on to her temper.

'Why, you little—' The woman came toward her, hands outstretched, talon-like fingernails extended.

Susannah interposed her bulk, and growled, 'Nobody gonna hurt my girl when I'm around! You back off!' Her arms were crossed in front of her like armor. The angry driver took a step backward.

A car drove up. 'Madam, if that is your vehicle, would you kindly— Beth! Susannah! What in the world is going on here?'

Elizabeth didn't even try to conceal how glad she was to see him. 'Fred, this woman nearly ran into Susannah, driving like a maniac, and then she—' She stopped. Her voice was shaking, and she was very afraid she was going to cry.

The woman backed off. 'Such a fuss over nothing! That . . . person walked right in front of me. She could have done terrible damage to my car, and as it is, my nerves will never be the same! I'm going to sue!'

'Ah. Then I've come along at just the right time. I am an attorney, madam.' He produced his card. 'Frederick Wilkins, with Carter, Sanders, and Smith. And your name, please?'

'Marjorie Woods— No! I don't have to give you my name! I haven't done anything wrong. It's that stuck-up Walker girl and that fat mammy of hers! You'll be hearing from my husband.' She stomped back to her car and started the engine. Fred hurried to move his car out of her way, but even so, she scraped the running board as she steered erratically past.

'Well, that was interesting,' said Fred mildly. 'I want to hear all about it later, but now we'd better see if Mr Jones has heard the commotion and fled.'

'I'll see to him,' said Susannah in full command mode. She surged ahead and spotted him just around the corner, looking warily either way. 'Joshua Jones, where you goin' to?' she bellowed.

'Miz Lewis! I ain't . . . I mean, Mr Bennett, he let me off kinda early, on account I gotta go home to my mama.'

'Yo' mama been safe in the arms o' Jesus a long time now. Don' you tell me no lies! An' don' think you can run away, neither. You gonna tell us a story, an' these white folks're takin' the trouble to write it down for you, so's you don' gotta go to the po-lice station. Sit!' She pointed to the bench he and Elizabeth had used the day before.

He sat.

Fred and his secretary approached. 'Mr Jones, I'm Fred Wilkins, a friend of Mrs Fairchild, and this is my secretary Mrs Lerner. Mrs Lerner, Mr Joshua Jones. Now, sir, if you can make room for her on that bench, she'll write down what you tell us.'

Joshua looked at the sidewalk and frowned. 'How I know she gonna put it down right? I cain't read.'

Fred smiled. 'Even I can't read what she writes down. She writes in something called shorthand, a way of writing very quickly. Only people who know shorthand can read it. So when we get back to the office she'll type it out in real English.'

'An' Joshua, don' you think these people gone try an' trick you.

They ain't that kind. You think I'd lie to you?' Susannah's hands were on her hips, her lower lip well extended.

Joshua cowered. 'No, ma'am.'

'Then ack like you got some gumption!'

Elizabeth blessed the moment she'd thought to bring Susannah along.

She started off the questioning by asking Joshua to tell again what he had told her yesterday, starting from the moment he first saw the man. Fred let the story flow for a few minutes and then interrupted with a question here and there. What did the man look like? Not just his clothes, but his face. Long, wide, wrinkled, scarred? Skin color. Dark, pale, yellowish, reddish? Ears. Did they stick out at all, or show any signs of his having been in a fight? Long neck (Fred stretched his as far as possible) or short (he hunched his shoulders and pulled his chin down)? The comical antics made Joshua relax and giggle a bit, as Fred had hoped.

Elizabeth ventured to interrupt. 'Mr Jones, I have a friend who's really good at drawing faces. Would you be willing to talk to her about how the man looked? She might be able to draw something that looked a little like him.'

Joshua had calmed down enough to look up at her. 'I kin draw faces, Miz Fairchild.'

'You can? How wonderful! If we bring you paper and pencil, could you draw a picture of this man?'

'I kin try. Maybe won't be no good.'

'It will be a big help. Now, let's see. Do you think your boss would mind if I used his phone to call my artist friend? She could bring you the right materials—'

'Ain't no need for that, ma'am. I got paper 'n' stuff right here. Mr Bennett, he let me draw when I ain't real busy.'

'Oh, can I come with you and see some of your drawings?' asked Elizabeth. *And make sure you don't panic and run.*

But he showed no inclination to run. His drawing pad and pencils were tucked in a little cubbyhole that was presumably his hideaway when he had no duties for a few minutes. It was cluttered, but cleaner than Elizabeth had expected. A motor garage, after all, can't be exactly pristine.

'May I see?' she asked.

He hesitated, and then opened the pad. 'I draw lots of stuff, not jus' people. This here's my best one.'

It was John Farson's mansion, Pleasant Home, drawn with such attention to detail that one could almost count the leaves on the trees, and such artistry that one could almost hear them rustle. Elizabeth was so astounded she could barely speak. 'But Joshua, this is . . . I am . . . you are an artist!'

He wriggled in embarrassment and tried to dig his toes into the floor. 'Jus' a colored boy likes to draw, thass all.'

She wanted to talk to him about going to art school, about selling his work, but this wasn't the time or place. 'You're much more than that, but we can talk about it later. Right now Mr Wilkins needs your drawing of the man you saw. Can you really do it from memory? It was more than a week ago.'

''Course.'

And he went back to the bench and proceeded to do just that, in about ten minutes, while his audience watched, enthralled. When he put his pencils down, he grimaced. 'I ain't got the right color pencils to do his shirt and tie. They was brighter'n that. And his eyes was a lighter brown. But the rest ain't bad. Only I didn' put in the . . . that stuff as was all over his suit.'

Elizabeth shuddered. Fred looked stunned. 'Alice, is there a printer in town that can reproduce this, in color?'

Mrs Lerner shook her head. 'Not in the village. There are several in Chicago. The process is very expensive, though.'

'That doesn't matter,' said Elizabeth firmly. 'We need copies up everywhere. Fred, you could take care of that?'

'If the police agree,' he said. 'It's in their hands, you know.'

'An' there's somethin' you haven' thought about, Miss Elizabeth.' Susannah's hands were on her hips again. 'You stick up this here pitcher all over town, somebody gonna know who drew it. An' Joshua, he live alone.'

'Not alone! I got my dog!'

'Yes, honey, but he a itty bitty thing couldn' scare off a alley cat. I'm thinkin' . . .' She looked meaningfully at Elizabeth.

'Certainly. We've plenty of extra room.' She turned to the boy. 'Joshua, we're afraid you might not be safe until this man is found and put in jail.'

'I thought you said I'd be safe after I told ever'thin'.'

'Yes, I said that, and I believed it. But that was before you made that drawing. If that man sees that, it's going to make him very angry, and I'm worried about you. Could I persuade you to come and stay with me and my parents and Susannah until it's all over?'

'Do you got a house like that?' He gestured toward the drawing pad.

'No, nothing like as big and grand as that. Just a nice, comfortable house.'

Susannah shot Elizabeth an amused look.

'Kin I bring my dog?'

'Of course.' Elizabeth crossed her fingers. They'd worry about the cats later. Right now they needed to get this boy to a safe place.

Fred stood. 'Then we're nearly done here. Just one more question, Mr Jones.'

'You kin call me Joshua,' he said shyly.

'Well then, Joshua, when the man left here, which way did he go? Or were you too far away from the garage door to see?'

'He went right on past, runnin' down the alley like the devil was after him, until he got to the street. Then he slowed down, like he didn' want nobody to notice him. And then he turned to go over to Marion Street an' I couldn' see him no more.'

'That's a start, anyway. What will help the most, though, is your amazing picture. Now, if you've finished your work here, I'll drive you home to get your clothes and toothbrush, and then to Mrs Fairchild's house. Susannah, I'm afraid I can't fit you and Elizabeth in along with the boy and my secretary, but I'll come back for you if that's all right. Then I need to catch the next train to Chicago to get this picture printed up.' He patted his briefcase, where he had stowed the precious portrait.

'The printing plants will have closed by the time you could get there,' said Elizabeth the practical. 'I suggest you take the picture to the police immediately. I'm sure Joshua can do another when he gets home, and maybe he has the proper colors there for the shirt and so on.'

Joshua nodded.

'You can take Susannah with you,' said Elizabeth. 'She can help Joshua collect his belongings. Mrs Lerner and I can walk—'

'Not alone!' The cry came from both Fred and Susannah. 'Honey, after the way that woman treated us, I'm not lettin' you go no place without me or Mr Fred goin' with you!'

'Susannah, we can't just sit here!'

'Mebbe your daddy waited for us. I'll go see.'

The two women sat back down on the bench. Fred paced, while young Joshua scanned the narrow street nervously. 'They not comin' to git me, are they?'

'No, Mr Jones,' Elizabeth soothed. 'We're looking after you.'

'I wish Miz Lewis would come back.'

And back she came a moment later, riding in Mr Walker's car. 'So we's all set, honey. I'm comin' with you, Joshua, in Mr Fred's car. You two ladies goin' with Miss Elizabeth's daddy. An' honey, you think you could make some iced tea when you gets home? Supper's all ready, but we all gonna be powerful thirsty.'

'I'll try, Susannah! Lucy showed me how to make tea.'

'You gotta make it real strong, 'cause the ice gonna water it down.'

Joshua was rocking back and forth, eager to be gone.

'Yes, young'un, I'm comin'. Back soon, honey.'

Finally they were all off.

THIRTY

T hey dropped Mrs Lerner off at the law office so she could type up the deposition, and then went home. Elizabeth was so tired she wanted only to drop into bed, but she'd promised that iced tea. She plodded to the kitchen and stopped, startled. 'Mary!'

She was standing in a corner. 'Yes'm. I come in. I knocked an' knocked, but wa'nt nobody home, an' the terrace door wa'nt locked, so I come in. I know I shouldn' of, but I didn' know what else to do.' She began to cry, trying to suppress deep sobs.

Elizabeth gently led her to a chair and pushed a handkerchief into her hand. 'Now you cry all you need to, and then you can tell me what's the matter.' She was very much afraid that she knew.

While she waited for the sobs to subside, she filled the kettle and put it on the gas range. The one thing she was sure she remembered about making tea was that the water had to be boiling. Did you make it in a teapot? But that surely wouldn't make enough.

And you shouldn't pour boiling water into the prized Waterford pitcher, should you?

The sobs had turned to sniffles. Elizabeth found a limp old tea towel and gave it to Mary in place of the sodden handkerchief. 'Now, then,' she said briskly. 'Can you tell me what's wrong?'

'My mama . . . she—'

'Susannah told me she was very sick. Did she . . . is she—?'

'She dead, Miss Elizabeth. They took her away, an' I was skeered to stay there by myself, an' I didn' know what to do, so I come here.' Sobs threatened again.

'And it was a very sensible thing to do. We were all busy, but Susannah will be home very soon, and when you're able to, I need your help. Do you know how to make iced tea? I promised Susannah I'd make some for supper, but all I know about tea is boiling water. Do I make it in a teapot or a pitcher? And how much tea should I use? I know it's one bag for a cup, but I don't know how much for a potful. And Susannah said to make it really strong.' She was talking, talking, talking to give Mary time to steady herself, and to give her something to think about besides her terrible loss.

'Miz Susannah, she make it in that big enamel soup kettle. I know how to do that!' She wiped her face one last time with the tea towel and stood up. Elizabeth handed her a towel she had dipped in cold water.

'Here, wash your face, and then if you can find that soup kettle? Quickly?'

The very strong tea was steeping when they heard Susannah come in the back door. 'All right, Mary, go upstairs and wash your face properly, and comb your hair. I'll tell Susannah you're here.' And pass on the news about her mother, and try to decide what to do with Joshua, and finish making the tea. She was reminded again of a one-armed paperhanger.

'Susannah, come into the kitchen a minute. Bring Joshua. We need to talk.' Her tone of voice cut off Susannah's questions. 'First of all, Mary's back. Her mother died a little while ago.'

'Oh, sweet Jesus! I knowed it was comin', but what she gonna do without her mama? Where is she?'

'I sent her up to her room to wash her face and tidy up a bit. She's been crying hard. And, oh dear, she helped me make the tea, and it's going to be way too strong. I forgot about it!'

Susannah took over. 'Joshua, you take that spoon – no, the big one hangin' right there – an' fish out them teabags from that pan. Careful, they's hot! Jus' dump 'em in the sink for now. An' then git some ice – it's in the Frigidaire, up on top in the freezer part – an' start putting it in, little at a time. They's more in the old ice-box in the shed. Now, Miss Elizabeth, I 'spect Mary's in no shape to set the tables, so you gonna have to. We jus' having potato salad an' ham an' cheese an' bread. Good thing your mama can't see. I'll finish up the tea, an' you tell your daddy supper in ten minutes. Soon's I can, I'll show Joshua where he gonna sleep. Oh, an' set a place at the big table for Mr Fred. He stayin' for supper.'

With Susannah firmly in charge, chaos turned into order. Elizabeth found Fred and recruited him to help with setting both tables, in the kitchen and the dining room. As they worked together, they talked quietly about Joshua.

'You know he's only seventeen? Been an orphan for three years and working at Lou Bennett's for two of those years. Oh, before I forget, I put his dog in the garage, in charge of Zeke. We'll introduce him to the cats later.'

'After we've put on armor.'

'Yes, there may be war. I wouldn't bet on Tige to win. As Susannah said, he's pretty little, a sort-of terrier. Cute as can be, and active, but no match for Ginger, I'd say.'

'Fred, what on earth are we going to do with him? After the murderer's safely put away, I mean?'

'I assume you mean Joshua, not his dog. The plan for now was to give him the little spare room near Susannah's, but with Mary back, that won't do.'

'A young man and a young woman right next door to each other. No. I'm sure they're both perfectly respectable, but . . . no.'

'So I'll have a quick word with Zeke. There's plenty of room for an extra bed in Zeke's rooms, and he'd be company for the boy. Man, I mean, but he seems so young.'

Elizabeth nodded. 'That's a really good idea. And I'm sure he'll be happier there. I think this house scares him.'

'He's been living in a tiny shed. He keeps it as clean as he can, but it was never meant to be a dwelling. I'll have to ask Susannah; she'll know the story. I'm guessing that his parents once lived in the neighboring house, but when they both died Joshua had to find someplace else to lay his head. The place is falling apart. Holes in the roof and the walls. No electricity, no plumbing. Pump and outhouse in the back yard. Rats, of course.'

'I suppose he rents it.'

Fred nodded. 'From a slumlord. I did a little checking when I went to the police station. The poor guy gets paid fairly well at the garage, but almost all his pay goes for that disgusting hovel. I'm hoping that . . .'

'That he never has to go back there. You know, I've been thinking about that. I know Zeke could use some help with the gardening. Mother keeps wanting more and more flower beds, and there's only Zeke to look after them. And he's not getting any younger. What if we could work out a barter arrangement? Joshua lives here, rent-free, if he'll help Zeke out in his spare time.'

'Do you think your parents would go for it?'

'Dad would be all for it, I know. And when Mother can get something for almost nothing, she's delighted.'

'Sounds like it might work. But what about Susannah? We both know she gets the final say about anything in this household.'

'She's already taken him under her wing, nagging him as much as she does me.'

'All right, I'll go find the boy and get him settled. And get him to work on that drawing!'

In very little more than the ten minutes Susannah had promised, they were all sitting down to their meal. Elizabeth had decreed that they would serve themselves, leaving Mary free to stay in the kitchen. They could hear chatter from the open kitchen door. 'Mary's beginning to cheer up,' said Elizabeth. 'I'm glad.'

'I had a word with Susannah,' Fred commented. 'Apparently Mary's mother has been slowly dying of consumption for months. Susannah says worry was the reason Mary was often absent-minded and clumsy, and she should do much better now.'

Mr Walker smiled. 'I'll bet that's not the only reason she's sounding happier. Don't know if you've noticed, but Mr Jones is a nice-looking young man.'

Elizabeth held up her hands in mock horror. 'Oh, my! Then it's a good thing he's sleeping in the garage!'

Her father was about to respond when he was interrupted by a thunderous pounding at the front door. Fred sprang up. 'I locked it when I came in, thank God. This sounds like trouble.

Mr Walker, see to the back door, will you? Beth, are there any others?'

'The terrace. But Fred, what is it?'

'Vengeance,' he replied briefly, and sprinted for the door.

Elizabeth ran to the kitchen, but Susannah was already in motion. 'I'm locking the terrace doors, honey. You check the windows. Joshua, grab that big fryin' pan and come with me.'

'I'm comin', too!' Mary ran after them as shouting began at the front door.

Elizabeth's heart was racing. This was so frighteningly familiar, so like the scene at Fred's house. The shouting from outside was horrible, profanity mixed with threats. Fred was just as loud, but his threats were legal ones, and phrased with less brimstone.

The law! Someone should call the police! She closed the last of the study windows and ran for the back hall, but her father was already at the phone.

But now noise was coming from the terrace. A woman's screaming voice. 'Lookee here, Herman! We got us a nest of 'em!'

She ran to the dining room. There were Susannah, Joshua, and Mary, three black faces glaring at – oh, dear heaven, it was that woman! Marjorie whatever. Her face was contorted with rage, and she was about to swing a baseball bat at the French doors. All glass!

'Daddy!' she cried. 'Help! They're going to get in!'

The woman moved the bat over her shoulder to prepare for a damaging blow, and suddenly lost her balance, spun around, and would have fallen to the flagstones but for an outstretched arm.

A dark arm. Zeke, who had pulled the bat away from her, had caught her, and then melted away into the shadows as a furious white man appeared. 'Where's that black bastard that was messin' with you?'

Mr Walker gently moved his servants away from the terrace door, opened it, and stepped out, Fred right beside him. 'Sir,' said Mr Walker, 'you will not use that kind of language in front of ladies. If this is your wife, she is unharmed. And you, sir, are shamefully drunk. The police are on their way. It would be wise to leave before they arrest you for public intoxication and disorderly contact, not to mention trespassing.'

'That nigger grabbed her, tried to drag her away! I'll find him and horsewhip him!'

'No, you won't!' The policeman came up from behind and turned the man to face him, waving his hand in front of his face to clear the whiskey fumes. 'You're coming with me.'

'Like hell I am! You go get that nigger that molested my wife!'

The policeman was joined by a second, who put handcuffs on the struggling man. 'Now you just come along. A night in the drunk tank won't hurt you.'

'You can't do that to my husband! This is Mr Woodson, you idiot! Don't you know who he is?'

'Yes, ma'am. He owns a furniture store in town. He's wealthy. He's also drunk and disorderly, he's trespassing, along with you, ma'am, and he's been making threats. We'll take you home, ma'am, where you can calm down.'

'And what about that nigger that tried to rape me? You're going to let him go?'

Elizabeth had had enough. 'Officer, the man she's speaking of is our gardener. He heard the disturbance and came up just in time to take away the baseball bat Mrs Woodson was about to use to break open our terrace doors. His motion caused her to lose balance, and she would have fallen hard if Zeke hadn't caught her. As soon as she was steady he went back to his rooms. He has an apartment over the garage. He took the bat with him, for which I'm grateful. Do you want it for evidence?'

'I suppose you're going to believe *her*,' stormed Mrs Woodson, 'just because she's rich and a nigger-lover and gets her name in the papers. I'll sue you all to hell and gone!'

'You do that, lady. Best of luck. Now, you letting us take you home, or what? I'd be real happy to take you to spend the night with your husband.'

Spluttering and complaining, she walked off with the policeman.

'I wonder where she'll end up,' murmured Elizabeth.

A third policeman appeared. 'Mr Walker, sir, I'm going to take a walk around your house to make sure that pair didn't do any damage.'

'They've trampled my wife's flower beds. She won't be at all happy about that when she comes home.'

'That probably comes under "malicious damage",' said Fred. 'I'll ask the court to extend his fine to include payment for their replacement.'

The policeman snorted. 'That'll probably just make him even madder at you. What was this all about tonight, anyway? Did he have some sort of quarrel with you?'

'Not exactly,' said Elizabeth. 'If there was any quarrel, it was between his wife and me, but it was petty. Or so I thought. Officer, I'll be happy to explain, but if there's no hurry, I'd much rather do it in the morning. It has been a long and trying day, and we're all very tired.'

'It'll keep, Mrs Fairchild. I'll just take that inspection tour, and get that bat from your gardener, and then I'll leave you in peace.'

THIRTY-ONE

F red finally went home, after Elizabeth and her father assured him, several times, that they would be perfectly safe. 'Well, then, I'll see you in the morning. I want to file charges against that precious pair, and I'd like to stop here first to collect that picture, if Joshua is able to draw it after tonight's brouhaha. Do you think it all scared him witless?'

'No, actually I think it gave him some self-confidence. He was helping. He was needed. I think he'll be eager to do that drawing for you. But you left the other at the station, didn't you?'

'Yes, but Joshua said a few things about it weren't quite right. I'm hoping, now that he has all his own materials, he'll produce an even better one. When does he have to leave for work, do you know?'

'Got to be there by nine sharp,' said Susannah, who was standing by to lock the door after Fred. 'I asked him when he wanted to have his breakfast, and after fussin' about him not needin' breakfast, we settled on eight.'

'Then tell him I'll pick him up at quarter to nine, and I'd like to take the picture with me. 'Night, love.' He kissed Elizabeth on the cheek and headed out the door before she could react.

Susannah was wise enough to make no comment, though her broad smile spoke volumes.

Dad was sitting in his big chair in the study, his eyes closed, a cup of coffee in front of him.

'Won't that keep you awake?' his daughter asked, dropping into a chair.

He opened his eyes. 'I doubt if anything short of a full-scale mortar attack would keep me awake tonight.' He finished the coffee. 'Want some?'

'No. I just want to go to bed and wake up in about a month, when all this is over.'

'Ought to be over sooner than that, now that remarkable young man has turned up.'

'He really is amazing, isn't he? You haven't seen any of his work yet, but he's a real artist. We're going to have to do something about that.'

'Yes. I'm thinking he ought to live with us permanently, if that suits him.'

Elizabeth gave a weary laugh. 'Fred and I talked about that. He says Joshua's living space is dreadful. We could hire him to help Zeke now and then, when he wasn't working at the filling station, and start him on some education. Did you know he can't read?'

'Doesn't surprise me. He's never been given a chance to learn. Didn't you say he's an orphan?'

'He has no one except his dog Tige. But of course Susannah has taken him firmly in hand, and Zeke will help out, too.'

'Not to mention Mary,' said Dad with a sly grin.

'Yes, well, we'll cross that bridge when we come to it. Do you think Mother will agree to the arrangement? I thought he could offer his help as payment for board and room, so it would cost very little.'

'Let me present the notion to her. If she thinks it was her idea, I'm sure she'll be fine with it.' He yawned. 'Bets, I simply can't stay awake any longer. Goodnight.'

Elizabeth woke at dawn. She sat up and rubbed the sleep out of her eyes, realizing to her surprise that she had slept undisturbed for the first time in what felt like weeks. It must have been her hope that the nightmare was nearing an end.

It certainly could have had nothing to do with Fred's parting kiss.

Of course not. The inner voice spoke in a distinctly sarcastic tone. She ignored it. Though she was remembering a pleasant dream or two . . . She ignored them too and began to plan her day.

It was going to be a busy one. First, she planned to accompany Fred to the police station. She wanted to know what was going to happen to yesterday's attackers. At the very least, she hoped Mr Woodson would have a terrible headache. And his wife would probably give him another when – if – he went home. Elizabeth couldn't quite understand why they had staged that scene, unless it was just unfocussed spite about her liberal bias, and her friendship with colored people. Hatred, she thought as she washed and dressed, was such a destructive attitude. The Woodsons, as members of the KKK, had for years had their hatred fed and nurtured by their fellows.

Well, their fellow racists, especially the women of the Walosas, wouldn't approve of their antics yesterday. They preferred non-violent methods of getting their point across. The subtle slur, the saccharine preaching about traditions and family values and sincere Christianity, the veiled threat, all these tactics were quite effective in achieving their ends. And if they weren't, their husbands could don their ridiculous robes and burn crosses. Loudly harassing individual families while intoxicated was definitely frowned upon. Especially the 'intoxicated' part, here in Oak Park.

One way and another, Elizabeth decided, the Woodsons would certainly get their comeuppance. She ran a brush through her hair and hurried downstairs.

It wasn't even seven o'clock yet, but the kitchen was already astir. Susannah was putting something in the oven. Mary was slicing bread for toast. Zeke was sitting at the table with a coffee cup in one hand and a pencil in the other hand. 'Now, boy, what's this?' He wrote something on the paper in front of him.

Joshua studied what he had written. 'C-a-t. That right, Mr Zeke?'

'Right! Now sound them out. What does it say?'

'Ssss-ay-t. Sayt? Don't make no sense.'

'No. Remember C makes two sounds. So does A. Here, I'll make the letters into a picture.' Cleverly Zeke wound the C and A around into a plump animal, and extended the T into a tail. 'Now what do you think?'

'It's a cat! K-aa-t! Oh!'

Joshua looked up and saw Elizabeth, who had been hovering just outside the door, delightedly watching Joshua's first reading lesson. His face took on its worried look as he jumped to his feet, but before he could stammer an apology, she swooped in and patted his shoulder. 'I'm proud of you, Joshua! You're doing very well. And look, they thought you were calling them.'

She pointed to the floor. Winding themselves around the legs of chairs and humans, they were purring loudly. 'Meet Ginger and Charlie, our two little beggars. They'll love you if you give them a little of your breakfast.'

Joshua looked apprehensive again. 'I don't know if they'll like Tige, though.'

'I don't either. We'll just have to see. Meanwhile we'd better try to keep them apart.' How, though? Well, that was a problem for later. 'Zeke, thank you for taking on this job. I wouldn't know how to begin.'

'My mama taught me to read this way. Reckon I can teach somebody as smart as this young 'un.'

'Smart enough to move this clutter out o' the way sos he can eat his breakfast? Miss Elizabeth, you want yours in here, too?'

'I'll see if Daddy's come down yet.'

She was forestalled by the sound of her father's voice. 'Something smells good,' he said, 'and I see the whole family is up and doing. Is there room for one more around this table?'

Joshua's eyes widened and Mary giggled nervously, but Susannah took it in stride. 'Shore is, Mister Walker. Zeke, you just fetch a chair from the dinin' room while I get my muffins out.'

'Dad, just wait till you see what Joshua's been doing!' She took the writing pad from the counter where Zeke had laid it. 'Look, Zeke's been teaching him to read! He already knows most of the alphabet, and he's beginning to put them together into words. Here, Joshua, show us what that animal is.' She pointed to Charlie.

Grinning widely, he picked up the pencil and wrote the three rather shaky letters. 'And I bet that one is called this.' And he painstakingly spelled out J-i-n-j-r.

'Oh, very good! We spell his name with a G, though. Sounds the same as J.' She wrote out G-i-n-g-e-r, and Joshua carefully copied it. He was about to ask how to spell Charlie's name when Susannah intervened.

'Now that's enough of that,' she commanded. 'You're gonna let my good food get cold. You can get back to your schoolin' this afternoon when you get back from work. You dig in, now, all of you.'

They had finished their meal before Elizabeth remembered about the drawing. 'Oh, heavens, Joshua, did you have time to make that drawing?'

'Yes, ma'am.' He stood and got the drawing pad he had put carefully on the countertop. 'It's better'n the other one, an' the colors are right.'

Elizabeth studied it. 'You're right. It is better. It has more life to it. I feel like that man could just walk right off the page.' She shuddered. 'I'm glad he can't! Joshua, you've done an amazing job. And a service to the community.'

He ducked his head in embarrassment. 'Jus' doin' what I like to do.'

'And what you're so very good at. Right. Now you help Susannah put your lunch together. Mr Wilkins will be here in a couple of minutes to take you to work.'

'I'm going' with him, Miss Elizabeth,' said Zeke firmly, looking her in the eye, 'to talk to his boss a little. He needs to be kept out o' sight for a few days.'

'Quite right, Zeke. I didn't think of that, but I'm glad you did. I don't know what we'd do without you and Susannah. Thank you!'

So there were four of them in Fred's car when they set out. Fred had assumed Elizabeth would get out with the other two at the garage, but she stayed in the car. 'I'm going with you to the police station,' she announced. 'I want to see their reaction when you give them that picture.'

'You think it'll knock their socks off? So do I. I'll have trouble getting it away from them to get the copies under way.'

'And this afternoon I'm taking a break from all this. Leslie and I are going for ice cream at Petersen's. But I may stay at the station with you for a while this morning, Fred. I want to know what's going to happen to the Woodsons. I hope they throw the book at both of them.'

'They will if I have anything to do with it,' said Fred, sounding very much like a lawyer. 'Or at least there's plenty to charge *him* with. As for his wife, though, there are very few laws against being a major nuisance.'

'There are social laws, though. I'm betting her friends will somehow fail to see her when they pass on the street and will forget to invite her to gatherings.'

'If she has any friends. Here we are.'

He helped her out of the car and up the stairs, holding his briefcase close to his side. They had to wait for a moment until they could see Sergeant Daniels, and when he came to the outer office he was accompanied by, of all people, Mr Woodson.

He was such a bedraggled specimen that Elizabeth could feel almost sorry for him. His head was plainly killing him. He squinted against the sunlight pouring through the station window. He walked as though his back hurt, and his clothes were rumpled and dirty. Elizabeth wrinkled up her nose at a stench she could swear was vomit.

'Sorry about this. I'm taking him over to the jail for a shower before he goes to court. His wife is supposed to be bringing him some clothes. I'll be back soon.'

'No need to hurry,' said Fred. 'I just wanted to drop this off to you.' He pulled out the picture.

'Hey!' Mr Woodson's voice was raspy, but nearly as loud as it had been the evening before. 'That's Carter! What're you doin' with a picture of my store manager? Gimmee that!'

THIRTY-TWO

Elizabeth was late for her ice cream date with Leslie. She'd forgotten all about it until Fred reminded her. Her mind was totally occupied with the events at the police station.

Woodson had immediately retracted his identification of the picture, but the scuffle when he tried to grab it brought the chief into the room. He immediately ordered Carter brought from the store to the station. His first comment was: 'Hey, who drew my picture? That's pretty good.'

'This is a picture of you?' asked the chief. 'Mr Woodson, you will be quiet.' He didn't add *Or else!*, but it was implied.

'Sure, it's me.' He had on the same shirt and tie, though his suit was brown. Presumably the tan one had been stained beyond hope.

'Then I arrest you, Mr Carter, for the murder of Enrico Antonelli on Thursday, June the fourth, in this village.'

At that Carter broke down and cried, claiming it was all Woodson's idea, and Woodson ranted and called for a lawyer, loudly refusing Fred, who didn't want the job anyway. It was very noisy and unpleasant, and Elizabeth was very glad when both men were taken into custody and she could take a deep breath again.

'What now?' she asked.

'They have to find a lawyer. The police have to find one, I mean. And it won't be an easy job, given Joshua's deposition, which is pretty damning. I wouldn't take it on myself, even if I weren't prejudiced against the two men. No one likes to take on a hopeless case.'

'I know everyone deserves to be defended, even when the thing is so obvious, but what on earth can the defense use in their favor?'

'The best thing, in the circumstances, would be for the two to plead guilty. Of course we don't have a motive yet, and a lawyer could claim that destroys the case. But what will probably happen is that the lawyer will try to discredit Joshua's testimony by claiming he's stupid and uneducated. Since many of the jury will be disposed to believe that, given his color, they might just get away with it.'

'Oh, no! Poor Joshua.'

'However' – he held up his hand – 'if they try that, I'll suggest that they bring witnesses like you and your father to testify in his favor. We'll just have to see. If it comes down to Walker and Fairchild versus the Walosas, I know who I'll bet on! Now, I have to talk to the chief some more, and I know you haven't had any lunch, but can I drive you to Petersen's and come back here?'

'Oh, golly! I forgot!'

'I wonder why. Anyway, you can get a huge banana split there to fill the void. Come along, my dear.'

Leslie looked at her watch when Elizabeth walked in. 'I thought you'd changed your mind.'

'No.' She sat down and heaved a big sigh. 'It's been quite a morning. I'll tell you all about it, but first can we get something to eat? Breakfast was sometime last week.'

She didn't actually like banana splits, but a double hot-fudge sundae with lots of whipped cream on top looked like heaven when it was set before her. Leslie let her take a few bites, and then said, 'I warn you, I'm growing dangerous. Tell!'

'To sum it up quickly, we caught the murderer.'

'No! Elizabeth Walker Fairchild, put down that spoon and tell all!'

'It'll take all afternoon,' Elizabeth warned.

'That's okay. The kids talked Grandma into a trip to the beach, so they're off my hands for ages.'

'Well.' She took another bite of the rich, creamy treat. 'The first real piece of luck came from Susannah.'

'Of course. Who else?'

Elizabeth told the story of Joshua seeing the man with the knife and the boy's incredible ability to draw the man from memory. 'Honestly, Leslie, he's an even better artist than you are, and you know you're really good. But you have to see Joshua's work.'

'I want to. But go on. Do you want another of those?' The sundae was gone, right down to the last drop of chocolate sauce.

'No, I guess not. But I'd love a strawberry ice cream soda.'

'Only if you tell the rest of the story!'

So she did, including the brouhaha of the night before at the Walker home and the explosive encounter today at the police station. 'And Fred's gone back to talk more to the police and give the prosecution some ideas. But the murderer's identified, he's in jail, and so's the one who egged him on, and we can all sleep tonight.'

'Especially Joshua.'

'Actually, with Susannah and Zeke around to look after him, I think he slept like a baby even last night.'

'And so will you. In an ice cream coma.'

They parted with a hug and a promise to see each other again soon, and Elizabeth walked home, surfeited and finally at ease.

Fred and Elizabeth walked from his car to their seat at the Ravinia park. It was a mild night for July. The full moon was just beginning to show against the twilit sky, and the low humidity meant the stars would sparkle later. The romance of the evening was somewhat impaired by the pervasive scent of citronella from the many candles that burned around the lawn, but they were necessary. Elizabeth had worn a voile jacket to cover her arms, just in case the defenses weren't sufficient. Mosquitoes seemed to love her.

'So you finally got the whole story?' she asked as they made their way across the lawn. 'About Woodson's involvement?'

'It's taken a while, because he didn't want to talk, but we've got most of it, anyway. It was a money matter, as you'd already figured out. It seems Woodson started financing Antonelli at an early stage of the antique shop.'

'Mrs Antonelli told Father Cole that he began by selling lovely things his family had brought from Italy. He hated to do it, but he was working as a laborer and making very little money.'

'Yes, and his little enterprise flourished, but of course he soon ran out of stock, and getting more required money he didn't have. The banks wouldn't lend to him, or at least that's what Woodson said.'

'That just might be true. He was Italian, which made him a pariah, but even if he'd been American, Dad says the antiques business is a very poor risk.'

'He's right about that. At any rate, Woodson had bought some of Antonelli's wares and wanted more. Apparently his wife loves that kind of thing. You wouldn't think it from her behavior, would you?'

Elizabeth chuckled.

'And when Antonelli told him that he didn't have the money for new stock, Woodson advanced some. And for a while things went swimmingly. Antonelli had a good eye. He made a handsome profit on almost everything, though he paid off the loan by giving Woodson pretty much what he wanted free of charge.'

'I hope he hid the really valuable things when that appalling man was in the shop!'

Fred laughed. 'Probably. He was an astute businessman.'

'I don't understand why Woodson would deal with him at all, though, with all his bigoted ideas about Italians.'

'My dear, Woodson didn't know Antonelli – Anthony, as we all knew him – was Italian! Very few people did, except the bankers who knew his real name. You didn't, for example. I didn't. Antonelli didn't exactly hide it, but he had no accent, and he was smart enough not to proclaim it from the housetops. At any rate, business soon became so good that he didn't need the loans anymore, and apparently Woodson had temporarily satisfied his wife's cravings.'

'But then something happened. His daughter's medical bills?'

'That's what I surmised. But no. He was able to pay those, according to his wife, but it left him without much of a cushion. No, what happened was the highboy. Oh, here we go.'

The orchestra had stopped tootling. The oboist gave them an A. A few more adjustments, and then the concertmaster signaled for silence, the orchestra rose, and the conductor walked on stage. Applause, bows, and the evening began.

Elizabeth loved *The Barber of Seville*. She loved the music, the farcical plot, the almost slapstick scenes, everything about the opera. But tonight she was eager for the intermission, which allowed her to talk.

'What do you mean, the highboy?' she demanded the moment the applause had died down.

'Let's stretch our legs for a bit, and I'll tell you.' He propelled her away from the crowd.

'Well?'

'Antonelli knew the highboy was coming up for auction, and he knew it would cost a lot. He went back to Woodson and asked if he could borrow the money. But Woodson didn't want the highboy. That sort of thing is not to Mrs Woodson's taste, it seems.'

Elizabeth made a face.

'But Antonelli said he would pay back the loan plus a handsome bonus, as soon as he sold the piece. Finally Woodson agreed.'

'The orchestra's coming back. Hurry!'

'It was a matter of timing. Antonelli went to the auction, bought the piece, and assumed it would be delivered soon and he could sell it for a huge profit. But the shipping was delayed. Antonelli became more and more frantic, as Woodson became more and more insistent about the money. Finally Woodson had enough, and sent his manager Carter to get the money any way he could.'

'And he panicked and pulled a knife. On the very day the highboy was delivered!'

They got to their seat just in time for the reappearance of the conductor. Elizabeth gave the rest of the opera what attention she could spare, but she still had questions.

'What on earth made Mr Carter kill Mr Antonelli?' she pursued as they walked back to the car after the final curtain call. 'Such a stupid thing to do.'

'We'll never know that, love. Carter claims it was self-defense. Antonelli rushed him, he says, and he got scared and pulled his knife, and then Antonelli stumbled and fell onto it.'

'What piffle!'

'I agree, and I imagine the jury will, too.'

'And what's going to happen to Mr Woodson, who started the whole thing?'

'Accessory before the fact, at the very least. There are a lot of charges against him besides that, though. His business dealings have not always been what they should be, so after the Antonelli case is dealt with, he'll be right back in court facing another jury. Now, what about some coffee before we head home? Or hot chocolate? It's turned a bit nippy.'

She agreed to coffee, so they stopped at their favorite little café. Fred ordered chocolate cake to go with it, and when they had been served, he said, 'It's a shame you were too occupied with murder to enjoy the opera tonight.'

'You noticed.'

'I notice most things about you.'

Elizabeth felt herself blush, not so much at the words as at the tone of voice. 'Sorry. I couldn't help it. I'll do better with *Butterfly*.' She sipped her coffee and tried for a change of subject. 'You haven't seen Joshua lately, have you? He's a changed man. He seems to have grown up in these few weeks. He's even managed to get on Mother's good side, and that's not easy. She's glad to be home, but she hates not being able to walk properly, and it hasn't improved her temper. She's quite tolerant with Joshua, though, and he with her.'

'His life has changed. He's happy, and well cared-for, maybe for the first time in his life. He's learning to read, and that gives him self-confidence. I do see him now and then, when I drop by the garage. And of course he's fallen in love. That changes a man, too.'

Elizabeth couldn't think of a reply.

Fred looked around. There were few customers so late in the evening, and no one was paying the least attention to them. He lowered his voice. 'Beth, you know I love you. I haven't asked you to marry me, because I knew you weren't ready yet for a commitment. But you've changed. And so have I. I think we could be very happy together. Will you marry me?'

She took a deep breath. 'Fred, I—I love you, too. You're my best friend, and I feel safe and comfortable with you. But I don't know if I'm ready even now. There are still lumps of ice inside me. I'm scared. Can you . . . can you wait for an answer?'

His broad smile was her answer. All he said was, 'Damn. I can't kiss you here. Hurry up and finish that stupid coffee!'

AUTHOR'S NOTE

I have made a few changes to St Edmund's Church, especially in its personnel. For nearly the first fifty years of its existence, until 1956, it was led by the Reverend Monsignor John J. Code, not by my Father Cole. Its parishioners are entirely fictitious, though I hope their caring attitude reflects historic reality. I have not dared make any changes to the magnificent architecture.

I have also run up buildings here and there, trying to put them where such structures might actually have been in the 1920s. In general, though, I've tried to be faithful to the layout of the village as it was then.

Oak Park in the twenty-first century is a diverse, liberal, and welcoming community. Sadly, this was not always true. The Walosas Club is a historical reality, as, of course, are Al Capone and his gangsters. I have no evidence that they ever clashed in Oak Park; that conflict is the product of my disordered imagination.

To balance those disagreeable people, the man John Farson stands in the history of the village as a broad-minded and generous supporter of all sorts of causes, a shining light in the sometimes bleak darkness of those times.

And are our own times much better?